AN ANTARCTIC MYSTERY

The *Tasman* to the rescue.

AN

ANTARCTIC MYSTERY

BY

JULES VERNE

TRANSLATED BY MRS. CASHEL HOEY

ILLUSTRATED

PHILADELPHIA

J. B. LIPPINCOTT COMPANY

1899

CONTENTS

CONTENTS

LIST OF ILLUSTRATIONS.

AN ANTARCTIC MYSTERY.

PART I.

CHAPTER I.

THE KERGUELEN ISLANDS.

No doubt the following narrative will be received with entire incredulity, but I think it well that the public should be put in possession of the facts narrated in "An Antarctic Mystery." The public is free to believe them or not, at its good pleasure.

No more appropriate scene for the wonderful and terrible adventures which I am about to relate could be imagined than the Desolation Islands, so called, in 1779, by Captain Cook. I lived there for several weeks, and I can affirm, on the evidence of my own eyes and my own experience, that the famous English explorer and navigator was happily inspired when he gave the islands that significant name.

Geographical nomenclature, however, insists on the name of Kerguelen, which is generally adopted for the group which lies in 49° 45′ south latitude, and 69° 6′ east longitude. This is just, because in 1772, Baron Kerguelen, a Frenchman, was the first to discover those islands in the southern part of the Indian Ocean. Indeed, the commander of the squadron on that voyage believed that he had found a new continent on the limit of the Antarctic seas, but in the course of a second expedition he recognized his error. There was only an archipelago. I may be believed when I assert that Desolation Islands is the only suitable name for this group of three hundred isles or islets in the midst of the vast expanse of ocean, which is constantly disturbed by austral storms.

Nevertheless, the group is inhabited, and the number of Europeans and Americans who formed the nucleus of the Kerguelen population at the date of the 2nd of August, 1839, had been augmented for two months past by a unit in my person. Just then I was waiting for an opportunity of leaving the place, having completed the geological and mineralogical studies which had brought me to the group in general and to Christmas Harbour in particular.

Christmas Harbour belongs to the most important islet of the archipelago, one that is about half as large as Corsica. It is safe, and easy, and free of access. Your ship may ride securely at single anchor in its waters, while the bay remains free from ice.

The Kerguelens possess hundreds of other fjords. Their coasts are notched and ragged, especially in the parts between the north and the south-east, where little islets abound. The soil, of volcanic origin, is composed of quartz, mixed with a bluish stone. In summer it is covered with green mosses, grey lichens, various hardy plants, especially wild saxifrage. Only one edible plant grows there, a kind of cabbage, not found anywhere else, and very bitter of flavour. Great flocks of royal and other penguins people these islets, finding good lodging on their rocky and mossy surface. These stupid birds, in their yellow and white feathers, with their heads thrown back and their wings like the sleeves of a monastic habit, look, at a distance, like monks in single file walking in procession along the beach.

The islands afford refuge to numbers of sea-calves, seals, and sea-elephants. The taking of those amphibious animals either on land or from the sea is profitable, and may lead to a trade which will bring a large number of vessels into these waters.

On the day already mentioned, I was accosted while strolling on the port by mine host of mine inn.

"Unless I am much mistaken, time is beginning to seem very long to you, Mr. Jeorling?"

The speaker was a big tall American who kept the only inn on the port.

"If you will not be offended, Mr. Atkins, I will acknowledge that I do find it long."

"Of course I won't be offended. Am I not as well used to answers of that kind as the rocks of the Cape to the rollers?"

"And you resist them equally well."

"Of course. From the day of your arrival at Christmas Harbour, when you came to the Green Cormorant, I said to myself that in a fortnight, if not in a week, you would have enough of it, and would be sorry you had landed in the Kerguelens."

"No, indeed, Mr. Atkins; I never regret anything I have done."

"That's a good habit, sir."

"Besides, I have gained knowledge by observing curious things here. I have crossed the rolling plains, covered with hard stringy mosses, and I shall take away curious mineralogical and geological specimens with me.

I have gone sealing, and taken sea-calves with your people. I have visited the rookeries where the penguin and the albatross live together in good fellowship, and that was well worth my while. You have given me now and again a dish of petrel, seasoned by your own hand, and very acceptable when one has a fine healthy appetite. I have found a friendly welcome at the Green Cormorant, and I am very much obliged to you. But, if I am right in my reckoning, it is two months since the Chilian two-master *Penâs* set me down at Christmas Harbour in mid-winter.

"And you want to get back to your own country, which is mine, Mr. Jeorling; to return to Connecticut, to Providence, our capital."

"Doubtless, Mr. Atkins, for I have been a globe-trotter for close upon three years. One must come to a stop and take root at some time."

"Yes, and when one has taken root, one puts out branches."

"Just so, Mr. Atkins. However, as I have no relations living, it is likely that I shall be the last of my line. I am not likely to take a fancy for marrying at forty."

"Well, well, that is a matter of taste. Fifteen years ago I settled down comfortably at Christmas Harbour with my Betsy; she has presented me with ten children, who in their turn will present me with grandchildren."

"You will not return to the old country?"

"What should I do there, Mr. Jeorling, and what could I ever have done there? There was nothing before me but poverty. Here, on the contrary, in these Islands of Desolation, where I have no reason to feel desolate, ease and competence have come to me and mine!"

"No doubt, and I congratulate you, Mr. Atkins, for you are a happy man. Nevertheless it is not impossible that the fancy may take you some day—"

Mr. Atkins answered by a vigorous and convincing shake of the head. It was very pleasant to hear this worthy American talk. He was completely acclimatized on his archipelago, and to the conditions of life there. He lived with his family as the penguins lived in their rookeries. His wife was a "valiant" woman of the Scriptural type, his sons were strong, hardy fellows, who did not know what sickness meant. His business was prosperous. The Green Cormorant had the custom of all the ships, whalers and others, that put in at Kerguelen. Atkins supplied them with everything they required, and no second inn existed at Christmas Harbour. His sons were carpenters, sail-makers, and fishers, and they hunted the amphibians in all the creeks during the hot season. In short, this was a family of honest folk who fulfilled their destiny without much difficulty.

"Once more, Mr. Atkins, let me assure you," I resumed, "I am delighted to have come to Kerguelen. I shall always remember the islands kindly. Nevertheless, I should not be sorry to find myself at sea again."

"Come, Mr. Jeorling, you must have a little patience," said the philosopher, "you must not forget that the fine days will soon be here. In five or six weeks—"

"Yes, and in the meantime, the hills and the plains, the rocks and the shores will be covered thick with snow, and the sun will not have strength to dispel the mists on the horizon."

"Now, there you are again, Mr. Jeorling! Why, the

wild grass is already peeping through the white sheet! Just look!"

"Yes, with a magnifying glass! Between ourselves, Atkins, could you venture to pretend that your bays are not still ice-locked in this month of August, which is the February of our northern hemisphere?"

"I acknowledge that, Mr. Jeorling. But again I say have patience! The winter has been mild this year. The ships will soon show up, in the east or in the west, for the fishing season is near."

"May Heaven hear you, Atkins, and guide the *Halbrane* safely into port."

"Captain Len Guy? Ah, he's a good sailor, although he's English—there are good people everywhere—and he takes in his supplies at the Green Cormorant."

"You think the *Halbrane*—"

"Will be signalled before a week, Mr. Jeorling, or, if not, it will be because there is no longer a Captain Len Guy; and if there is no longer a Captain Len Guy, it is because the *Halbrane* has sunk in full sail between the Kerguelens and the Cape of Good Hope."

Thereupon Mr. Atkins walked away, with a scornful gesture, indicating that such an eventuality was out of all probability.

My intention was to take my passage on board the *Halbrane* so soon as she should come to her moorings in Christmas Harbour. After a rest of six or seven days, she would set sail again for Tristan d'Acunha, where she was to discharge her cargo of tin and copper. I meant to stay in the island for a few weeks of the fine season, and from thence set out for Connecticut. Nevertheless, I did not fail to take into due account the share that belongs to chance in human affairs, for it is wise, as Edgar Poe has said, always "to reckon with the unforeseen, the unexpected, the inconceivable, which have a very large share (in those affairs), and chance ought always to be a matter of strict calculation."

Each day I walked about the port and its neighbourhood. The sun was growing strong. The rocks were emerging by degrees from their winter clothing of snow; moss of a wine-like colour was springing up on the basalt cliffs, strips of seaweed fifty yards long were floating on the sea, and on the plain the lyella, which is of Andean origin, was pushing up its little points, and the only leguminous plant of the region, that gigantic cabbage already mentioned, valuable for its anti-scorbutic properties, was making its appearance.

I had not come across a single land mammal—sea mammals swarm in these waters—not even of the batrachian or reptilian kinds. A few insects only—butterflies or others—and even these did not fly, for before they could use their wings, the atmospheric currents carried the tiny bodies away to the surface of the rolling waves.

"And the *Halbrane?*" I used to say to Atkins each morning.

"The *Halbrane*, Mr. Jeorling," he would reply with complacent assurance, "will surely come into port to-day, or, if not to-day, to-morrow."

In my rambles on the shore, I frequently routed a crowd of amphibians, sending them plunging into the newly-released waters. The penguins, heavy and impassive creatures, did not disappear at my approach; they took no notice; but the black petrels, the puffins, black and white, the grebes and others, spread their wings at sight of me.

One day I witnessed the departure of an albatross, saluted by the very best croaks of the penguins, no doubt as a friend whom they were to see no more. Those powerful birds can fly for two hundred leagues without resting for a moment, and with such rapidity that they sweep through vast spaces in a few hours. The departing albatross sat motionless upon a high rock, at the end of the bay of Christmas Harbour, looking at the waves as they dashed violently against the beach.

Suddenly, the bird rose with a great sweep into the air, its claws folded beneath it, its head stretched out like the prow of a ship, uttering its shrill cry: a few moments later it was reduced to a black speck in the vast height and disappeared behind the misty curtain of the south.

CHAPTER II.

THE SCHOONER *HALBRANE.*

THE *Halbrane* was a schooner of three hundred tons, and a fast sailer. On board there was a captain, a mate, or lieutenant, a boatswain, a cook, and eight sailors; in all twelve men, a sufficient number to work the ship. Solidly built, copper-bottomed, very manageable, well suited for navigation between the fortieth and sixtieth parallels of south latitude, the *Halbrane* was a credit to the ship-yards of Birkenhead.

All this I learned from Atkins, who adorned his narrative with praise and admiration of its theme. Captain Len Guy, of Liverpool, was three-fifths owner of the vessel, which he had commanded for nearly six years. He traded in the southern seas of Africa and America, going from one group of islands to another and from continent to continent. His ship's company was but a dozen men, it is true, but she was used for the purposes of trade only; he would have required a more numerous crew, and all the implements, for taking seals and other amphibia. The *Halbrane* was not defenceless, however; on the contrary, she was heavily armed, and this was well, for those southern seas were not too safe; they were frequented at that period by pirates, and on approaching the isles the *Halbrane* was put into a condition to resist attack. Besides, the men always slept with one eye open.

One morning—it was the 27th of August—I was roused out of my bed by the rough voice of the innkeeper and the tremendous thumps he gave my door.

"Mr. Jeorling, are you awake?"

"Of course I am, Atkins. How should I be otherwise, with all that noise going on? What's up?"

"A ship six miles out in the offing, to the nor'east, steering for Christmas!"

"Will it be the *Halbrane?*"

"We shall know that in a short time, Mr. Jeorling. At any rate it is the first boat of the year, and we must give it a welcome."

I dressed hurriedly and joined Atkins on the quay, where I found him in the midst of a group engaged in eager discussion. Atkins was indisputably the most considerable and considered man in the archipelago—consequently he secured the best listeners. The matter in dispute was whether the schooner in sight was or was not the *Halbrane*. The majority maintained that she was not, but Atkins was positive she was, although on this occasion he had only two backers.

The dispute was carried on with warmth, the host of the Green Cormorant defending his view, and the dissentients maintaining that the fast-approaching schooner was either English or American, until she was near enough to hoist her flag and the Union Jack went fluttering up into the sky. Shortly after the *Halbrane* lay at anchor in the middle of Christmas Harbour.

The captain of the *Halbrane*, who received the demonstrative greeting of Atkins very coolly, it seemed to me,

The approach of the *Halbrane*.

was about forty-five, red-faced, and solidly built, like his schooner ; his head was large, his hair was already turning grey, his black eyes shone like coals of fire under his thick eyebrows, and his strong white teeth were set like rocks in his powerful jaws ; his chin was lengthened by a coarse red beard, and his arms and legs were strong and firm. Such was Captain Len Guy, and he impressed me with the notion that he was rather impassive than hard, a shut-up sort of person, whose secrets it would not be easy to get at. I was told the very same day that my impression was correct, by a person who was better informed than Atkins, although the latter pretended to great intimacy with the captain. The truth was that nobody had penetrated that reserved nature.

I may as well say at once that the person to whom I have alluded was the boatswain of the *Halbrane*, a man named Hurliguerly, who came from the Isle of Wight. This person was about forty-four, short, stout, strong, and bow-legged ; his arms stuck out from his body, his head was set like a ball on a bull neck, his chest was broad enough to hold two pairs of lungs (and he seemed to want a double supply, for he was always puffing, blowing, and talking); he had droll roguish eyes, with a network of wrinkles under them. A noteworthy detail was an ear-ring, one only, which hung from the lobe of his left ear. What a contrast to the captain of the schooner, and how did two such dissimilar beings contrive to get on together? They had contrived it, somehow, for they had been at sea in each other's company for fifteen years, first in the brig *Power*, which had been replaced by the schooner *Halbrane*, six years before the beginning of this story.

Atkins had told Hurliguerly on his arrival that I would take passage on the *Halbrane*, if Captain Len Guy consented to my doing so, and the boatswain presented himself on the following morning without any notice or introduction. He already knew my name, and he accosted me as follows:

"Mr. Jeorling, I salute you."

"I salute you in my turn, my friend. What do you want?"

"To offer you my services."

"On what account?"

"On account of your intention to embark on the *Halbrane*."

"Who are you?"

"I am Hurliguerly, the boatswain of the *Halbrane*, and besides, I am the faithful companion of Captain Len Guy, who will listen to me willingly, although he has the reputation of not listening to anybody."

"Well, my friend, let us talk, if you are not required on board just now."

"I have two hours before me, Mr. Jeorling. Besides, there's very little to be done to-day. If you are free, as I am—"

He waved his hand towards the port.

"Cannot we talk very well here?" I observed.

"Talk, Mr. Jeorling, talk standing up, and our throats dry, when it is so easy to sit down in a corner of the Green Cormorant in front of two glasses of whisky."

"I don't drink."

"Well, then, I'll drink for both of us. Oh! don't imagine you are dealing with a sot! No! never more than is good for me, but always as much!"

I followed the man to the tavern, and while Atkins was busy on the deck of the ship, discussing the prices of his purchases and sales, we took our places in the eating-room of his inn. And first I said to Hurliguerly: "It was on Atkins that I reckoned to introduce me to Captain Len Guy, for he knows him very intimately, if I am not mistaken."

"Pooh! Atkins is a good sort, and the captain has an esteem for him. But he can't do what I can. Let me act for you, Mr. Jeorling."

"Is it so difficult a matter to arrange, boatswain, and is there not a cabin on board the *Halbrane?* The smallest would do for me, and I will pay—"

"All right, Mr. Jeorling! There is a cabin, which has never been used, and since you don't mind putting your hand in your pocket if required—however—between ourselves—it will take somebody sharper than you think, and who isn't good old Atkins, to induce Captain Len Guy to take a passenger. Yes, indeed, it will take all the smartness of the good fellow who now drinks to your health, regretting that you don't return the compliment!"

What a wink it was that accompanied this sentiment! And then the man took a short black pipe out of the pocket of his jacket, and smoked like a steamer in full blast.

"Mr. Hurliguerly?" said I.

"Mr. Jeorling."

"Why does your captain object to taking me on his ship?"

"Because he does not intend to take anybody on board his ship. He never has taken a passenger."

"But, for what reason, I ask you."

"Oh! because he wants to go where he likes, to turn about if he pleases and go the other way without accounting for his motives to anybody. He never leaves these southern seas, Mr. Jeorling; we have been going these many years between Australia on the east and America on the west; from Hobart Town to the Kerguelens, to Tristan d'Acunha, to the Falklands, only taking time anywhere to sell our cargo, and sometimes dipping down into the Antarctic Sea. Under these circumstances, you understand, a passenger might be troublesome, and besides, who would care to embark on the *Halbrane?* she does not like to flout the breezes, and goes wherever the wind drives her."

"The *Halbrane* positively leaves the Kerguelens in four days?"

"Certainly."

"And this time she will sail westward for Tristan l'Acunha?"

"Probably."

"Well, then, that probability will be enough for me, and since you offer me your services, get Captain Len Guy to accept me as a passenger."

"It's as good as done."

"All right, Hurliguerly, and you shall have no reason to repent of it."

"Eh! Mr. Jeorling," replied this singular mariner, shaking his head as though he had just come out of the sea, "I have never repented of anything, and I know well that I shall not repent of doing you a service. Now, if you will allow me, I shall take leave of you, without waiting for Atkins to return, and get on board."

With this, Hurliguerly swallowed his last glass of

whisky at a gulp—I thought the glass would have gone down with the liquor—bestowed a patronizing smile on me, and departed.

An hour later, I met the innkeeper on the port, and told him what had occurred.

"Ah! that Hurliguerly!" said he, "always the old story. If you were to believe him, Captain Len Guy wouldn't blow his nose without consulting him. He's a queer fellow, Mr. Jeorling, not bad, not stupid, but a great hand at getting hold of dollars or guineas! If you fall into his hands, mind your purse, button up your pocket, and don't let yourself be done."

"Thanks for your advice, Atkins. Tell me, you have been talking with Captain Len Guy; have you spoken about me?"

"Not yet, Mr. Jeorling. There's plenty of time. The *Halbrane* has only just arrived, and—"

"Yes, yes, I know. But you understand that I want to be certain as soon as possible."

"There's nothing to fear. The matter will be all right. Besides, you would not be at a loss in any case. When the fishing season comes, there will be more ships in Christmas Harbour than there are houses around the Green Cormorant. Rely on me. I undertake your getting a passage."

Now, these were fair words, but, just as in the case of Hurliguerly, there was nothing in them. So, notwithstanding the fine promises of the two, I resolved to address myself personally to Len Guy, hard to get at though he might be, so soon as I should meet him alone.

The next day, in the afternoon, I saw him on the quay,

and approached him. It was plain that he would have preferred to avoid me. It was impossible that Captain Len Guy, who knew every dweller in the place, should not have known that I was a stranger, even supposing that neither of my would-be patrons had mentioned me to him.

His attitude could only signify one of two things—either my proposal had been communicated to him, and he did not intend to accede to it; or neither Hurliguerly nor Atkins had spoken to him since the previous day. In the latter case, if he held aloof from me, it was because of his morose nature; it was because he did not choose to enter into conversation with a stranger.

At the moment when I was about to accost him, the *Halbrane's* lieutenant rejoined his captain, and the latter availed himself of the opportunity to avoid me. He made a sign to the officer to follow him, and the two walked away at a rapid pace.

"This is serious," said I to myself. "It looks as though I shall find it difficult to gain my point. But, after all t only means delay. To-morrow morning I will go on board the *Halbrane*. Whether he likes it or whether he doesn't, this Len Guy will have to hear what I've got to say, and to give me an answer, yes or no!"

Besides, the captain of the *Halbrane* might come at dinner-time to the Green Cormorant, where the ship's people usually took their meals when ashore. So I waited, and did not go to dinner until late. I was disappointed, however, for neither the captain nor anyone belonging to the ship patronized the Green Cormorant that day. I had to dine alone, exactly as I had been doing every day for two months.

After dinner, about half-past seven, when it was dark, I went out to walk on the port, keeping on the side of the houses. The quay was quite deserted; not a man of the *Halbrane's* crew was ashore. The ship's boats were alongside, rocking gently on the rising tide. I remained there until nine, walking up and down the edge in full view of the *Halbrane*. Gradually the mass of the ship became indistinct, there was no movement and no light. I returned to the inn, where I found Atkins smoking his pipe near the door.

"Atkins," said I, "it seems that Captain Len Guy does not care to come to your inn very often?"

"He sometimes comes on Sunday, and this is Saturday, Mr. Jeorling."

"You have not spoken to him?"

"Yes, I have."

Atkins was visibly embarrassed.

"You have informed him that a person of your acquaintance wished to take passage on the *Halbrane*?"

"Yes."

"What was his answer?"

"Not what either you or I would have wished, Mr. Jeorling."

"He refuses?"

"Well, yes, I suppose it was refusing; what he said was: 'My ship is not intended to carry passengers. I never have taken any, and I never intend to do so.'"

CHAPTER III.

CAPTAIN LEN GUY.

I SLEPT ill. Again and again I "dreamed that I was dreaming." Now—this is an observation made by Edgar Poe—when one suspects that one is dreaming, the waking comes almost instantly. I woke then, and every time in a very bad humour with Captain Len Guy. The idea of leaving the Kerguelens on the *Halbrane* had full possession of me, and I grew more and more angry with her disobliging captain. In fact, I passed the night in a fever of indignation, and only recovered my temper with daylight. Nevertheless I was determined to have an explanation with Captain Len Guy about his detestable conduct. Perhaps I should fail to get anything out of that human hedgehog, but at least I should have given him a piece of my mind.

I went out at eight o'clock in the morning. The weather was abominable. Rain, mixed with snow, a storm coming over the mountains at the back of the bay from the west, clouds scurrying down from the lower zones, an avalanche of wind and water. It was not likely that Captain Len Guy had come ashore merely to enjoy such a wetting and blowing.

No one on the quay; of course not. As for my getting on board the *Halbrane*, that could not be done without hailing one of her boats, and the boatswain would not venture to send it for me.

"Besides," I reflected, "on his quarter-deck the captain is at home, and neutral ground is better for what I want to say to him, if he persists in his unjustifiable refusal. I will watch him this time, and if his boat touches the quay, he shall not succeed in avoiding me."

I returned to the Green Cormorant, and took up my post behind the window panes, which were dimmed by the hissing rain. There I waited, nervous, impatient, and in a state of growing irritation. Two hours wore away thus. Then, with the instability of the winds in the Kerguelens, the weather became calm before I did. I opened my window, and at the same moment a sailor stepped into one of the boats of the *Halbrane* and laid hold of a pair of oars, while a second man seated himself in the back, but without taking the tiller ropes. The boat touched the landing-place and Captain Len Guy stepped on shore.

In a few seconds I was out of the inn, and confronted him.

"Sir," said I in a cold hard tone.

Captain Len Guy looked at me steadily, and I was struck by the sadness of his eyes, which were as black as ink. Then in a very low voice he asked:

"You are a stranger?"

"A stranger at the Kerguelens? Yes."

"Of English nationality?"

"No. American."

He saluted me, and I returned the curt gesture.

"Sir," I resumed, "I believe Mr. Atkins of the Green Cormorant has spoken to you respecting a proposal of mine. That proposal, it seems to me, deserved a favourable reception on the part of a—"

"The proposal to take passage on my ship?" interposed Captain Len Guy.

"Precisely."

"I regret, sir, I regret that I could not agree to your request."

"Will you tell me why?"

"Because I am not in the habit of taking passengers. That is the first reason."

"And the second, captain?"

"Because the route of the *Halbrane* is never settled beforehand. She starts for one port and goes to another, just as I find it to my advantage. You must know that I am not in the service of a shipowner. My share in the schooner is considerable, and I have no one but myself to consult in respect to her."

"Then it entirely depends on you to give me a passage?"

"That is so, but I can only answer you by a refusal —to my extreme regret."

"Perhaps you will change your mind, captain, when you know that I care very little what the destination of your schooner may be. It is not unreasonable to suppose that she will go somewhere—"

"Somewhere indeed." I fancied that Captain Len Guy threw a long look towards the southern horizon.

"To go here or to go there is almost a matter of indifference to me. What I desired above all was to get away from Kerguelen at the first opportunity that should offer."

Captain Len Guy made me no answer; he remained in silent thought, but did not endeavour to slip away from me.

"You are doing me the honour to listen to me?" I asked him sharply.

"Yes, sir."

"I will then add that, if I am not mistaken, and if the route of your ship has not been altered, it was your intention to leave Christmas Harbour for Tristan d'Acunha."

"Perhaps for Tristan d'Acunha, perhaps for the Cape, perhaps for the Falklands, perhaps for elsewhere."

"Well, then, Captain Guy, it is precisely elsewhere that I want to go," I replied ironically, and trying hard to control my irritation.

Then a singular change took place in the demeanour of Captain Len Guy. His voice became more sharp and harsh. In very plain words he made me understand that it was quite useless to insist, that our interview had already lasted too long, that time pressed, and he had business at the port; in short that we had said all that we could have to say to each other.

I had put out my arm to detain him—to seize him would be a more correct term—and the conversation, ill begun, seemed likely to end still more ill, when this odd person turned towards me and said in a milder tone,—

"Pray understand, sir, that I am very sorry to be unable to do what you ask, and to appear disobliging to an American. But I could not act otherwise. In the course of the voyage of the *Halbrane* some unforeseen incident might occur to make the presence of a passenger inconvenient—even one so accommodating as yourself. Thus I might expose myself to the risk of being unable to profit by the chances which I seek."

"I have told you, captain, and I repeat it, that although

my intention is to return to America and to Connecticut, I don't care whether I get there in three months or in six, or by what route; it's all the same to me, and even were your schooner to take me to the Antarctic seas—"

"The Antarctic seas!" exclaimed Captain Len Guy, with a question in his tone. And his look searched my thoughts with the keenness of a dagger.

"Why do you speak of the Antarctic seas?" he asked, taking my hand.

"Well, just as I might have spoken of the 'Hyperborean seas' from whence an Irish poet has made Sebastian Cabot address some lovely verses to his 'Lady.'[1] I spoke of the South Pole as I might have spoken of the North."

Captain Len Guy did not answer, and I thought I saw tears glisten in his eyes. Then, as though he would escape from some harrowing recollection which my words had evoked, he said,—

"Who would venture to seek the South Pole?"

"It would be difficult to reach, and the experiments would be of no practical use," I replied. "Nevertheless there are men sufficiently adventurous to embark in such an enterprise."

"Yes—adventurous is the word!" muttered the captain.

"And now," I resumed, "the United States is again making an attempt with Wilkes's fleet, the *Vancouver*, the *Peacock*, the *Flying Fish*, and others."

"The United States, Mr. Jeorling? Do you mean to say that an expedition has been sent by the Federal Government to the Antarctic seas?"

"The fact is certain, and last year, before I left America,

[1] Thomas D'Arcy McGee.

I learned that the vessels had sailed. That was a year ago, and it is very possible that Wilkes has gone farther than any of the preceding explorers."

Captain Len Guy had relapsed into silence, and came out of his inexplicable musing only to say abruptly,—

"You come from Connecticut, sir?"

"From Connecticut."

"And more specially?"

"From Providence."

"Do you know Nantucket Island?"

"I have visited it several times."

"You know, I think," said the captain, looking straight into my eyes, "that Nantucket Island was the birth-place of Arthur Gordon Pym, the hero of your famous romance-writer Edgar Poe."

"Yes. I remember that Poe's romance starts from Nantucket."

"Romance, you say? That was the word you used?"

"Undoubtedly, captain."

"Yes, and that is what everybody says! But, pardon me, I cannot stay any longer. I regret that I cannot alter my mind with respect to your proposal. But, at any rate, you will only have a few days to wait. The season is about to open. Trading ships and whalers will put in at Christmas Harbour, and you will be able to make a choice, with the certainty of going to the port you want to reach. I am very sorry, sir, and I salute you."

With these words Captain Len Guy walked quickly away, and the interview ended differently from what I had expected, that is to say in formal, although polite, fashion.

As there is no use in contending with the impossible, I

gave up the hope of a passage on the *Halbrane*, but continued to feel angry with her intractable captain. And why should I not confess that my curiosity was aroused? I felt that there was something mysterious about this sullen mariner, and I should have liked to find out what it was.

That day, Atkins wanted to know whether Captain Len Guy had made himself less disagreeable. I had to acknowledge that I had been no more fortunate in my negotiations than my host himself, and the avowal surprised him not a little. He could not understand the captain's obstinate refusal. And—a fact which touched him more nearly—the Green Cormorant had not been visited by either Len Guy or his crew since the arrival of the *Halbrane*. The men were evidently acting upon orders. So far as Hurliguerly was concerned, it was easy to understand that after his imprudent advance he did not care to keep up useless relations with me. I knew not whether he had attempted to shake the resolution of his chief; but I was certain of one thing; if he had made any such effort it had failed.

During the three following days, the 10th, 11th, and 12th of August, the work of repairing and re-victualling the schooner went on briskly; but all this was done with regularity, and without such noise and quarrelling as seamen at anchor usually indulge in. The *Halbrane* was evidently well commanded, her crew well kept in hand, discipline strictly maintained.

The schooner was to sail on the 15th of August, and on the eve of that day I had no reason to think that Captain Len Guy had repented him of his categorical refusal. Indeed, I had made up my mind to the disappointment, and had no longer any angry feeling about it. When Captain Len Guy and myself met on the quay, we took no notice of each other; nevertheless, I fancied there was some hesitation in his manner; as though he would have liked to speak to me. He did not do so, however, and I was not disposed to seek a further explanation.

At seven o'clock in the evening of the 14th of August, the island being already wrapped in darkness, I was walking on the port after I had dined, walking briskly too, for it was cold, although dry weather. The sky was studded with stars and the air was very keen. I could not stay out long, and was returning to mine inn, when a man crossed my path, paused, came back, and stopped in front of me. It was the captain of the *Halbrane*.

"Mr. Jeorling," he began, "the *Halbrane* sails to-morrow morning, with the ebb tide."

"What is the good of telling me that," I replied, "since you refuse—"

"Sir, I have thought over it, and if you have not changed your mind, come on board at seven o'clock."

"Really, captain," I replied, "I did not expect this relenting on your part."

"I repeat that I have thought over it, and I add that the *Halbrane* shall proceed direct to Tristan d'Acunha. That will suit you, I suppose?"

"To perfection, captain. To-morrow morning, at seven o'clock, I shall be on board."

"Your cabin is prepared."

"The cost of the voyage—"

"We can settle that another time," answered the captain, "and to your satisfaction. Until to-morrow, then—"

"Until to-morrow."

I stretched out my arm, to shake hands with him upon our bargain. Perhaps he did not perceive my movement in the darkness, at all events he made no response to it, but walked rapidly away and got into his boat.

I was greatly surprised, and so was Atkins, when I found him in the eating-room of the Green Cormorant and told him what had occurred. His comment upon it was characteristic.

"This queer captain," he said, "is as full of whims as a spoilt child! It is to be hoped he will not change his mind again at the last moment."

The next morning at daybreak I bade adieu to the Green Cormorant, and went down to the port, with my kind-hearted host, who insisted on accompanying me to the ship, partly in order to make his mind easy respecting the sincerity of the captain's repentance, and partly that he might take leave of him, and also of Hurliguerly. A boat was waiting at the quay, and we reached the ship in a few minutes.

The first person whom I met on the deck was Hurliguerly; he gave me a look of triumph, which said as plainly as speech: "Ha! you see now. Our hard-to-manage captain has given in at last. And to whom do you owe this, but to the good boatswain who did his best for you, and did not boast overmuch of his influence?"

Was this the truth? I had strong reasons for doubting it. After all, what did it matter?

Captain Len Guy came on deck immediately after my arrival; this was not surprising, except for the fact that he did not appear to remark my presence.

Going aboard the *Halbrane*.

Atkins then approached the captain and said in a pleasant tone,—

"We shall meet next year!"

"If it please God, Atkins."

They shook hands. Then the boatswain took a hearty leave of the innkeeper, and was rowed back to the quay.

Before dark the white summits of Table Mount and Havergal, which rise, the former to two, the other to three thousand feet above the level of the sea, had disappeared from our view.

CHAPTER IV.

FROM THE KERGUELEN ISLES TO PRINCE EDWARD ISLAND.

NEVER did a voyage begin more prosperously, or a passenger start in better spirits. The interior of the *Halbrane* corresponded with its exterior. Nothing could exceed the perfect order, the Dutch cleanliness of the vessel. The captain's cabin, and that of the lieutenant, one on the port, the other on the starboard side, were fitted up with a narrow berth, a cupboard anything but capacious, an arm-chair, a fixed table, a lamp hung from the ceiling, various nautical instruments, a barometer, a thermometer, a chronometer, and a sextant in its oaken box. One of the two other cabins was prepared to receive me. It was eight feet in length, five in breadth. I was accustomed to the exigencies of sea life, and could do with its narrow proportions, also with its furniture—a table, a cupboard, a cane-bottomed arm-chair, a washing-stand on an iron pedestal, and a berth to which a less accommodating passenger would doubtless have objected. The passage would be a short one, however, so I took possession of that cabin, which I was to occupy for only four, or at the worst five weeks, with entire content.

The eight men who composed the crew were named

respectively Martin Holt, sailing-master; Hardy, Rogers, Drap, Francis, Gratian, Burg, and Stern—sailors all between twenty-five and thirty-five years old—all Englishmen, well trained, and remarkably well disciplined by a hand of iron.

Let me set it down here at the beginning, the exceptionally able man whom they all obeyed at a word, a gesture, was not the captain of the *Halbrane*; that man was the second officer, James West, who was then thirty-two years of age.

James West was born on the sea, and had passed his childhood on board a lighter belonging to his father, and on which the whole family lived. All his life he had breathed the salt air of the English Channel, the Atlantic, or the Pacific. He never went ashore except for the needs of his service, whether of the State or of trade. If he had to leave one ship for another he merely shifted his canvas bag to the latter, from which he stirred no more. When he was not sailing in reality he was sailing in imagination. After having been ship's boy, novice, sailor, he became quartermaster, master, and finally lieutenant of the *Halbrane*, and he had already served for ten years as second in command under Captain Len Guy.

James West was not even ambitious of a higher rise; he did not want to make a fortune; he did not concern himself with the buying or selling of cargoes; but everything connected with that admirable instrument a sailing ship, James West understood to perfection.

The personal appearance of the lieutenant was as follows: middle height, slightly built, all nerves and muscles, strong limbs as agile as those of a gymnast, the true sailor's "look," but of very unusual far-sightedness and surprising penetration, sunburnt face, hair thick and short, beardless cheeks and chin, regular features, the whole expression denoting energy, courage, and physical strength at their utmost tension.

James West spoke but rarely—only when he was questioned. He gave his orders in a clear voice, not repeating them, but so as to be heard at once, and he was understood. I call attention to this typical officer of the Merchant Marine, who was devoted body and soul to Captain Len Guy as to the schooner *Halbrane*. He seemed to be one of the essential organs of his ship, and if the *Halbrane* had a heart it was in James West's breast that it beat.

There is but one more person to be mentioned; the ship's cook—a negro from the African coast named Endicott, thirty years of age, who had held that post for eight years. The boatswain and he were great friends, and indulged in frequent talks.

Life on board was very regular, very simple, and its monotony was not without a certain charm. Sailing is repose in movement, a rocking in a dream, and I did not dislike my isolation. Of course I should have liked to find out why Captain Len Guy had changed his mind with respect to me; but how was this to be done? To question the lieutenant would have been loss of time. Besides, was he in possession of the secrets of his chief? It was no part of his business to be so, and I had observed that he did not occupy himself with anything outside of it. Not ten words were exchanged between him and me during the two meals which we took in common daily. I must acknowledge, however, that I frequently caught the captain's eyes fixed upon me, as though he longed to question me, as though he had something to learn from me, whereas it was I, on the contrary, who had something to learn from him. But we were both silent.

Had I felt the need of talking to somebody very strongly, I might have resorted to the boatswain, who was always disposed to chatter; but what had he to say that could interest me? He never failed to bid me good morning and good evening in most prolix fashion, but beyond these courtesies I did not feel disposed to go.

The good weather lasted, and on the 18th of August, in the afternoon, the look-out discerned the mountains of the Crozet group. The next day we passed Possession Island, which is inhabited only in the fishing season. At this period the only dwellers there are flocks of penguins, and the birds which whalers call "white pigeons."

The approach to land is always interesting at sea. It occurred to me that Captain Len Guy might take this opportunity of speaking to his passenger; but he did not.

We should see land, that is to say the peaks of Marion and Prince Edward Islands, before arriving at Tristan d'Acunha, but it was there the *Halbrane* was to take in a fresh supply of water. I concluded therefore that the monotony of our voyage would continue unbroken to the end. But, on the morning of the 20th of August, to my extreme surprise, Captain Len Guy came on deck, approached me, and said, speaking very low,—

"Sir, I have something to say to you."

"I am ready to hear you, captain."

"I have not spoken until to-day, for I am naturally taciturn." Here he hesitated again, but after a pause, continued with an effort,—

"Mr. Jeorling, have you tried to discover my reason for changing my mind on the subject of your passage?"

"I have tried, but I have not succeeded, captain. Perhaps, as I am not a compatriot of yours, you—"

"It is precisely because you are an American that I decided in the end to offer you a passage on the *Halbrane*."

"Because I am an American?"

"Also, because you come from Connecticut."

"I don't understand."

"You will understand if I add that I thought it possible, since you belong to Connecticut, since you have visited Nantucket Island, that you might have known the family of Arthur Gordon Pym."

"The hero of Edgar Poe's romance?"

"The same. His narrative was founded upon the manuscript in which the details of that extraordinary and disastrous voyage across the Antarctic Sea was related."

I thought I must be dreaming when I heard Captain Len Guy's words. Edgar Poe's romance was nothing but a fiction, a work of imagination by the most brilliant of our American writers. And here was a sane man treating that fiction as a reality.

I could not answer him. I was asking myself what manner of man was this one with whom I had to deal.

"You have heard my question?" persisted the captain.

"Yes, yes, captain, certainly, but I am not sure that I quite understand."

"I will put it to you more plainly. I ask you whether in Connecticut you personally knew the Pym family who lived in Nantucket Island? Arthur Pym's father was one of the principal merchants there, he was a Navy contractor.

It was his son who embarked in the adventures which he related with his own lips to Edgar Poe—"

"Captain! Why, that story is due to the powerful imagination of our great poet. It is a pure invention."

"So, then, you don't believe it, Mr. Jeorling?" said the captain, shrugging his shoulders three times.

"Neither I nor any other person believes it, Captain Guy, and you are the first I have heard maintain that it was anything but a mere romance."

"Listen to me, then, Mr. Jeorling, for although this 'romance'—as you call it—appeared only last year, it is none the less a reality. Although eleven years have elapsed since the facts occurred, they are none the less true, and we still await the 'word' of an enigma which will perhaps never be solved."

Yes, he was mad; but by good fortune West was there to take his place as commander of the schooner. I had only to listen to him, and as I had read Poe's romance over and over again, I was curious to hear what the captain had to say about it.

"And now," he resumed in a sharper tone and with a shake in his voice which denoted a certain amount of nervous irritation, "it is possible that you did not know the Pym family, that you have never met them either at Providence or at Nantucket—"

"Or elsewhere."

"Just so! But don't commit yourself by asserting that the Pym family never existed, that Arthur Gordon is only a fictitious personage, and his voyage an imaginary one! Do you think any man, even your Edgar Poe, could have been capable of inventing, of creating—?"

The increasing vehemence of Captain Len Guy warned

me of the necessity of treating his monomania with respect, and accepting all he said without discussion.

"Now," he proceeded, "please to keep the facts which I am about to state clearly in your mind; there is no disputing about facts. You may deduce any results from them you like. I hope you will not make me regret that I consented to give you a passage on the *Halbrane*."

This was an effectual warning, so I made a sign of acquiescence. The matter promised to be curious. He went on,—

"When Edgar Poe's narrative appeared in 1838, I was at New York. I immediately started for Baltimore, where the writer's family lived; the grandfather had served as quarter-master-general during the War of Independence. You admit, I suppose, the existence of the Poe family, although you deny that of the Pym family?"

I said nothing, and the captain continued, with a dark glance at me,—

"I inquired into certain matters relating to Edgar Poe. His abode was pointed out to me and I called at the house. A first disappointment! He had left America, and I could not see him. Unfortunately, being unable to see Edgar Poe, I was unable to refer to Arthur Gordon Pym in the case. That bold pioneer of the Antarctic regions was dead! As the American poet had stated, at the close of the narrative of his adventures, Gordon's death had already been made known to the public by the daily press."

What Captain Len Guy said was true; but, in common with all the readers of the romance, I had taken this declaration for an artifice of the novelist. My notion was that, as he either could not or dared not wind up so extraordinary a work of imagination, Poe had given it to be understood that he had not received the last three chapters from Arthur Pym, whose life had ended under sudden and deplorable circumstances which Poe did not make known.

"Then," continued the captain, "Edgar Poe being absent, Arthur Pym being dead, I had only one thing to do; to find the man who had been the fellow-traveller of Arthur Pym, that Dirk Peters who had followed him to the very verge of the high latitudes, and whence they had both returned—how? This is not known. Did they come back in company? The narrative does not say, and there are obscure points in that part of it, as in many other places. However, Edgar Poe stated explicitly that Dirk Peters would be able to furnish information relating to the non-communicated chapters, and that he lived at Illinois. I set out at once for Illinois; I arrived at Springfield; I inquired for this man, a half-breed Indian. He lived in the hamlet of Vandalia; I went there, and met with a second disappointment. He was not there, or rather, Mr. Jeorling, he was *no longer* there. Some years before this Dirk Peters had left Illinois, and even the United States, to go—nobody knows where. But I have talked, at Vandalia, with people who had known him, with whom he lived, to whom he related his adventures, but did not explain the final issue. Of that he alone holds the secret."

What! This Dirk Peters had really existed? He still lived? I was on the point of letting myself be carried away by the statements of the captain of the *Halbrane!* Yes, another moment, and, in my turn, I should have made a fool of myself. This poor mad fellow imagined that he had gone to Illinois and seen people at Vandalia who had known Dirk Peters, and that the latter had disappeared No wonder, since he had never existed, save in the brain of the novelist!

Nevertheless I did not want to vex Len Guy, and perhaps drive him still more mad. Accordingly I appeared entirely convinced that he was speaking words of sober seriousness, even when he added,—

"You are aware that in the narrative mention is made by the captain of the schooner on which Arthur Pym had embarked, of a bottle containing a sealed letter, which was deposited at the foot of one of the Kerguelen peaks?"

"Yes, I recall the incident."

"Well, then, in one of my latest voyages I sought for the place where that bottle ought to be. I found it and the letter also. That letter stated that the captain and Arthur Pym intended to make every effort to reach the uttermost limits of the Antarctic Sea!"

"You found that bottle?"

"Yes!"

"And the letter?"

"Yes!"

I looked at Captain Len Guy. Like certain monomaniacs he had come to believe in his own inventions. I was on the point of saying to him, "Show me that letter," but I thought better of it. Was he not capable of having written the letter himself? And then I answered,—

"It is much to be regretted, captain, that you were unable to come across Dirk Peters at Vandalia! He would at least have informed you under what conditions he and Arthur Pym returned from so far. Recollect, now, in the last chapter but one they are both there. Their boat is in front of the thick curtain of white mist; it dashes into the gulf of the cataract just at the moment when a veiled human form rises. Then there is nothing more; nothing but two blank lines—"

"Decidedly, sir, it *is* much to be regretted that I could not lay my hand on Dirk Peters! It would have been interesting to learn what was the outcome of these adventures. But, to my mind, it would have been still more interesting to have ascertained the fate of the others."

"The others?" I exclaimed almost involuntarily. "Of whom do you speak?"

"Of the captain and crew of the English schooner which picked up Arthur Pym and Dirk Peters after the frightful shipwreck of the *Grampus*, and brought them across the Polar Sea to Tsalal Island—"

"Captain," said I, just as though I entertained no doubt of the authenticity of Edgar Poe's romance, "is it not the case that all these men perished, some in the attack on the schooner, the others by the infernal device of the natives of Tsalal?"

"Who can tell?" replied the captain in a voice hoarse from emotion. "Who can say but that some of the unfortunate creatures survived, and contrived to escape from the natives?"

"In any case," I replied, "it would be difficult to admit that those who had survived could still be living."

"And why?"

"Because the facts we are discussing are eleven years old."

"Sir," replied the captain, "since Arthur Pym and Dirk Peters were able to advance beyond Tsalal Island farther than the eighty-third parallel, since they found means of living in the midst of those Antarctic lands, why should not their companions, if they were not all killed by the natives, if they were so fortunate as to reach the neighbouring islands sighted during the voyage—why should not those unfortunate countrymen of mine have contrived to live there? Why should they not still be there, awaiting their deliverance?"

"Your pity leads you astray, captain," I replied. "It would be impossible."

"Impossible, sir! And if a fact, on indisputable evidence, appealed to the whole civilized world; if a material proof of the existence of these unhappy men, imprisoned at the ends of the earth, were furnished, who would venture to meet those who would fain go to their aid with the cry of 'Impossible!'"

Was it a sentiment of humanity, exaggerated to the point of madness, that had roused the interest of this strange man in those shipwrecked folk who never had suffered shipwreck, for the good reason that they never had existed?

Captain Len Guy approached me anew, laid his hand on my shoulder and whispered in my ear,—

"No, sir, no! the last word has not been said concerning the crew of the *Jane*."

Then he promptly withdrew.

The *Jane* was, in Edgar Poe's romance, the name of the ship which had rescued Arthur Pym and Dirk Peters from the wreck of the *Grampus*, and Captain Len Guy had now uttered it for the first time. It occurred to me then that Guy was the name of the captain of the *Jane*, an English ship; but what of that? The captain of the *Jane* never lived but in the imagination of the novelist, he and the skipper of the *Halbrane* have nothing in common except a name which is frequently to be found in England. But, on thinking of the similarity, it struck me that the poor captain's brain had been turned by this very thing. He had conceived the notion that he was of kin to the unfortunate captain of the *Jane!* And this had brought him to his present state, this was the source of his passionate pity for the fate of the imaginary shipwrecked mariners!

It would have been interesting to discover whether James West was aware of the state of the case, whether his chief had ever talked to him of the follies he had revealed to me. But this was a delicate question, since it involved the mental condition of Captain Len Guy; and besides, any kind of conversation with the lieutenant was difficult. On the whole I thought it safer to restrain my curiosity. In a few days the schooner would reach Tristan d'Acunha, and I should part with her and her captain for good and all. Never, however, could I lose the recollection that I had actually met and sailed with a man who took the fictions of Edgar Poe's romance for sober fact. Never could I have looked for such an experience!

On the 22nd of August the outline of Prince Edward's Island was sighted, south latitude 46° 55′, and 37° 46′ east longitude. We were in sight of the island for twelve hours, and then it was lost in the evening mists.

On the following day the *Halbrane* headed in the direction of the north-west, towards the most northern parallel of the southern hemisphere which she had to attain in the course of that voyage.

CHAPTER V.

EDGAR POE'S ROMANCE.

In this chapter I have to give a brief summary of Edgar Poe's romance, which was published at Richmond under the title of

THE ADVENTURES OF ARTHUR GORDON PYM.

We shall see whether there was any room for doubt that the adventures of this hero of romance were imaginary. But indeed, among the multitude of Poe's readers, was there ever one, with the sole exception of Len Guy, who believed them to be real? The story is told by the principal personage. Arthur Pym states in the preface that on his return from his voyage to the Antarctic seas he met, among the Virginian gentlemen who took an interest in geographical discoveries, Edgar Poe, who was then editor of the *Southern Literary Messenger* at Richmond, and that he authorized the latter to publish the first part of his adventures in that journal "under the cloak of fiction." That portion having been favourably received, a volume containing the complete narrative was issued with the signature of Edgar Poe.

Arthur Gordon Pym was born at Nantucket, where he

attended the Bedford School until he was sixteen years old. Having left that school for Mr. Ronald's, he formed a friendship with one Augustus Barnard, the son of a ship's captain. This youth, who was eighteen, had already accompanied his father on a whaling expedition in the southern seas, and his yarns concerning that maritime adventure fired the imagination of Arthur Pym. Thus it was that the association of these youths gave rise to Pym's irresistible vocation to adventurous voyaging, and to the instinct that especially attracted him towards the high zones of the Antarctic region. The first exploit of Augustus Barnard and Arthur Pym was an excursion on board a little sloop, the *Ariel*, a two-decked boat which belonged to the Pyms. One evening the two youths, both being very tipsy, embarked secretly, in cold October weather, and boldly set sail in a strong breeze from the south-west. The *Ariel*, aided by the ebb tide, had already lost sight of land when a violent storm arose. The imprudent young fellows were still intoxicated. No one was at the helm, not a reef was in the sail. The masts were carried away by the furious gusts, and the wreck was driven helplessly before the wind. Then came a great ship which passed over the *Ariel* as the *Ariel* would have passed over a floating feather.

Arthur Pym gives the fullest details of the rescue of his companion and himself after this collision, under conditions of extreme difficulty. At length, thanks to the second officer of the *Penguin*, from New London, which arrived on the scene of the catastrophe, the comrades were picked up, with life all but extinct, and taken back to Nantucket.

This adventure, to which I cannot deny an appearance of veracity, was an ingenious preparation for the chapters that were to follow, and indeed, up to the day on which Pym penetrates into the polar circle, the narrative might conceivably be regarded as authentic. But, beyond the polar circle, above the austral icebergs, it is quite another thing, and, if the author's work be not one of pure imagination, I am—well, of any other nationality than my own. Let us get on.

Their first adventure had not cooled the two youths, and eight months after the affair of the *Ariel*—June, 1827—the brig *Grampus* was fitted out by the house of Lloyd and Vredenburg for whaling in the southern seas. This brig was an old, ill-repaired craft, and Mr. Barnard, the father of Augustus, was its skipper. His son, who was to accompany him on the voyage, strongly urged Arthur to go with him, and the latter would have asked nothing better, but he knew that his family, and especially his mother, would never consent to let him go.

This obstacle, however, could not stop a youth not much given to submit to the wishes of his parents. His head was full of the entreaties and persuasion of his companion, and he determined to embark secretly on the *Grampus*, for Mr. Barnard would not have authorized him to defy the prohibition of his family. He announced that he had been invited to pass a few days with a friend at New Bedford, took leave of his parents and left his home. Forty-eight hours before the brig was to sail, he slipped on board unperceived, and got into a hiding-place which had been prepared for him unknown alike to Mr. Barnard and the crew.

The cabin occupied by Augustus communicated by a trap-door with the hold of the *Grampus*, which was crowded with barrels, bales, and the innumerable components of a cargo. Through the trap-door Arthur Pym reached his hiding-place, which was a huge wooden chest with a sliding side to it. This chest contained a mattress, blankets, a jar of water, ship's biscuit, smoked sausage, a roast quarter of mutton, a few bottles of cordials and liqueurs, and also writing-materials. Arthur Pym, supplied with a lantern, candles, and tinder, remained three days and nights in his retreat. Augustus Barnard had not been able to visit him until just before the *Grampus* set sail.

An hour later, Arthur Pym began to feel the rolling and pitching of the brig. He was very uncomfortable in the chest, so he got out of it, and in the dark, while holding on by a rope which was stretched across the hold to the trap of his friend's cabin, he was violently sea-sick in the midst of the chaos. Then he crept back into his chest, ate, and fell asleep.

Several days elapsed without the reappearance of Augustus Barnard. Either he had not been able to get down into the hold again, or he had not ventured to do so, fearing to betray the presence of Arthur Pym, and thinking the moment for confessing everything to his father had not yet come.

Arthur Pym, meanwhile, was beginning to suffer from the hot and vitiated atmosphere of the hold. Terrible nightmares troubled his sleep. He was conscious of raving, and in vain sought some place amid the mass of cargo where he might breathe a little more easily. In one of these fits of delirium he imagined that he was gripped in the claws of an African lion,[1] and in a paroxysm of terror he was

[1] The American "lion" is only a small species of puma, and not formidable enough to terrify a Nantucket youth.

about to betray himself by screaming, when he lost consciousness.

The fact is that he was not dreaming at all. It was not a lion that Arthur Pym felt crouching upon his chest, it was his own dog, Tiger, a young Newfoundland. The animal had been smuggled on board by Augustus Barnard unperceived by anybody—(this, at least, is an unlikely occurrence). At the moment of Arthur's coming out of his swoon the faithful Tiger was licking his face and hands with lavish affection.

Now the prisoner had a companion. Unfortunately, the said companion had drunk the contents of the water jar while Arthur was unconscious, and when Arthur Pym felt thirsty, he discovered that there was " not a drop to drink ! " His lantern had gone out during his prolonged faint ; he could not find the candles and the tinder-box, and he then resolved to rejoin Augustus Barnard at all hazards. He came out of the chest, and although faint from inanition and trembling with weakness, he felt his way in the direction of the trap-door by means of the rope. But, while he was approaching, one of the bales of cargo, shifted by the rolling of the ship, fell down and blocked up the passage. With immense but quite useless exertion he contrived to get over this obstacle, but when he reached the trap-door under Augustus Barnard's cabin he failed to raise it, and on slipping the blade of his knife through one of the joints he found that a heavy mass of iron was placed upon the trap, as though it were intended to condemn him beyond hope. He had to renounce his attempt and drag himself back towards the chest, on which he fell, exhausted, while Tiger covered him with caresses.

The master and the dog were desperately thirsty, and when Arthur stretched out his hand, he found Tiger lying on his back, with his paws up and his hair on end. He then felt Tiger all over, and his hand encountered a string passed round the dog's body. A strip of paper was fastened to the string under his left shoulder.

Arthur Pym had reached the last stage of weakness. Intelligence was almost extinct. However, after several fruitless attempts to procure a light, he succeeded in rubbing the paper with a little phosphorus—(the details given in Edgar Poe's narrative are curiously minute at this point)—and then by the glimmer that lasted less than a second he discerned just seven words at the end of a sentence. Terrifying words these were: *blood—remain hidden—life depends on it.*

What did these words mean? Let us consider the situation of Arthur Pym, at the bottom of the ship's hold, between the boards of a chest, without light, without water, with only ardent liquor to quench his thirst! And this warning to remain hidden, preceded by the word "blood"—that supreme word, king of words, so full of mystery, of suffering, of terror! Had there been strife on board the *Grampus?* Had the brig been attacked by pirates? Had the crew mutinied? How long had this state of things lasted?

It might be thought that the marvellous poet had exhausted the resources of his imagination in the terror of such a situation; but it was not so. There is more to come!

Arthur Pym lay stretched upon his mattress, incapable of thought, in a sort of lethargy; suddenly he became aware of a singular sound, a kind of continuous whistling breathing. It was Tiger, panting, Tiger with eyes that glared in the midst of the darkness, Tiger with gnashing teeth—Tiger gone mad. Another moment and the dog had sprung upon Arthur Pym, who, wound up to the highest pitch of horror, recovered sufficient strength to ward off his fangs, and wrapping around him a blanket which Tiger had torn with his white teeth, he slipped out of the chest, and shut the sliding side upon the snapping and struggling brute.

Arthur Pym contrived to slip through the stowage of the hold, but his head swam, and, falling against a bale, he let his knife drop from his hand.

Just as he felt himself breathing his last sigh he heard his name pronounced, and a bottle of water was held to his lips. He swallowed the whole of its contents, and experienced the most exquisite of pleasures.

A few minutes later, Augustus Barnard, seated with his comrade in a corner of the hold, told him all that had occurred on board the brig.

Up to this point, I repeat, the story is admissible, but we have not yet come to the events which "surpass all probability by their marvellousness."

The crew of the *Grampus* numbered thirty-six men, including the Barnards, father and son. After the brig had put to sea on the 20th of June, Augustus Barnard had made several attempts to rejoin Arthur Pym in his hiding-place, but in vain. On the third day a mutiny broke out on board, headed by the ship's cook, a negro like our Endicott; but he, let me say at once, would never have thought of heading a mutiny.

Numerous incidents are related in the romance—the massacre of most of the sailors who remained faithful to

Captain Barnard, then the turning adrift of the captain and four of those men in a small whaler's boat when the ship was abreast of the Bermudas. These unfortunate persons were never heard of again.

Augustus Barnard would not have been spared, but for the intervention of the sailing-master of the *Grampus*. This sailing-master was a half-breed named Dirk Peters, and was the person whom Captain Len Guy had gone to look for in Illinois!

The *Grampus* then took a south-east course under the command of the mate, who intended to pursue the occupation of piracy in the southern seas.

These events having taken place, Augustus Barnard would again have joined Arthur Pym, but he had been shut up in the forecastle in irons, and told by the ship's cook that he would not be allowed to come out until "the brig should be no longer a brig." Nevertheless, a few days afterwards, Augustus contrived to get rid of his fetters, to cut through the thin partition between him and the hold, and, followed by Tiger, he tried to reach his friend's hiding-place. He could not succeed, but the dog had scented Arthur Pym, and this suggested to Augustus the idea of fastening a note to Tiger's neck bearing the words:

"I scrawl this with blood—remain hidden—your life depends on it—"

This note, as we have already learned, Arthur Pym had received. Just as he had arrived at the last extremity of distress his friend reached him.

Augustus added that discord reigned among the mutineers. Some wanted to take the *Grampus* towards the Cape Verde Islands; others, and Dirk Peters was of this number, were bent on sailing to the Pacific Isles.

Tiger was not mad. He was only suffering from terrible thirst, and soon recovered when it was relieved.

The cargo of the *Grampus* was so badly stowed away that Arthur Pym was in constant danger from the shifting of the bales, and Augustus, at all risks, helped him to remove to a corner of the 'tween decks.

The half-breed continued to be very friendly with the son of Captain Barnard, so that the latter began to consider whether the sailing-master might not be counted on in an attempt to regain possession of the ship.

They were just thirty days out from Nantucket when, on the 4th of July, an angry dispute arose among the mutineers about a little brig signalled in the offing, which some of them wanted to take and others would have allowed to escape. In this quarrel a sailor belonging to the cook's party, to which Dirk Peters had attached himself, was mortally injured. There were now only thirteen men on board, counting Arthur Pym.

Under these circumstances a terrible storm arose, and the *Grampus* was mercilessly knocked about. This storm raged until the 9th of July, and on that day, Dirk Peters having manifested an intention of getting rid of the mate, Augustus Barnard readily assured him of his assistance, without, however, revealing the fact of Arthur Pym's presence on board. Next day, one of the cook's adherents, a man named Rogers, died in convulsions, and, beyond all doubt, of poison. Only four of the cook's party then remained, of these Dirk Peters was one. The mate had five, and would probably end by carrying the day over the cook's party.

There was not an hour to lose. The half-breed having informed Augustus Barnard that the moment for action had arrived, the latter told him the truth about Arthur Pym.

While the two were in consultation upon the means to be employed for regaining possession of the ship, a tempest was raging, and presently a gust of irresistible force struck the *Grampus* and flung her upon her side, so that on righting herself she shipped a tremendous sea, and there was considerable confusion on board. This offered a favourable opportunity for beginning the struggle, although the mutineers had made peace among themselves. The latter numbered nine men, while the half-breed's party consisted only of himself, Augustus Barnard and Arthur Pym. The ship's master possessed only two pistols and a hanger. It was therefore necessary to act with prudence.

Then did Arthur Pym (whose presence on board the mutineers could not suspect) conceive the idea of a trick which had some chance of succeeding. The body of the poisoned sailor was still lying on the deck; he thought it likely, if he were to put on the dead man's clothes and appear suddenly in the midst of those superstitious sailors, that their terror would place them at the mercy of Dirk Peters. It was still dark when the half-breed went softly towards the ship's stern, and, exerting his prodigious strength to the utmost, threw himself upon the man at the wheel and flung him over the poop.

Augustus Barnard and Arthur Pym joined him instantly, each armed with a belaying-pin. Leaving Dirk Peters in the place of the steersman, Arthur Pym, so disguised as to present the appearance of the dead man, and his comrade, posted themselves close to the head of the forecastle gangway. The mate, the ship's cook, all the others were there, some sleeping, the others drinking or talking; guns and pistols were within reach of their hands.

The tempest raged furiously; it was impossible to stand on the deck.

At that moment the mate gave the order for Augustus Barnard and Dirk Peters to be brought to the forecastle. This order was transmitted to the man at the helm, no other than Dirk Peters, who went down, accompanied by Augustus Barnard, and almost simultaneously Arthur Pym made his appearance.

The effect of the apparition was prodigious. The mate, terrified on beholding the resuscitated sailor, sprang up, beat the air with his hands, and fell down dead. Then Dirk Peters rushed upon the others, seconded by Augustus Barnard, Arthur Pym, and the dog Tiger. In a few moments all were strangled or knocked on the head,—save Richard Parker, the sailor, whose life was spared.

And now, while the tempest was in full force, only four men were left to work the brig, which was labouring terribly with seven feet of water in her hold. They had to cut down the mainmast, and, when morning came, the mizen. That day was truly awful, the night was more awful still! If Dirk Peters and his companions had not lashed themselves securely to the remains of the rigging, they must have been carried away by a tremendous sea, which drove in the hatches of the *Grampus*.

Then follows in the romance a minute record of the series of incidents ensuing upon this situation, from the 14th of July to the 7th of August; the fishing for victuals in the submerged hold, the coming of a mysterious brig laden with corpses, which poisoned the atmosphere and passed on like a huge coffin, the sport of a wind of death:

the torments of hunger and thirst; the impossibility of reaching the provision store; the drawing of lots by straws —the shortest gave Richard Parker to be sacrificed for the life of the other three—the death of that unhappy man, who was killed by Dirk Peters and devoured; lastly, the finding in the hold of a jar of olives and a small turtle.

Owing to the displacement of her cargo the *Grampus* rolled and pitched more and more. The frightful heat caused the torture of thirst to reach the extreme limit of human endurance, and on the 1st of August, Augustus Barnard died. On the 3rd, the brig foundered in the night, and Arthur Pym and the half-breed, crouching upon the upturned keel, were reduced to feed upon the barnacles with which the bottom was covered, in the midst of a crowd of waiting, watching sharks. Finally, after the shipwrecked mariners of the *Grampus* had drifted no less than twenty-five degrees towards the south, they were picked up by the schooner *Jane*, of Liverpool, Captain William Guy.

Evidently, reason is not outraged by an admission of the reality of these facts, although the situations are strained to the utmost limits of possibility; but that does not surprise us, for the writer is the American magician-poet, Edgar Poe. But from this moment onwards we shall see that no semblance of reality exists in the succession of incidents.

Arthur Pym and Dirk Peters were well treated on board the English schooner *Jane.* In a fortnight, having recovered from the effects of their sufferings, they remembered them no more. With alternations of fine and bad weather the *Jane* sighted Prince Edward's Island on the 13th of October, then the Crozet Islands, and afterwards the Kerguelens, which I had left eleven days ago.

Three weeks were employed in chasing sea-calves, these furnished the *Jane* with a goodly cargo. It was during this time that the captain of the *Jane* buried the bottle in which his namesake of the *Halbrane* claimed to have found a letter containing William Guy's announcement of his intention to visit the austral seas.

On the 12th of November, the schooner left the Kerguelens, and after a brief stay at Tristan d'Acunha she sailed to reconnoitre the Auroras in 35° 15′ of south latitude, and 37° 38′ of west longitude. But these islands were not to be found, and she did not find them.

On the 12th of December the *Jane* headed towards the Antarctic pole. On the 26th, the first icebergs came in sight beyond the seventy-third degree.

From the 1st to the 14th of January, 1828, the movements were difficult, the polar circle was passed in the midst of ice-floes, the icebergs' point was doubled and the ship sailed on the surface of an open sea—the famous open sea where the temperature is 47° Fahrenheit, and the water is 34°.

Edgar Poe, every one will allow, gives free rein to his fancy at this point. No navigator had ever reached latitudes so high—not even James Weddell of the British Navy, who did not get beyond the seventy-fourth parallel in 1822. But the achievement of the *Jane*, although difficult of belief, is trifling in comparison with the succeeding incidents which Arthur Pym, or rather Edgar Poe, relates with simple earnestness. In fact he entertained no doubt of reaching the pole itself.

In the first place, not a single iceberg is to be seen on this fantastic sea. Innumerable flocks of birds skim its surface, among them is a pelican which is shot. On a floating piece of ice is a bear of the Arctic species and of gigantic size. At last land is signalled. It is an island of a league in circumference, to which the name of Bennet Islet was given, in honour of the captain's partner in the ownership of the *Jane*.

Naturally, in proportion as the schooner sailed southwards the variation of the compass became less, while the temperature became milder, with a sky always clear and a uniform northerly breeze. Needless to add that in that latitude and in the month of January there was no darkness.

The *Jane* pursued her adventurous course, until, on the 18th of January, land was sighted in latitude 83° 20′ and longitude 43° 5′.

This proved to be an island belonging to a numerous group scattered about in a westerly direction.

The schooner approached and anchored off the shore. Arms were placed in the boats, and Arthur Pym got into one of the latter with Dirk Peters. The men rowed shorewards, but were stopped by four canoes carrying armed men, "new men" the narrative calls them. These men showed no hostile intentions, but cried out continuously "anamoo" and "lamalama." When the canoes were alongside the schooner, the chief, Too-Wit, was permitted to go on board with twenty of his companions. There was profound astonishment on their part then, for they took the ship for a living creature, and lavished caresses on the rigging, the masts, and the bulwarks. Steered between the reefs by these natives, she crossed a bay with a bottom of black sand, and cast anchor within a mile of the beach. Then William Guy, leaving the hostages on board, stepped ashore amid the rocks.

If Arthur Pym is to be believed, this was Tsalal Island! Its trees resembled none of the species in any other zone of our planet. The composition of the rocks revealed a stratification unknown to modern mineralogists. Over the bed of the streams ran a liquid substance without any appearance of limpidity, streaked with distinct veins, which did not reunite by immediate cohesion when they were parted by the blade of a knife!

Klock-Klock, which we are obliged to describe as the chief "town" of the island, consisted of wretched huts entirely formed of black skins; it possessed domestic animals resembling the common pig, a sort of sheep with a black fleece, twenty kinds of fowls, tame albatross, ducks, and large turtles in great numbers.

On arriving at Klock-Klock, Captain William Guy and his companions found a population—which Arthur Pym estimated at ten thousand souls, men, women, and children—if not to be feared, at least to be kept at a distance, so noisy and demonstrative were they. Finally, after a long halt at the hut of Too-Wit, the strangers returned to the shore, where the "bêche-de-mer"—the favourite food of the Chinese—would provide enormous cargoes; for the succulent mollusk is more abundant there than in any other part of the austral regions.

Captain William Guy immediately endeavoured to come to an understanding with Too-Wit on this matter, requesting him to authorize the construction of sheds in which some of the men of the *Jane* might prepare the bêche-de-mer, while the schooner should hold on her course towards the Pole. Too-Wit accepted this proposal willingly, and made a bargain by which the natives were to give their labour in the gathering-in of the precious mollusk.

At the end of a month, the sheds being finished, three men were told off to remain at Tsalal. The natives had not given the strangers cause to entertain the slightest suspicion of them. Before leaving the place, Captain William Guy wished to return once more to the village of Klock-Klock, having, from prudent motives, left six men on board, the guns charged, the bulwark nettings in their place, the anchor hanging at the forepeak—in a word, all in readiness to oppose an approach of the natives. Too-Wit, escorted by a hundred warriors, came out to meet the visitors. Captain William Guy and his men, although the place was propitious to an ambuscade, walked in close order, each pressing upon the other. On the right, a little in advance, were Arthur Pym, Dirk Peters, and a sailor named Allen. Having reached a spot where a fissure traversed the hill-side, Arthur Pym turned into it in order to gather some hazel nuts which hung in clusters upon stunted bushes. Having done this, he was returning to the path, when he perceived that Allen and the half-breed had accompanied him. They were all three approaching the mouth of the fissure, when they were thrown down by a sudden and violent shock. At the same moment the crumbling masses of the hill slid down upon them, and they instantly concluded that they were doomed to be buried alive.

Alive—all three? No! Allen had been so deeply covered by the sliding soil that he was already smothered, but Arthur Pym and Dirk Peters contrived to drag themselves on their knees, and opening a way with their bowie knives, to a projecting mass of harder clay, which had resisted the movement from above, and from thence they climbed to a natural platform at the extremity of a wooded ravine. Above them they could see the blue sky-roof, and from their position were enabled to survey the surrounding country.

An artificial landslip, cunningly contrived by the natives, had taken place. Captain William Guy and his twenty-eight companions had disappeared; they were crushed beneath more than a million tons of earth and stones.

The plain was swarming with natives who had come, no doubt, from the neighbouring islets, attracted by the prospect of pillaging the *Jane*. Seventy boats were being paddled towards the ship. The six men on board fired on them, but their aim was uncertain in the first volley; a second, in which mitraille and grooved bullets were used, produced terrible effect. Nevertheless, the *Jane* being boarded by the swarming islanders, her defenders were massacred, and she was set on fire.

Finally a terrific explosion took place—the fire had reached the powder store—killing a thousand natives and mutilating as many more, while the others fled, uttering the cry of *tékéli-li! tékéli-li!*

During the following week, Arthur Pym and Dirk Peters, living on nuts and bitterns' flesh, escaped discovery by the natives, who did not suspect their presence. They found themselves at the bottom of a sort of dark abyss including several planes, but without issue, hollowed out from the hillside, and of great extent. The two men could not live in the midst of these successive abysses, and after several attempts they let themselves slide on one of the slopes of the hill. Instantly, six savages rushed upon them; but, thanks to their pistols, and the extraordinary strength of the half-breed, four of the assailants were killed. The fifth was dragged away by the fugitives, who reached a boat which had been pulled up on the beach and was laden with three huge turtles. A score of natives pursued and vainly tried to stop them; the former were driven off, and the boat was launched successfully and steered for the south.

Arthur Pym was then navigating beyond the eighty-fourth degree of south latitude. It was the beginning of March, that is to say, the antarctic winter was approaching. Five or six islands, which it was prudent to avoid, were visible towards the west. Arthur Pym's opinion was that the temperature would become more mild by degrees as they approached the pole. They tied together two white shirts which they had been wearing, and hoisted them to do duty as a sail. At sight of these shirts the native, who answered to the name of Nu-Nu, was terrified. For eight days this strange voyage continued, favoured by a mild wind from the north, in permanent daylight, on a sea without a fragment of ice, indeed, owing to the high and even temperature of the water, no ice had been seen since the parallel of Bennet Island.

Then it was that Arthur Pym and Dirk Peters entered upon a region of novelty and wonder. Above the horizon line rose a broad bar of light grey vapour, striped with long luminous rays, such as are projected by the polar aurora. A very strong current came to the aid of the breeze. The boat sailed rapidly upon a liquid surface of milky aspect, exceedingly hot, and apparently agitated from beneath. A fine white ash-dust began to fall, and this increased the terror of Nu-Nu, whose lips trembled over his two rows of black ivory.

On the 9th of March this rain of ashes fell in redoubled volume, and the temperature of the water rose so high that the hand could no longer bear it. The immense curtain of vapour, spread over the distant perimeter of the southern horizon resembled a boundless cataract falling noiselessly from the height of some huge rampart lost in the height of the heavens.

Twelve days later, it was darkness that hung over these waters, darkness furrowed by luminous streaks darting from the milky depths of the Antarctic Ocean, while the incessant shower of ash-dust fell and melted in its waters.

The boat approached the cataract with an impetuous velocity whose cause is not explained in the narrative of Arthur Pym. In the midst of this frightful darkness a flock of gigantic birds, of livid white plumage, swept by, uttering their eternal *tékéli-li*, and then the savage, in the supreme throes of terror, gave up the ghost.

Suddenly, in a mad whirl of speed, the boat rushed into the grasp of the cataract, where a vast gulf seemed ready to swallow it up. But before the mouth of this gulf there stood a veiled human figure, of greater size than any inhabitant of this earth, and the colour of the man's skin was the perfect whiteness of snow.

Such is the strange romance conceived by the more than human genius of the greatest poet of the New World.

CHAPTER VI.

AN OCEAN WAIF.

THE navigation of the *Halbrane* went on prosperously with the help of the sea and the wind. In fifteen days, if this state of things lasted, she might reach Tristan d'Acunha. Captain Len Guy left the working of the ship to James West, and well might he do so; there was nothing to fear with such a seaman as he.

"Our lieutenant has not his match afloat," said Hurliguerly to me one day. "He ought to be in command of a flag-ship."

"Indeed," I replied, "he seems to be a true son of the sea."

"And then, our *Halbrane*, what a craft! Congratulate yourself, Mr. Jeorling, and congratulate yourself also that I succeeded in bringing the captain to change his mind about you."

"If it was you who obtained that result, boatswain, I thank you heartily."

"And so you ought, for he was plaguily against it, was our captain, in spite of all old man Atkins could say. But I managed to make him hear reason."

"I shan't forget it, boatswain, I shan't forget it, since, thanks to your intervention, instead of moping at

Kerguelen I hope shortly to get within sight of Tristan d'Acunha."

"In a few days, Mr. Jeorling. Only think, sir, according to what I hear tell, they are making ships in England and America with machines in their insides, and wheels which they use as a duck uses its paddles. All right, we shall know what's the good of them when they come into use. My notion is, however, that those ships will never be able to fight with a fine frigate sailing with a fresh breeze."

. . . .

It was the 3rd of September. If nothing occurred to delay us, our schooner would be in sight of port in three days. The chief island of the group is visible on clear days at a great distance.

That day, between ten and eleven o'clock in the morning, I was walking backwards and forwards on the deck, on the windward side. We were sliding smoothly over the surface of an undulating sea. The *Halbrane* resembled an enormous bird, one of the gigantic albatross kind described by Arthur Pym—which had spread its sail-like wings, and was carrying a whole ship's crew towards space.

James West was looking out through his glasses to starboard at an object floating two or three miles away, and several sailors, hanging over the side, were also curiously observing it.

I went forward and looked attentively at the object. It was an irregularly formed mass about twelve yards in length, and in the middle of it there appeared a shining lump.

"That is no whale," said Martin Holt, the sailing-master. "It would have blown once or twice since we have been looking at it."

"Certainly!" assented Hardy. "Perhaps it is the carcase of some deserted ship."

"May the devil send it to the bottom!" cried Roger. "It would be a bad job to come up against it in the dark; it might send us down before we could know what had happened."

"I believe you," added Drap, "and these derelicts are more dangerous than a rock, for they are now here and again there, and there's no avoiding them."

Hurliguerly came up at this moment and planted his elbows on the bulwark, alongside of mine.

"What do you think of it, boatswain?" I asked.

"It is my opinion, Mr. Jeorling," replied the boatswain, "that what we see there is neither a blower nor a wreck, but merely a lump of ice."

"Hurliguerly is right," said James West; "it is a lump of ice, a piece of an iceberg which the currents have carried hither."

"What?" said I, "to the forty-fifth parallel?"

"Yes, sir," answered West, "that has occurred, and the ice sometimes gets up as high as the Cape, if we are to take the word of a French navigator, Captain Blosseville, who met one at this height in 1828."

"Then this mass will melt before long," I observed, feeling not a little surprised that West had honoured me by so lengthy a reply.

"It must indeed be dissolved in great part already," he continued, "and what we see is the remains of a mountain of ice which must have weighed millions of tons."

Captain Len Guy now appeared, and perceiving the

group of sailors around West, he came forward. A few words were exchanged in a low tone between the captain and the lieutenant, and the latter passed his glass to the former, who turned it upon the floating object, now at least a mile nearer to us.

"It is ice," said he, "and it is lucky that it is dissolving! The *Halbrane* might have come to serious grief by collision with it in the night"

I was struck by the fixity of his gaze upon the object, whose nature he had so promptly declared: he continued to contemplate it for several minutes, and I guessed what was passing in the mind of the man under the obsession of a fixed idea. This fragment of ice, torn from the southern icebergs, came from those waters wherein his thoughts continually ranged. He wanted to see it more near, perhaps at close quarters, it might be to take away some bits of it. At an order from West the schooner was directed towards the floating mass; presently we were within two cables'-length, and I could examine it.

The mound in the centre was melting rapidly; before the end of the day nothing would remain of the fragment of ice which had been carried by the currents so high up as the forty-fifth parallel.

Captain Len Guy gazed at it steadily, but he now needed no glass, and presently we all began to distinguish a second object which little by little detached itself from the mass, according as the melting process went on—a black shape, stretched on the white ice.

What was our surprise, mingled with horror, when we saw first an arm, then a leg, then a trunk, then a head appear, forming a human body, not in a state of nakedness, but clothed in dark garments.

For a moment I even thought that the limbs moved, that the hands were stretched towards us.

The crew uttered a simultaneous cry. No! this body was not moving, but it was slowly slipping off the icy surface.

I looked at Captain Len Guy. His face was as livid as that of the corpse that had drifted down from the far latitudes of the austral zone. What could be done was done to recover the body of the unfortunate man, and who can tell whether a faint breath of life did not animate it even then? In any case his pockets might perhaps contain some document that would enable his identity to be established. Then, accompanied by a last prayer, those human remains should be committed to the depths of the ocean, the cemetery of sailors who die at sea.

A boat was let down. I followed it with my eyes as it neared the side of the ice fragment eaten by the waves.

Hurliguerly set foot upon a spot which still offered some resistance. Gratian got out after him, while Francis kept the boat fast by the chain. The two crept along the ice until they reached the corpse, then drew it to them by the arms and legs and so got it into the boat. A few strokes of the oars and the boatswain had rejoined the schooner. The corpse, completely frozen, having been laid at the foot of the mizen mast, Captain Len Guy approached and examined it long and closely, as though he sought to recognize it.

It was the corpse of a sailor, dressed in coarse stuff, woollen trousers and a patched jersey; a belt encircled his waist twice. His death had evidently occurred some months previously, probably very soon after the unfortunate man had been carried away by the drift. He was about forty, with slightly grizzled hair, a mere skeleton covered with skin. He must have suffered agonies of hunger.

Captain Len Guy lifted up the hair, which had been preserved by the cold, raised the head, gazed upon the scaled eyelids, and finally said with a sort of sob,—

"Patterson! Patterson!"

"Patterson?" I exclaimed.

The name, common as it was, touched some chord in my memory. When had I heard it uttered? Had I read it anywhere?

At this moment, James West, on a hint from the boatswain, searched the pockets of the dead man, and took out of them a knife, some string, an empty tobacco box, and lastly a leather pocket-book furnished with a metallic pencil.

"Give me that," said the captain. Some of the leaves were covered with writing, almost entirely effaced by the damp. He found, however, some words on the last page which were still legible, and my emotion may be imagined when I heard him read aloud in a trembling voice: "The *Jane* . . . Tsalal island . . . by eighty-three . . . There . . . eleven years . . . Captain . . . five sailors surviving . . . Hasten to bring them aid."

And under these lines was a name, a signature, the name of Patterson!

Then I remembered! Patterson was the second officer of the *Jane*, the mate of that schooner which had picked up Arthur Pym and Dirk Peters on the wreck of the *Grampus*, the *Jane* having reached Tsalal Island; the *Jane* which was attacked by natives and blown up in the midst of those waters.

So then it was all true? Edgar Poe's work was that of

an historian, not a writer of romance? Arthur Gordon Pym's journal had actually been confided to him! Direct relations had been established between them! Arthur Pym existed, or rather he had existed, he was a real being! And he had died, by a sudden and deplorable death under circumstances not revealed before he had completed the narrative of his extraordinary voyage! And what parallel had he reached on leaving Tsalal Island with his companion, Dirk Peters, and how had both of them been restored to their native land, America?

I thought my head was turning, that I was going mad—I who accused Captain Guy of being insane! No! I had not heard aright! I had misunderstood! This was a mere phantom of my fancy!

And yet, how was I to reject the evidence found on the body of the mate of the *Jane*, that Patterson whose words were supported by ascertained dates? And above all, how could I retain a doubt, after James West, who was the most self-possessed among us, had succeeded in deciphering the following fragments of sentences:—

"Drifting since the 3rd of June north of Tsalal Island. . . . Still there . . . Captain William Guy and five of the men of the *Jane*—the piece of ice I am on is drifting across the iceberg . . . food will soon fail me. . . . Since the 13th of June . . . my last resources exhausted . . . to-day . . . 16th of June . . . I am going to die."

So then for nearly three months Patterson's body had lain on the surface of this ice-waif which we had met on our way from the Kerguelens to Tristan d'Acunha! Ah! why had we not saved the mate of the *Jane!*

I had to yield to evidence. Captain Len Guy, who knew Patterson, had recognized him in this frozen corpse!

It was indeed he who accompanied the captain of the *Jane* when he had interred that bottle, containing the letter which I had refused to believe authentic, at the Kerguelens. Yes! for eleven years, the survivors of the English schooner had been cast away there without any hope of succour.

Len Guy turned to me and said,—

"Do you believe—*now?*"

"I believe," said I, falteringly; "but Captain William Guy of the *Jane*, and Captain Len Guy of the *Halbrane*—"

"Are brothers!" he cried in a loud voice, which was heard by all the crew.

Then we turned our eyes once more to the place where the lump of ice had been floating; but the double influence of the solar rays and the waters in this latitude had produced its effect, no trace of the dead man's last refuge remained on the surface of the sea.

CHAPTER VII.

TRISTAN D'ACUNHA.

FOUR days later, the *Halbrane* neared that curious island of Tristan d'Acunha, which may be described as the big boiler of the African seas. By that time I had come to realize that the "hallucination" of Captain Len Guy was a truth, and that he and the captain of the *Jane* (also a reality) were connected with each other by this ocean waif from the authentic expedition of Arthur Pym. My last doubts were buried in the depths of the ocean with the body of Patterson.

And now, what was Captain Len Guy going to do? There was not a shadow of doubt on that point. He would take the *Halbrane* to Tsalal Island, as marked upon Patterson's note-book. His lieutenant, James West, would go whithersoever he was ordered to go; his crew would not hesitate to follow him, and would not be stopped by any fear of passing the limits assigned to human power, for the soul of their captain and the strength of their lieutenant would be in them.

This, then, was the reason why Captain Len Guy refused to take passengers on board his ship, and why he had told me that his routes never were certain; he was always hoping that an opportunity for venturing into the sea of ice might arise. Who could tell indeed, whether he would not have sailed for the south at once without putting in at Tristan d'Acunha, if he had not wanted water? After what I had said before I went on board the *Halbrane*, I should have had no right to insist on his proceeding to the island for the sole purpose of putting me ashore. But a supply of water was indispensable, and besides, it might be possible there to put the schooner in a condition to contend with the icebergs and gain the open sea—since open it was beyond the eighty-second parallel—in fact to attempt what Lieutenant Wilkes of the American Navy was then attempting.

The navigators knew at this period, that from the middle of November to the beginning of March was the limit during which some success might be looked for. The temperature is more bearable then, storms are less frequent, the icebergs break loose from the mass, the ice wall has holes in it, and perpetual day reigns in that distant region.

Tristan d'Acunha lies to the south of the zone of the regular south-west winds. Its climate is mild and moist. The prevailing winds are west and north-west, and, during the winter—August and September—south. The island was inhabited, from 1811, by American whale fishers. After them, English soldiers were installed there to watch the St. Helena seas, and these remained until after the death of Napoleon, in 1821. Several years later the group of islands populated by Americans and Dutchmen from the Cape acknowledged the suzerainty of Great Britain, but this was not so in 1839. My personal observation at that date convinced me that the possession of Tristan d'Acunha was not worth disputing. In the sixteenth century the islands were called the Land of Life.

On the 5th of September, in the morning, the towering volcano of the chief island was signalled ; a huge snow-covered mass, whose crater formed the basin of a small lake. Next day, on our approach, we could distinguish a vast heaped-up lava field. At this distance the surface of the water was striped with gigantic seaweeds, vegetable ropes, varying in length from six hundred to twelve hundred feet, and as thick as a wine barrel.

Here I should mention that for three days subsequent to the finding of the fragment of ice, Captain Len Guy came on deck for strictly nautical purposes only, and I had no opportunities of seeing him except at meals, when he maintained silence, that not even James West could have enticed him to break. I made no attempt to do this, being convinced that the hour would come when Len Guy would again speak to me of his brother, and of the efforts which he intended to make to save him and his companions. Now, I repeat, the season being considered, that hour had not come, when the schooner cast anchor on the 6th of September at Ansiedling, in Falmouth Bay, precisely in the place indicated in Arthur Pym's narrative as the moorings of the *Jane*.

At the period of the arrival of the *Jane*, an ex-corporal of the English artillery, named Glass, reigned over a little colony of twenty-six individuals, who traded with the Cape, and whose only vessel was a small schooner. At our arrival this Glass had more than fifty subjects, and was, as Arthur Pym remarked, quite independent of the British Government. Relations with the ex-corporal were established on the arrival of the *Halbrane*, and he proved very friendly and obliging. West, to whom the captain left the business of refilling the water tanks and taking in supplies of fresh meat and vegetables, had every reason to be satisfied with Glass, who, no doubt, expected to be paid, and was paid, handsomely.

The day after our arrival I met ex-corporal Glass, a vigorous, well-preserved man, whose sixty years had not impaired his intelligent vivacity. Independently of his trade with the Cape and the Falklands, he did an important business in seal-skins and the oil of marine animals, and his affairs were prosperous. As he appeared very willing to talk, I entered briskly into conversation with this self-appointed Governor of a contented little colony, by asking him,—

"Do many ships put in to Tristan d'Acunha?"

"As many as we require," he replied, rubbing his hands together behind his back, according to his invariable custom.

"In the fine season?"

"Yes, in the fine season, if indeed we can be said to have any other in these latitudes."

"I congratulate you, Mr. Glass. But it is to be regretted that Tristan d'Acunha has not a single port. If you possessed a landing-stage, now?"

"For what purpose, sir, when nature has provided us with such a bay as this, where there is shelter from gales, and it is easy to lie snug right up against the rocks? No, Tristan has no port, and Tristan can do without one."

Why should I have contradicted this good man? He was proud of his island, just as the Prince of Monaco is justly proud of his tiny principality.

I did not persist, and we talked of various things. He offered to arrange for me an excursion to the depths of the thick forests, which clothed the volcano up to the middle of the central cove.

I thanked him, but declined his offer, preferring to employ my leisure on land in some mineralogical studies. Besides, the *Halbrane* was to set sail so soon as she had taken in her provisions.

"Your captain is in a remarkable hurry!" said Governor Glass.

"You think so?"

"He is in such haste that his lieutenant does not even talk of buying skins or oil from me."

"We require only fresh victuals and fresh water, Mr. Glass."

"Very well," replied the Governor, who was rather annoyed, "what the *Halbrane* will not take other vessels will."

Then he resumed,—

"And where is your schooner bound for on leaving us?"

"For the Falklands, no doubt, where she can be repaired."

"You, sir, are only a passenger, I suppose?"

"As you say, Mr. Glass, and I had even intended to remain at Tristan d'Acunha for some weeks. But I have had to relinquish that project."

"I am sorry to hear it, sir. We should have been happy to offer you hospitality while awaiting the arrival of another ship."

"Such hospitality would have been most valuable to me," I replied, "but unfortunately I cannot avail myself of it."

In fact, I had finally resolved not to quit the schooner, but to embark for America from the Falkland Isles without much delay. I felt sure that Captain Len Guy would not refuse to take me to the islands. I informed Mr. Glass of my intention, and he remarked, still in a tone of annoyance,—

"As for your captain, I have not even seen the colour of his hair."

"I don't think he has any intention of coming ashore."

"Is he ill?"

"Not to my knowledge. But it does not concern you, since he has sent his lieutenant to represent him."

"Oh, *he's* a cheerful person! One may extract two words from him occasionally. Fortunately, it is easier to get coin out of his pocket than speech out of his lips."

"That's the important thing, Mr. Glass."

"You are right, sir—Mr. Jeorling, of Connecticut, I believe?"

I assented.

"So! I know *your* name, while I have yet to learn that of the captain of the *Halbrane*."

"His name is Guy—Len Guy."

"An Englishman?"

"Yes—an Englishman."

"He might have taken the trouble to pay a visit to a countryman of his, Mr. Jeorling! But stay! I had some dealings formerly with a captain of that name. Guy, Guy—"

"William Guy?" I asked, quickly.

"Precisely. William Guy."

"Who commanded the *Jane?*"

"The *Jane?* Yes. The same man."

"An English schooner which put in at Tristan d'Acunha eleven years ago?"

"Eleven years, Mr. Jeorling. I had been settled in the island where Captain Jeffrey, of the *Berwick*, of London, found me in the year 1824, for full seven years. I perfectly recall this William Guy, as if he were before me. He was a fine, open-hearted fellow, and I sold him a cargo of seal-skins. He had the air of a gentleman, rather proud, but good-natured."

"And the *Jane?*"

"I can see her now at her moorings in the same place as the *Halbrane*. She was a handsome vessel of one hundred and eighty tons, very slender for'ards. She belonged to the port of Liverpool."

"Yes; that is true, all that is true."

"And is the *Jane* still afloat, Mr. Jeorling?"

"No, Mr. Glass."

"Was she lost?"

"The fact is only too true, and the greater part of her crew with her."

"Will you tell me how this happened?"

"Willingly. On leaving Tristan d'Acunha the *Jane* headed for the bearings of the Aurora and other islands, which William Guy hoped to recognize from information—"

"That came from me," interrupted the ex-corporal. "And those other islands, may I learn whether the *Jane* discovered them?"

"No, nor the Auroras either, although William Guy remained several weeks in those waters, running from east to west, with a look-out always at the masthead."

"He must have lost his bearings, Mr. Jeorling, for, if several whalers, who were well deserving of credit, are to be believed, these islands do exist, and it was even proposed to give them my name."

"That would have been but just," I replied politely.

"It will be very vexatious if they are not discovered some day," added the Governor, in a tone which indicated that he was not devoid of vanity.

"It was then," I resumed, "that Captain Guy resolved to carry out a project he had long cherished, and in which he was encouraged by a certain passenger who was on board the *Jane*—"

"Arthur Gordon Pym," exclaimed Glass, "and his companion, one Dirk Peters; the two had been picked up at sea by the schooner."

"You knew them, Mr. Glass?" I asked eagerly.

"Knew them, Mr. Jeorling? I should think I did, indeed! That Arthur Pym was a strange person, always wanting to rush into adventures—a real rash American, quite capable of starting off to the moon! Has he gone there at last?"

"No, not quite, Mr. Glass, but, during her voyage, the schooner, it seems, did clear the polar circle, and pass the ice-wall. She got farther than any ship had ever done before."

"What a wonderful feat!"

"Yes. Unfortunately, the *Jane* did not return. Arthur Pym and William Guy escaped the doom of the *Jane* and the most of her crew. They even got back to America, how I do not know. Afterwards Arthur Pym died, but under what circumstances I am ignorant. As for the half-breed, after having retired to Illinois, he went off one day without a word to anyone, and no trace of him has been found."

"And William Guy?" asked Mr. Glass.

I related the finding of the body of Patterson, the mate

of the *Jane*, and I added that everything led to the belief that the captain of the *Jane* and five of his companions were still living on an island in the austral regions, at less than six degrees from the Pole.

"Ah, Mr. Jeorling," cried Glass, "if some day William Guy and his sailors might be saved! They seemed to me to be such fine fellows."

"That is just what the *Halbrane* is certainly going to attempt, so soon as she is ready, for her captain, Len Guy, is William Guy's own brother."

"Is it possible? Well, although I do not know Captain Len Guy, I venture to assert that the brothers do not resemble each other—at least in their behaviour to the Governor of Tristan d'Acunha!"

It was plain that the Governor was profoundly mortified, but no doubt he consoled himself by the prospect of selling his goods at twenty-five per cent. above their value.

One thing was certain: Captain Len Guy had no intention of coming ashore. This was the more singular, inasmuch as he could not be unaware that the *Jane* had put in at Tristan d'Acunha before proceeding to the southern seas. Surely he might be expected to put himself in communication with the last European who had shaken hands with his brother!

Nevertheless, Captain Len Guy remained persistently on board his ship, without even going on deck; and, looking through the glass skylight of his cabin, I saw him perpetually stooping over the table, which was covered with open books and out-spread charts. No doubt the charts were those of the austral latitudes, and the books were narratives of the precursors of the *Jane* in those mysterious regions of the south.

On the table lay also a volume which had been read and re-read a hundred times. Most of its pages were dogs'-eared and their margins were filled with pencilled notes. And on the cover shone the title in brightly gilded letters :

THE ADVENTURES OF ARTHUR GORDON PYM.

CHAPTER VIII.

BOUND FOR THE FALKLANDS.

ON the 8th of September, in the evening, I had taken leave of His Excellency the Governor-General of the Archipelago of Tristan d'Acunha—for such is the official title bestowed upon himself by that excellent fellow, Glass, ex-corporal of artillery in the British Army. On the following day, before dawn, the *Halbrane* sailed.

After we had rounded Herald Point, the few houses of Ansiedlung disappeared behind the extremity of Falmouth Bay. A fine breeze from the east carried us along gaily.

During the morning we left behind us in succession Elephant Bay, Hardy Rock, West Point, Cotton Bay, and Daly's Promontory; but it took the entire day to lose sight of the volcano of Tristan d'Acunha, which is eight thousand feet high; its snow-clad bulk was at last veiled by the shades of evening.

During that week our voyage proceeded under the most favourable conditions; if these were maintained, the end of the month of September ought to bring us within sight of the first peaks of the Falkland Group; and so, very sensibly towards the south; the schooner having descended from the thirty-eighth parallel to the fifty-fifth degree of latitude.

The most daring, or, perhaps I ought to say, the most lucky of those discoverers who had preceded the *Halbrane*, under the command of Captain Len Guy, in the Antarctic seas, had not gone beyond—Kemp, the sixty-sixth parallel; Ballerry, the sixty-seventh; Biscoe, the sixty-eighth; Bellinghausen and Morrell, the seventieth; Cook, the seventy-first; Weddell, the seventy-fourth. And it was beyond the eighty-third, nearly five hundred and fifty miles farther, that we must go to the succour of the survivors of the *Jane!*

I confess that for a practical man of unimaginative temperament, I felt strangely excited; a nervous restlessness had taken possession of me. I was haunted by the figures of Arthur Pym and his companions, lost in Antarctic ice-deserts. I began to feel a desire to take part in the proposed undertaking of Captain Len Guy. I thought about it incessantly. As a fact there was nothing to recall me to America. It is true that whether I should get the consent of the commander of the *Halbrane* remained to be seen; but, after all, why should he refuse to keep me as a passenger? Would it not be a very "human" satisfaction to him to give me material proof that he was in the right, by taking me to the very scene of a catastrophe that I had regarded as fictitious, showing me the remains of the *Jane* at Tsalal, and landing me on that selfsame island which I had declared to be a myth?

Nevertheless, I resolved to wait, before I came to any definite determination, until an opportunity of speaking to the captain should arise.

After an interval of unfavourable weather, during which the *Halbrane* made but slow progress, on the 4th of October, in the morning, the aspect of the sky and the sea

Cook's route was effectually barred by ice-floes.

underwent a marked change. The wind became calm, the waves abated, and the next day the breeze veered to the north-west. This was very favourable to us, and in ten days, with a continuance of such fortunate conditions, we might hope to reach the Falklands.

It was on the 11th that the opportunity of an explanation with Captain Len Guy was presented to me, and by himself, for he came out of his cabin, advanced to the side of the ship where I was seated, and took his place at my side.

Evidently he wished to talk to me, and of what, if not the subject which entirely absorbed him? He began by saying:

"I have not yet had the pleasure of a chat with you, Mr. Jeorling, since our departure from Tristan d'Acunha!"

"To my regret, captain," I replied, but with reserve, for I wanted him to make the running.

"I beg you to excuse me," he resumed, "I have so many things to occupy me and make me anxious. A plan of campaign to organize, in which nothing must be unforeseen or unprovided for. I beg you not to be displeased with me—"

"I am not, I assure you."

"That is all right, Mr. Jeorling; and now that I know you, that I am able to appreciate you, I congratulate myself upon having you for a passenger until our arrival at the Falklands."

"I am very grateful, captain, for what you have done for me, and I feel encouraged to—"

The moment seemed propitious to my making my proposal, when Captain Len Guy interrupted me.

"Well, Mr. Jeorling," he asked, "are you now convinced of the reality of the voyage of the *Jane*, or do you still regard Edgar Poe's book as a work of pure imagination?"

"I do not so regard it, captain."

"You no longer doubt that Arthur Pym and Dirk Peters have really existed, or that my brother William Guy and five of his companions are living?"

"I should be the most incredulous of men, captain, to doubt either fact, and my earnest desire is that the favour of Heaven may attend you and secure the safety of the shipwrecked mariners of the *Jane*."

"I will do all in my power, Mr. Jeorling, and by the blessing of God I shall succeed."

"I hope so, captain. Indeed, I am certain it will be so, and if you consent—"

"Is it not the case that you talked of this matter with one Glass, an English ex-corporal, who sets up to be Governor of Tristan d'Acunha?" inquired the captain, without allowing me to finish my sentence.

"That is so," I replied, "and what I learned from Glass has contributed not a little to change my doubts into certainty."

"Ah! he has satisfied you?"

"Yes. He perfectly remembers to have seen the *Jane*, eleven years ago, when she had put in at Tristan d'Acunha."

"The *Jane*—and my brother?"

"He told me that he had personal dealings with Captain William Guy."

"And he traded with the *Jane*?"

"Yes, as he has just been trading with the *Halbrane*."

"She was moored in this bay?"

"In the same place as your schooner."

"And—Arthur Pym—Dirk Peters?"

"He was with them frequently."

"Did he ask what had become of them?"

"Oh yes, and I informed him of the death of Arthur Pym, whom he regarded as a foolhardy adventurer, capable of any daring folly."

"Say a madman, and a dangerous madman, Mr. Jeorling. Was it not he who led my unfortunate brother into that fatal enterprise?"

"There is, indeed, reason to believe so from his narrative."

"And never to forget it!" added the captain in a tone of agitation.

"This man, Glass," I resumed, "also knew Patterson, the mate of the *Jane*."

"He was a fine, brave, faithful fellow, Mr. Jeorling, and devoted, body and soul, to my brother."

"As West is to you, captain."

"Does Glass know where the shipwrecked men from the *Jane* are now?"

"I told him, captain, and also all that you have resolved to do to save them."

I did not think proper to add that Glass had been much surprised at Captain Guy's abstaining from visiting him, as, in his absurd vanity, he held the commander of the *Halbrane* bound to do, nor that he did not consider the Governor of Tristan d'Acunha bound to take the initiative.

"I wish to ask you, Mr. Jeorling, whether you think everything in Arthur Pym's journal, which has been published by Edgar Poe, is exactly true?"

"I think there is some need for doubt," I answered "the singular character of the hero of those adventures being taken into consideration—at least concerning the phenomena of the island of Tsalal. And we know that Arthur Pym was mistaken in asserting that Captain William Guy and several of his companions perished in the landslip of the hill at Klock-Klock."

"Ah! but he does not assert this, Mr. Jeorling! He says only that, when he and Dirk Peters had reached the opening through which they could discern the surrounding country, the seat of the artificial earthquake was revealed to them. Now, as the whole face of the hill was rushing into the ravine, the fate of my brother and twenty-nine of his men could not be doubtful to his mind. He was, most naturally, led to believe that Dirk Peters and himself were the only white men remaining alive on the island. He said nothing but this—nothing more. These were only suppositions—very reasonable, are they not?"

"I admit that, fully, captain."

"But now, thanks to Patterson's note-book, we are certain that my brother and five of his companions escaped from the landslip contrived by the natives."

"That is quite clear, captain. But, as to what became of the survivors of the *Jane*, whether they were taken by the natives of Tsalal and kept in captivity, or remained free, Patterson's note-book says nothing, nor does it relate under what circumstances he himself was carried far away from them."

"All that we shall learn, Mr. Jeorling. Yes, we shall know all. The main point is that we are quite sure my brother and five of his sailors were living less than four months ago on some part of Tsalal Island. There is now no question of a romance signed 'Edgar Poe,' but of a veracious narrative signed 'Patterson.'"

"Captain," said I, "will you let me be one of your company until the end of the campaign of the *Halbrane* in the Antarctic seas?"

Captain Len Guy looked at me with a glance as penetrating as a keen blade. Otherwise he did not appear surprised by the proposal I had made; perhaps he had been expecting it—and he uttered only the single word:

"Willingly."

CHAPTER IX.

FITTING OUT THE *HALBRANE*.

ON the 15th of October, our schooner cast anchor in Port Egmont, on the north of West Falkland. The group is composed of two islands, one the above-named, the other Soledad or East Falkland. Captain Len Guy gave twelve hours' leave to the whole crew. The next day the proceedings were to begin by a careful and minute inspection of the vessel's hull and keel, in view of the contemplated prolonged navigation of the Antarctic seas. That day Captain Len Guy went ashore, to confer with the Governor of the group on the subject of the immediate re-victualling of the schooner. He did not intend to make expense a consideration, because the whole adventure might be wrecked by an unwise economy. Besides I was ready to aid with my purse, as I told him, and I intended that we should be partners in the cost of this expedition.

James West remained on board all day, according to his custom in the absence of the captain, and was engaged until evening in the inspection of the hold. I did not wish to go ashore until the next day. I should have ample time while we remained in port to explore Port Egmont and its surroundings, and to study the geology and mineralogy of the island. Hurliguerly regarded the opportunity as highly favourable for the rencwal of talk with me, and availed himself of it accordingly. He accosted me as follows:

"Accept my sincere compliments, Mr. Jeorling."

"And wherefore, boatswain?"

"On account of what I have just heard—that you are to come with us to the far end of the Antarctic seas."

"Oh! not so far, I imagine, and if it is not a matter of going beyond the eighty-fourth parallel—"

"Who can tell," replied the boatswain, "at all events the *Halbrane* will make more degrees of latitude than any other ship before her."

"We shall see."

"And does that not alarm you, Mr. Jeorling?"

"Not in the very least."

"Nor us, rest assured. No, no! You see, Mr. Jeorling, our captain is a good one, although he is no talker. You only need to take him the right way! First he gives you the passage to Tristan d'Acunha that he refused you at first, and now he extends it to the pole."

"The pole is not the question, boatswain."

"Ah! it will be reached at last, some day."

"The thing has not yet been done. And, besides, I don't take much interest in the pole, and have no ambition to conquer it. In any case it is only to Tsalal Island—"

"Tsalal Island, of course. Nevertheless, you will acknowledge that our captain has been very accommodating to you, and—"

"And therefore I am much obliged to him, boatswain, and," I hastened to add, "to you also; since it is to your influence I owe my passage."

"Very likely." Hurliguerly, a good fellow at bottom, as

I afterwards learned, discerned a little touch of irony in my tone; but he did not appear to do so; he was resolved to persevere in his patronage of me. And, indeed, his conversation could not be otherwise than profitable to me, for he was thoroughly acquainted with the Falkland Islands. The result was that on the following day I went ashore adequately prepared to begin my perquisitions. At that period the Falklands were not utilized as they have been since.

It was at a later date that Port Stanley—described by Elisée Réclus, the French geographer, as "ideal"—was discovered. Port Stanley is sheltered at every point of the compass, and could contain all the fleets of Great Britain.

If I had been sailing for the last two months with bandaged eyes, and without knowing whither the *Halbrane* was bound, and had been asked during the first few hours at our moorings, "Are you in the Falkland Isles or in Norway?" I should have puzzled how to answer the question. For here were coasts forming deep creeks, the steep hills with peaked sides, and the coast-ledges faced with grey rock. Even the seaside climate, exempt from great extremes of cold and heat, is common to the two countries. Besides, the frequent rains of Scandinavia visit Magellan's region in like abundance. Both have dense fogs, and, in spring and autumn, winds so fierce that the very vegetables in the fields are frequently rooted up.

A few walks inland would, however, have sufficed to make me recognize that I was still separated by the equator from the waters of Northern Europe. What had I found to observe in the neighbourhood of Port Egmont after my explorations of the first few days? Nothing but the signs of a sickly vegetation, nowhere arborescent. Here and there a few shrubs grew, in place of the flourishing firs of the Norwegian mountains, and the surface of a spongy soil which sinks and rises under the foot is carpeted with mosses, fungi, and lichens. No! this was not the enticing country where the echoes of the sagas resound, this was not the poetic realm of Wodin and the Valkyries.

On the deep waters of the Falkland Strait, which separates the two principal isles, great masses of extraordinary aquatic vegetation floated, and the bays of the Archipelago, where whales were already becoming scarce, were frequented by other marine mammals of enormous size—seals, twenty-five feet long by twenty in circumference, and great numbers of sea elephants, wolves, and lions, of proportions no less gigantic. The uproar made by these animals, by the females and their young especially, surpasses description. One would think that herds of cattle were bellowing on the beach. Neither difficulty nor danger attends the capture, or at least the slaughter of the marine beasts. The sealers kill them with a blow of a club when they are lying in the sands on the strand. These are the special features that differentiate Scandinavia from the Falklands, not to speak of the infinite number of birds which rose on my approach, grebe, cormorants, black-headed swans, and above all, tribes of penguins, of which hundreds of thousands are massacred every year.

One day, when the air was filled with a sound of braying, sufficient to deafen one, I asked an old sailor belonging to Port Egmont,—

"Are there asses about here?"

"Sir," he replied, "those are not asses that you hear, but penguins."

The asses themselves, had any been there, would have been deceived by the braying of these stupid birds. I pursued my investigations some way to the west of the bay. West Falkland is more extensive than its neighbour, La Soledad, and possesses another fort at the southern point of Byron's Sound—too far off for me to go there.

I could not estimate the population of the Archipelago even approximately. Probably, it did not then exceed from two to three hundred souls, mostly English, with some Indians, Portuguese, Spaniards, Gauchos from the Argentine Pampas, and natives from Tierra del Fuego. On the other hand, the representatives of the ovine and bovine races were to be counted by tens of thousands. More than five hundred thousand sheep yield over four hundred thousand dollars' worth of wool yearly. There are also horned cattle bred on the islands; these seem to have increased in size, while the other quadrupeds, for instance, horses, pigs, and rabbits, have decreased. All these live in a wild state, and the only beast of prey is the dog-fox, a species peculiar to the fauna of the Falklands.

Not without reason has this island been called "a cattle farm." What inexhaustible pastures, what an abundance of that savoury grass, the tussock, does nature lavish on animals there! Australia, though so rich in this respect, does not set a better spread table before her ovine and bovine pensioners.

The Falklands ought to be resorted to for the re-victualling of ships. The groups are of real importance to navigators making for the Strait of Magellan, as well as to those who come to fish in the vicinity of the polar regions.

When the work on the hull was done, West occupied himself with the masts and the rigging, with the assistance of Martin Holt, our sailing master, who was very clever at this kind of industry.

On the 21st of October, Captain Len Guy said to me:

"You shall see, Mr. Jeorling, that nothing will be neglected to ensure the success of our enterprise. Everything that can be foreseen has been foreseen, and if the *Halbrane* is to perish in some catastrophe, it will be because it is not permitted to human beings to go against the designs of God."

"I have good hopes, captain, as I have already said. Your vessel and her crew are worthy of confidence. But, supposing the expedition should be much prolonged, perhaps the supply of provisions—"

"We shall carry sufficient for two years, and those shall be of good quality. Port Egmont has proved capable of supplying us with everything we require."

"Another question, if you will allow me?"

"Put it, Mr. Jeorling, put it."

"Shall you not need a more numerous crew for the *Halbrane*? Though you have men enough for the working of the ship, suppose you find you have to attack or to defend in the Antarctic waters? Let us not forget that, according to Arthur Pym's narrative, there were thousands of natives on Tsalal Island, and if your brother—if his companions are prisoners—"

"I hope, Mr. Jeorling, our artillery will protect the *Halbrane* better than the *Jane* was protected by her guns. To tell the truth, the crew we have would not be sufficient for an expedition of this kind. I have been arranging for recruiting our forces."

"Will it be difficult?"

"Yes and no; for the Governor has promised to help me."

"I surmise, captain, that recruits will have to be attracted by larger pay."

"Double pay, Mr. Jeorling, and the whole crew must have the same."

"You know, captain, I am disposed, and, indeed, desirous to contribute to the expenses of the expedition. Will you kindly consider me as your partner?"

"All that shall be arranged, Mr. Jeorling, and I am very grateful to you. The main point is to complete our armament with the least possible delay. We must be ready to clear out in a week."

The news that the schooner was bound for the Antarctic seas had produced some sensation in the Falklands, at Port Egmont, and in the ports of La Soledad. At that season a number of unoccupied sailors were there, awaiting the passing of the whaling-ships to offer their services, for which they were very well paid in general. If it had been only for a fishing campaign on the borders of the Polar Circle, between the Sandwich Islands and New Georgia, Captain Len Guy would have merely had to make a selection. But the projected voyage was a very different thing; and only the old sailors of the *Halbrane* were entirely indifferent to the dangers of such an enterprise, and ready to follow their chief whithersoever it might please him to go.

In reality it was necessary to treble the crew of the schooner. Counting the captain, the mate, the boatswain, the cook and myself, we were thirteen on board. Now, thirty-two or thirty-four men would not be too many for us, and it must be remembered that there were thirty-eight on board the *Jane*.

In this emergency the Governor exerted himself to the utmost, and thanks to the largely-extra pay that was offered, Captain Len Guy procured his full tale of seamen. Nine recruits signed articles for the duration of the campaign, which could not be fixed beforehand, but was not to extend beyond Tsalal Island.

The crew, counting every man on board except myself, numbered thirty-one, and a thirty-second for whom I bespeak especial attention. On the eve of our departure, Captain Len Guy was accosted at the angle of the port by an individual whom he recognized as a sailor by his clothes, his walk, and his speech.

This individual said, in a rough and hardly intelligible voice,—

"Captain, I have to make a proposal to you."

"What is it?"

"Have you still a place?"

"For a sailor?"

"For a sailor."

"Yes and no."

"Is it yes?"

"It is yes, if the man suits me."

"Will you take me?"

"You are a seaman?"

"I have served the sea for twenty-five years."

"Where?"

"In the Southern Seas."

"Far?"

"Yes, far, far."

"Your age?"

"Forty-four years."

"And you are at Port Egmont?"

"I shall have been there three years, come Christmas."

"Did you expect to get on a passing whale-ship?"

"No."

"Then what were you doing here?"

"Nothing, and I did not think of going to sea again."

"Then why seek a berth?"

"Just an idea. The news of the expedition your schooner is going on was spread. I desire, yes, I desire to take part in it—with your leave, of course."

"You are known at Port Egmont?"

"Well known, and I have incurred no reproach since I came here."

"Very well," said the captain. "I will make inquiry respecting you."

"Inquire, captain, and if you say yes, my bag shall be on board this evening."

"What is your name?"

"Hunt."

"And you are—?"

"An American."

This Hunt was a man of short stature, his weather beaten face was brick red, his skin of a yellowish-brown like an Indian's, his body clumsy, his head very large, his legs were bowed, his whole frame denoted exceptional strength, especially the arms, which terminated in huge hands. His grizzled hair resembled a kind of fur.

A particular and anything but prepossessing character was imparted to the physiognomy of this individual by the extraordinary keenness of his small eyes, his almost lipless mouth, which stretched from ear to ear, and his long teeth, which were dazzlingly white; their enamel being intact, for he had never been attacked by scurvy, the common scourge of seamen in high latitudes.

Hunt had been living in the Falklands for three years; he lived alone on a pension, no one knew from whence this was derived. He was singularly uncommunicative, and passed his time in fishing, by which he might have lived, not only as a matter of sustenance, but as an article of commerce.

The information gained by Captain Len Guy was necessarily incomplete, as it was confined to Hunt's conduct during his residence at Port Egmont. The man did not fight, he did not drink, and he had given many proofs of his Herculean strength. Concerning his past nothing was known, but undoubtedly he had been a sailor. He had said more to Len Guy than he had ever said to anybody; but he kept silence respecting the family to which he belonged, and the place of his birth. This was of no importance; that he should prove to be a good sailor was all we had to think about. Hunt obtained a favourable reply, and came on board that same evening.

On the 27th, in the morning, in the presence of the authorities of the Archipelago, the *Halbrane's* anchor was lifted, the last good wishes and the final adieus were exchanged, and the schooner took the sea. The same evening Capes Dolphin and Pembroke disappeared in the mists of the horizon.

Thus began the astonishing adventure undertaken by these brave men, who were driven by a sentiment of humanity towards the most terrible regions of the Antarctic realm.

CHAPTER X.

THE OUTSET OF THE ENTERPRISE.

HERE was I, then, launched into an adventure which seemed likely to surpass all my former experiences. Who would have believed such a thing of me. But I was under a spell which drew me towards the unknown, that unknown of the polar world whose secrets so many daring pioneers had in vain essayed to penetrate. And this time, who could tell but that the sphinx of the Antarctic regions would speak for the first time to human ears!

The new crew had firstly to apply themselves to learning their several duties, and the old—all fine fellows—aided them in the task. Although Captain Len Guy had not had much choice, he seemed to have been in luck. These sailors, of various nationalities, displayed zeal and good will. They were aware, also, that the mate was a man whom it would not do to vex, for Hurliguerly had given them to understand that West would break any man's head who did not go straight. His chief allowed him full latitude in this respect.

"A latitude," he added, "which is obtained by taking the altitude of the eye with a shut fist."

I recognized my friend the boatswain in the manner of this warning to all whom it might concern.

The new hands took the admonition seriously, and there was no occasion to punish any of them. As for Hunt, while he observed the docility of a true sailor in all his duties, he always kept himself apart, speaking to none, and even slept on the deck, in a corner, rather than occupy a bunk in the forecastle with the others.

Captain Len Guy's intention was to take the Sandwich Isles for his point of departure towards the south, after having made acquaintance with New Georgia, distant eight hundred miles from the Falklands. Thus the schooner would be in longitude on the route of the *Jane*.

On the 2nd of November this course brought us to the bearings which certain navigators have assigned to the Aurora Islands, 30° 15′ of latitude and 47° 33′ of east longitude.

Well, then, notwithstanding the affirmations—which I regarded with suspicion—of the captains of the *Aurora* in 1762, of the *Saint Miguel*, in 1769, of the *Pearl*, in 1779, of the *Prinicus* and the *Dolores*, in 1790, of the *Atrevida*, in 1794, which gave the bearings of the three islands of the group, we did not perceive a single indication of land in the whole of the space traversed by us. It was the same with regard to the alleged islands of the conceited Glass. Not a single little islet was to be seen in the position he had indicated, although the look-out was most carefully kept. It is to be feared that his Excellency the Governor of Tristan d'Acunha will never see his name figuring in geographical nomenclature.

It was now the 6th of November. Our passage promised to be shorter than that of the *Jane*. We had no need to hurry, however. Our schooner would arrive

Taking in sail under difficulties.

before the gates of the iceberg wall would be open. For three days the weather caused the working of the ship to be unusually laborious, and the new crew behaved very well; thereupon the boatswain congratulated them. Hurliguerly bore witness that Hunt, for all his awkward and clumsy build, was in himself worth three men.

"A famous recruit," said he.

"Yes, indeed," I replied, "and gained just at the last moment."

"Very true, Mr. Jeorling! But what a face and head he has, that Hunt!"

"I have often met Americans like him in the regions of the Far West," I answered, "and I should not be surprised if this man had Indian blood in his veins. Do you ever talk with Hunt?"

"Very seldom, Mr. Jeorling. He keeps himself to himself, and away from everybody. And yet, it is not for want of mouth. I never saw anything like his! And his hands! Have you seen his hands? Be on your guard, Mr. Jeorling, if ever he wants to shake hands with you."

"Fortunately, boatswain, Hunt does not seem to be quarrelsome. He appears to be a quiet man who does not abuse his strength."

"No—except when he is setting a halyard. Then I am always afraid the pulley will come down and the yard with it."

Hunt certainly was a strange being, and I could not resist observing him with curiosity, especially as it struck me that he regarded me at times with a curious intentness.

On the 10th of November, at about two in the afternoon, the look-out shouted,—

"Land ahead, starboard!"

An observation had just given 55° 7′ latitude and 41° 13′ longitude. This land could only be the Isle de Saint Pierre—its British names are South Georgia, New Georgia, and King George's Island—and it belongs to the circumpolar regions.

It was discovered by the Frenchman, Barbe, in 1675, before Cook; but, although he came in second, the celebrated navigator gave it the series of names which it still bears.

The schooner took the direction of this island, whose snow-clad heights—formidable masses of ancient rock—rise to an immense altitude through the yellow fogs of the surrounding space.

New Georgia, situated within five hundred leagues of Magellan Straits, belongs to the administrative domain of the Falklands. The British administration is not represented there by anyone, the island is not inhabited, although it is habitable, at least in the summer season.

On the following day, while the men were gone in search of water, I walked about in the vicinity of the bay. The place was an utter desert, for the period at which sealing is pursued there had not arrived. New Georgia, being exposed to the direct action of the Antarctic polar current, is freely frequented by marine mammals. I saw several droves of these creatures on the rocks, the strand, and within the rock-grottoes of the coast. Whole "smalas" of penguins, standing motionless in interminable rows, brayed their protest against the invasion of an intruder—I allude to myself.

Innumerable larks flew over the surface of the waters and the sands; their song awoke my memory of lands more favoured by nature. It is fortunate that these birds do not want branches to perch on; for there does not exist a tree in New Georgia. Here and there I found a few phanerogams, some pale-coloured mosses, and especially tussock grass in such abundance that numerous herds of cattle might be fed upon the island.

On the 12th November the *Halbrane* sailed once more, and having doubled Charlotte Point at the extremity of Royal Bay, she headed in the direction of the Sandwich Islands, four hundred miles from thence.

So far we had not encountered floating ice. The reason was that the summer sun had not detached any, either from the icebergs or the southern lands. Later on, the current would draw them to the height of the fiftieth parallel, which, in the southern hemisphere, is that of Paris or Quebec. But we were much impeded by huge banks of fog which frequently shut out the horizon. Nevertheless, as these waters presented no danger, and there was nothing to fear from ice packs or drifting icebergs, the *Halbrane* was able to pursue her route towards the Sandwich Islands comfortably enough. Great flocks of clangorous birds, breasting the wind and hardly moving their wings, passed us in the midst of the fogs, petrels, divers, halcyons, and albatross, bound landwards, as though to show us the way.

Owing, no doubt, to these mists, we were unable to discern Traversey Island. Captain Len Guy, however, thought some vague streaks of intermittent light which were perceived in the night, between the 14th and 15th, probably proceeded from a volcano which might be that of Traversey, as the crater frequently emits flames.

On the 17th November the schooner reached the

Archipelago to which Cook gave the name of Southern Thule in the first instance, as it was the most southern land that had been discovered at that period. He afterwards baptized it Sandwich Isles.

James West repaired to Thule in the large boat, in order to explore the approachable points, while Captain Len Guy and I descended on the Bristol strand.

We found absolutely desolate country; the only inhabitants were melancholy birds of Antarctic species. Mosses and lichens cover the nakedness of an unproductive soil. Behind the beach a few firs rise to a considerable height on the bare hill-sides, from whence great masses occasionally come crashing down with a thundering sound. Awful solitude reigns everywhere. There was nothing to attest the passage of any human being, or the presence of any shipwrecked persons on Bristol Island.

West's exploration at Thule produced a precisely similar result. A few shots fired from our schooner had no effect but to drive away the crowd of petrels and divers, and to startle the rows of stupid penguins on the beach.

While Captain Len Guy and I were walking, I said to him,—

"You know, of course, what Cook's opinion on the subject of the Sandwich group was when he discovered it. At first he believed he had set foot upon a continent. According to him, the mountains of ice carried out of the Antarctic Sea by the drift were detached from that continent. He recognized afterwards that the Sandwiches only formed an Archipelago, but, nevertheless, his belief that a polar continent farther south exists, remained firm and unchanged."

"I know that is so, Mr. Jeorling," replied the captain,

"but if such a continent exists, we must conclude that there is a great gap in its coast, and that Weddell and my brother each got in by that gap at six years' interval. That our great navigator had not the luck to discover this passage is easy to explain; he stopped at the seventy-first parallel! But others found it after Captain Cook, and others will find it again."

"And we shall be of the number, captain."

"Yes—with the help of God! Cook did not hesitate to assert that no one would ever venture farther than he had gone, and that the Antarctic lands, if any such existed, would never be seen, but the future will prove that he was mistaken. They have been seen so far as the eighty-fourth degree of latitude—"

"And who knows," said I, "perhaps beyond that, by Arthur Pym."

"Perhaps, Mr. Jeorling. It is true that we have not to trouble ourselves about Arthur Pym, since he, at least, and Dirk Peters also, returned to America."

"But—supposing he did not return?"

"I consider that we have not to face that eventuality," replied Captain Len Guy.

CHAPTER XI.

FROM THE SANDWICH ISLANDS TO THE POLAR CIRCLE.

THE *Halbrane*, singularly favoured by the weather, sighted the New South Orkneys group in six days after she had sailed from the Sandwich Islands. This archipelago was discovered by Palmer, an American, and Bothwell, an Englishman, jointly, in 1821-22. Crossed by the sixty-first parallel, it is comprehended between the forty-fourth and the forty-seventh meridian.

On approaching, we were enabled to observe contorted masses and steep cliffs on the north side, which became less rugged as they neared the coast, at whose edge lay enormous ice-floes, heaped together in formidable confusion; these, before two months should have expired, would be drifted towards the temperate waters. At that season the whaling ships would appear to carry on the taking of the great blowing creatures, while some of their crews would remain on the islands to capture seals and sea-elephants.

In order to avoid the strait, which was encumbered with islets and ice-floes, Captain Len Guy first cast anchor at the south-eastern extremity of Laurie Island, where he passed the day on the 24th; then, having rounded Cape Dundas, he sailed along the southern coast of Coronation

Island, where the schooner anchored on the 25th. Our close and careful researches produced no result as regarded the sailors of the *Jane.*

The islands and islets were peopled by multitudes of birds. Without taking the penguins into account, those guano-covered rocks were crowded with white pigeons, a species of which I had already seen some specimens. These birds have rather short, conical beaks, and red-rimmed eyelids; they can be knocked over with little difficulty. As for the vegetable kingdom in the New South Orkneys, it is represented only by grey lichen and some scanty sea-weeds. Mussels are found in great abundance all along the rocks; of these we procured an ample supply.

The boatswain and his men did not lose the opportunity of killing several dozens of penguins with their sticks, not from a ruthless instinct of destruction, but from the legitimate desire to procure fresh food.

"Their flesh is just as good as chicken, Mr. Jeorling," said Hurliguerly. "Did you not eat penguin at the Kerguelens?"

"Yes, boatswain, but it was cooked by Atkins."

"Very well, then; it will be cooked by Endicott here, and you will not know the difference."

And in fact we in the saloon, like the men in the fore-castle, were regaled with penguin, and acknowledged the merits of our excellent sea-cook.

The *Halbrane* sailed on the 26th of November, at six o'clock in the morning, heading south. She reascended the forty-third meridian; this we were able to ascertain very exactly by a good observation. This route it was that Weddell and then William Guy had followed, and, provided the schooner did not deflect either to the east or the west, she must inevitably come to Tsalal Island. The difficulties of navigation had to be taken into account, of course.

The wind, continuing to blow steadily from the west, was in our favour, and if the present speed of the *Halbrane* could be maintained, as I ventured to suggest to Captain Len Guy, the voyage from the South Orkneys to the Polar Circle would be a short one. Beyond, as I knew, we should have to force the gate of the thick barrier of icebergs, or to discover a breach in that ice-fortress.

"So that, in less than a month, captain—" I suggested, tentatively.

"In less than a month I hope to have found the iceless sea which Weddell and Arthur Pym describe so fully, beyond the ice-wall, and thenceforth we need only sail on under ordinary conditions to Bennet Island in the first place, and afterwards to Tsalal Island. Once on that 'wide open sea,' what obstacle could arrest or even retard our progress?"

"I can foresee none, captain, so soon as we shall get to the back of the ice-wall. The passage through is the difficult point; it must be our chief source of anxiety, and if only the wind holds—"

"It will hold, Mr. Jeorling. All the navigators of the austral seas have been able to ascertain, as I myself have done, the permanence of this wind."

"That is true, and I rejoice in the assurance, captain. Besides, I acknowledge, without shrinking from the admission, that I am beginning to be superstitious."

"And why not, Mr. Jeorling? What is there unreasonable in admitting the intervention of a supernatural power in the most ordinary circumstances of life? And we, who sail the *Halbrane*, should we venture to doubt it? Recall to your mind our meeting with the unfortunate Patterson on our ship's course, the fragment of ice carried into the waters where we were, and dissolved immediately afterwards. Were not these facts providential? Nay, I go farther still, and am sure that, after having done so much to guide us towards our compatriots, God will not abandon us—"

"I think as you think, captain. No, His intervention is not to be denied, and I do not believe that chance plays the part assigned to it by superficial minds upon the stage of human life. All the facts are united by a mysterious chain.'

"A chain, Mr. Jeorling, whose first link, so far as we are concerned, is Patterson's ice-block, and whose last will be Tsalal Island. Ah! My brother! my poor brother! Left there for eleven years, with his companions in misery, without being able to entertain the hope that succour ever could reach them! And Patterson carried far away from them, under we know not what conditions, they not knowing what had become of him! If my heart is sick when I think of these catastrophes, Mr. Jeorling, at least it will not fail me unless it be at the moment when my brother throws himself into my arms."

So then we two were agreed in our trust in Providence. It had been made plain to us in a manifest fashion that God had entrusted us with a mission, and we would do all that might be humanly possible to accomplish it.

The schooner's crew, I ought to mention, were animated by the like sentiments, and shared the same hopes. I allude to the original seamen who were so devoted to their captain. As for the new ones, they were probably indifferent to the result of the enterprise, provided it should secure the profits promised to them by their engagement.

At least, I was assured by the boatswain that such was the case, but with the exception of Hunt. This man had apparently not been induced to take service by the bribe of high wages or prize money. He was absolutely silent on that and every other subject.

"If he does not speak to you, boatswain," I said, "neither does he speak to me."

"Do you know, Mr. Jeorling, what it is my notion that man has already done?"

"Tell me, Hurliguerly."

"Well, then, I believe he has gone far, far into the southern seas, let him be as dumb as a fish about it. Why he *is* dumb is his own affair. But if that sea-hog of a man has not been inside the Antarctic Circle and even the ice wall by a good dozen degrees, may the first sea we ship carry me overboard."

"From what do you judge, boatswain?"

"From his eyes, Mr. Jeorling, from his eyes. No matter at what moment, let the ship's head be as it may, those eyes of his are always on the south, open, unwinking, fixed like guns in position."

Hurliguerly did not exaggerate, and I had already remarked this. To employ an expression of Edgar Poe's, Hunt had eyes like a falcon's.

"When he is not on the watch," resumed the boatswain, "that savage leans all the time with his elbows on the side, as motionless as he is mute. His right place would be at the end of our bow, where he would do for a figure-head to the *Halbrane*, and a very ugly one at that! And then, when he is at the helm, Mr. Jeorling, just observe him! His enormous hands clutch the handles as though they were fastened to the wheel; he gazes at the binnacle as though the magnet of the compass were drawing his eyes. I pride myself on being a good steersman, but as for being the equal of Hunt, I'm not! With him, not for an instant does the needle vary from the sailing-line, however rough a lurch she may give. I am sure that if the binnacle lamp were to go out in the night Hunt would not require to relight it. The fire in his eyes would light up the dial and keep him right."

For several days our navigation went on in unbroken monotony, without a single incident, and under favourable conditions. The spring season was advancing, and whales began to make their appearance in large numbers.

In these waters a week would suffice for ships of heavy tonnage to fill their casks with the precious oil. Thus the new men of the crew, and especially the Americans, did not conceal their regret for the captain's indifference in the presence of so many animals worth their weight in gold, and more abundant than they had ever seen whales at that period of the year. The leading malcontent was Hearne, a sealing-master, to whom his companions were ready to listen. He had found it easy to get the upper hand of the other sailors by his rough manner and the surly audacity that was expressed by his whole personality. Hearne was an American, and forty-five years of age. He was an active, vigorous man, and I could see him in my mind's eye, standing up on his double bowed whaling-boat brandishing the harpoon, darting it into the flank of a whale, and paying out the rope. He must have been fine to see. Granted his passion for this business, I could not be surprised that his discontent showed itself upon occasion.

In any case, however, our schooner was not fitted out

for fishing, and the implements of whaling were not on board.

One day, about three o'clock in the afternoon, I had gone forward to watch the gambols of a "school" of the huge sea mammals. Hearne was pointing them out to his companions, and muttering in disjointed phrases,—

"There, look there! That's a fin-back! There's another, and another; three of them with their dorsal fins five or six feet high. Just see them swimming between two waves, quietly, making no jumps. Ah! if I had a harpoon, I bet my head that I could send it into one of the four yellow spots they have on their bodies. But there's nothing to be done in this traffic-box; one cannot stretch one's arms. Devil take it! In these seas it is fishing we ought to be at, not—"

Then, stopping short, he swore a few oaths, and cried out, "And that other whale!"

"The one with a hump like a dromedary?" asked a sailor.

"Yes. It is a humpback," replied Hearne. "Do you make out its wrinkled belly, and also its long dorsal fin? They're not easy to take, those humpbacks, for they go down into great depths and devour long reaches of your lines. Truly, we deserve that he should give us a switch of his tail on our side, since we don't send a harpoon into his."

"Look out! Look out!" shouted the boatswain. This was not to warn us that we were in danger of receiving the formidable stroke of the humpback's tail which the sealing-master had wished us. No, an enormous blower had come alongside the schooner, and almost on the instant a spout of ill-smelling water was ejected from its

"There, look there! That's a fin-back!"

blow-hole with a noise like a distant roar of artillery. The whole foredeck to the main hatch was inundated.

"That's well done!" growled Hearne, shrugging his shoulders, while his companions shook themselves and cursed the humpback.

Besides these two kinds of cetacea we had observed several right-whales, and these are the most usually met with in the southern seas. They have no fins, and their blubber is very thick. The taking of these fat monsters of the deep is not attended with much danger. The right-whales are vigorously pursued in the southern seas, where the little shell fish called "whales' food" abound. The whales subsist entirely upon these small crustaceans.

Presently, one of these right-whales, measuring sixty feet in length—that is to say, the animal was the equivalent of a hundred barrels of oil—was seen floating within three cables' lengths of the schooner.

"Yes! that's a right-whale," exclaimed Hearne. "You might tell it by its thick, short spout. See, that one on the port side, like a column of smoke, that's the spout of a right-whale! And all this is passing before our very noses—a dead loss! Why, it's like emptying money-bags into the sea not to fill one's barrels when one can. A nice sort of captain, indeed, to let all this merchandise be lost, and do such wrong to his crew!"

"Hearne," said an imperious voice, "go up to the main-top. You will be more at your ease there to reckon the whales."

"But, sir—"

"No reply, or I'll keep you up there until to-morrow. Come—be off at once."

And as he would have got the worst of an attempt at resistance, the sealing-master obeyed in silence.

The season must have been abnormally advanced, for although we continued to see a vast number of testaceans, we did not catch sight of a single whaling-ship in all this fishing-ground.

I hasten to state that, although we were not to be tempted by whales, no other fishing was forbidden on board the *Halbrane*, and our daily bill of fare profited by the boatswain's trawling lines, to the extreme satisfaction of stomachs weary of salt meat. Our lines brought us goby, salmon, cod, mackerel, conger, mullet, and parrot-fish.

The birds which we saw, and which came from every point of the horizon, were those I have already mentioned, petrels, divers, halcyons, and pigeons in countless flocks. I also saw—but beyond aim—a giant petrel; its dimensions were truly astonishing. This was one of those called "quebrantahnesos" by the Spaniards. This bird of the Magellanian waters is very remarkable; its curved and slender wings have a span of from thirteen to fourteen feet, equal to that of the wings of the great albatross. Nor is the latter wanting among these powerful winged creatures; we saw the dusky-plumed albatross of the cold latitudes, sweeping towards the glacial zone.

On the 30th of November, after observation taken at noon, it was found that we had reached 66° 23′ 3″ of latitude.

The *Halbrane* had then crossed the Polar Circle which circumscribes the area of the Antarctic zone.

CHAPTER XII.

BETWEEN THE POLAR CIRCLE AND THE ICE WALL.

SINCE the *Halbrane* has passed beyond the imaginary curve drawn at twenty-three and a half degrees from the Pole, it seems as though she had entered a new region, "that region of Desolation and Silence," as Edgar Poe says; that magic person of splendour and glory in which the *Eleanora's* singer longed to be shut up to all eternity; that immense ocean of light ineffable.

It is my belief—to return to less fanciful hypotheses—that the Antarctic region, with a superficies of more than five millions of square miles, has remained what our spheroid was during the glacial period. In the summer, the southern zone, as we all know, enjoys perpetual day, owing to the rays projected by the orb of light above its horizon in his spiral ascent. Then, so soon as he has disappeared, the long night sets in, a night which is frequently illumined by the polar aurora or Northern Lights.

It was then in the season of light that our schooner was about to sail in these formidable regions. The permanent brightness would not fail us before we should have reached Tsalal Island, where we felt no doubt of finding the men of the *Jane*.

When Captain Len Guy, West, and the old sailors of the crew learned that the schooner had cleared the sixty-sixth parallel of latitude, their rough and sunburnt faces shone with satisfaction. The next day, Hurliguerly accosted me on the deck with a broad smile and a cheerful manner.

"So then, Mr. Jeorling," said he, "we've left the famous 'Circle' behind us!"

"Not far enough, boatswain, not far enough!"

"Oh, that will come! But I am disappointed."

"In what way?"

"Because we have not done what is usual on board ships on crossing the Line!"

"You regret that?"

"Certainly I do, and the *Halbrane* might have been allowed the ceremony of a southern baptism."

"A baptism? And whom would you have baptized, boatswain, seeing that all our men, like yourself, have already sailed beyond this parallel?"

"We! Oh, yes! But you! Oh, no, Mr. Jeorling. And why, may I ask, should not that ceremony be performed in your honour?"

"True, boatswain; this is the first time in the course of my travels that I have been in so high a latitude."

"And you should have been rewarded by a baptism, Mr. Jeorling. Yes, indeed, but without any big fuss—no drum and trumpet about it, and leaving out old Father Neptune with his masquerade. If you would permit me to baptize you—"

"So be it, Hurliguerly," said I, putting my hand into my pocket. "Baptize as you please. Here is something to drink my health with at the nearest tavern."

"Then that will be Bennet Islet or Tsalal Island, provided there are any taverns in those savage islands, and any Atkinses to keep them."

"Tell me, boatswain—I always get back to Hunt—does he seem so much pleased to have passed the Polar Circle as the *Halbrane's* old sailors are?"

"Who knows? There's nothing to be got out of him one way or another. But, as I have said before, if he has not already made acquaintance with the ice-barrier."

"What makes you think so?"

"Everything and nothing, Mr. Jeorling. One feels these things; one doesn't think them. Hunt is an old sea-dog, who has carried his canvas bag into every corner of the world."

The boatswain's opinion was mine also, and some inexplicable presentiment made me observe Hunt constantly, for he occupied a large share of my thoughts.

Early in December the wind showed a north-west tendency, and that was not good for us, but we would have no serious right to complain so long as it did not blow due south-west. In the latter case the schooner would have been thrown out of her course, or at least she would have had a struggle to keep in it, and it was better for us, in short, not to stray from the meridian which we had followed since our departure from the New South Orkneys. Captain Len Guy was made anxious by this alteration in the wind, and besides, the speed of the *Halbrane* was manifestly lessened, for the breeze began to soften on the 4th, and in the middle of the night it died away.

In the morning the sails hung motionless and shrivelled along the masts. Although not a breath reached us, and the surface of the ocean was unruffled, the schooner was rocked from side to side by the long oscillations of the swell coming from the west.

"The sea feels something," said Captain Len Guy to me, "and there must be rough weather on that side," he added, pointing westward.

"The horizon is misty," I replied; "but perhaps the sun towards noon—"

"The sun has no strength in this latitude, Mr. Jeorling, not even in summer. Jem!"

West came up to us.

"What do you think of the sky?"

"I do not think well of it. We must be ready for anything and everything, captain."

"Has not the look-out given warning of the first drifting ice?" I asked.

"Yes," replied Captain Len Guy, "and if we get near the icebergs the damage will not be to them. Therefore, if prudence demands that we should go either to the east or to the west, we shall resign ourselves, but only in case of absolute necessity."

The watch had made no mistake. In the afternoon we sighted masses, islets they might be called, of ice, drifting slowly southward, but these were not yet of considerable extent or altitude. These packs were easy to avoid; they could not interfere with the sailing of the *Halbrane*. But, although the wind had hitherto permitted her to keep on her course, she was not advancing, and it was exceedingly disagreeable to be rolling about in a rough and hollow sea which struck our ship's sides most unpleasantly.

About two o'clock it was blowing a hurricane from all the points of the compass. The schooner was terribly knocked about, and the boatswain had the deck cleared of everything that was movable by her rolling and pitching.

Fortunately, the cargo could not be displaced, the stowage having been effected with perfect forecast of nautical eventualities. We had not to dread the fate of the *Grampus*, which was lost owing to negligence in her lading. It will be remembered that the brig turned bottom upwards, and that Arthur Pym and Dirk Peters remained for several days crouching on its keel.

Besides, the schooner's pumps did not give a drop of water; the ship was perfectly sound in every part, owing to the efficient repairs that had been done during our stay at the Falklands. The temperature had fallen rapidly, and hail, rain, and snow thickened and darkened the air. At ten o'clock in the evening—I must use this word, although the sun remained always above the horizon—the tempest increased, and the captain and his lieutenant, almost unable to hear each other's voices amid the elemental strife, communicated mostly by gestures, which is as good a mode as speech between sailors.

I could not make up my mind to retire to my cabin, and, seeking the shelter of the roundhouse, I remained on deck, observing the weather phenomena, and the skill, certainty, celerity, and effect with which the crew carried out the orders of the captain and West. It was a strange and terrible experience for a landsman, even one who had seen so much of the sea and seamanship as I had. At the moment of a certain difficult manœuvre, four men had to climb to the crossbars of the fore-mast in order to reef the mainsail. The first who sprang to the ratlines was Hunt. The second was Martin Holt; Burry and one of the recruits followed them. I could not have believed that any man could display such skill and agility as Hunt's. His hands and feet hardly caught the ratlines. Having reached the crossbars first, he stretched himself on the ropes to the end of the yard, while Holt went to the other end, and the two recruits remained in the middle.

While the men were working, and the tempest was raging round us, a terrific lurch of the ship to starboard under the stroke of a mountainous wave, flung everything on the deck into wild confusion, and the sea rushed in through the scupper-holes. I was knocked down, and for some moments was unable to rise.

So great had been the incline of the schooner that the end of the yard of the mainsail was plunged three or four feet into the crest of a wave. When it emerged Martin Holt, who had been astride on it, had disappeared. A cry was heard, uttered by the sailing-master, whose arm could be seen wildly waving amid the whiteness of the foam. The sailors rushed to the side and flung out one a rope, another a cask, a third a spar—in short, any object of which Martin Holt might lay hold. At the moment when I struggled up to my feet I caught sight of a massive substance which cleft the air and vanished in the whirl of the waves.

Was this a second accident? No! it was a voluntary action, a deed of self-sacrifice. Having finished his task, Hunt had thrown himself into the sea, that he might save Martin Holt.

"Two men overboard!"

Yes, two—one to save the other. And were they not about to perish together?

The two heads rose to the foaming surface of the water. Hunt was swimming vigorously, cutting through the waves, and was nearing Martin Holt.

Hunt to the rescue.

"They are lost! both lost!" exclaimed the captain. "The boat, West, the boat!"

"If you give the order to lower it," answered West, "I will be the first to get into it, although at the risk of my life. But I must have the order."

In unspeakable suspense the ship's crew and myself had witnessed this scene. None thought of the position of the *Halbrane*, which was sufficiently dangerous; all eyes were fixed upon the terrible waves. Now fresh cries, the frantic cheers of the crew, rose above the roar of the elements. Hunt had reached the drowning man just as he sank out of sight, had seized hold of him, and was supporting him with his left arm, while Holt, incapable of movement, swayed helplessly about like a weed. With the other arm Hunt was swimming bravely and making way towards the schooner.

A minute, which seemed endless, passed. The two men, the one dragging the other, were hardly to be distinguished in the midst of the surging waves.

At last Hunt reached the schooner, and caught one of the lines hanging over the side.

In a minute Hunt and Martin Holt were hoisted on board; the latter was laid down at the foot of the foremast, and the former was quite ready to go to his work. Holt was speedily restored by the aid of vigorous rubbing; his senses came back, and he opened his eyes.

"Martin Holt," said Captain Len Guy, who was leaning over him, "you have been brought back from very far—"

"Yes, yes, captain," answered Holt, as he looked about him with a searching gaze, "but who saved me?"

"Hunt," cried the boatswain, "Hunt risked his life for you."

As the latter was hanging back, Hurliguerly pushed him towards Martin Holt, whose eyes expressed the liveliest gratitude.

"Hunt," said he, "you have saved me. But for you I should have been lost. I thank you."

Hunt made no reply.

"Hunt," resumed Captain Len Guy, "don't you hear?"

The man seemed not to have heard.

"Hunt," said Martin Holt again, "come near to me. I thank you. I want to shake hands with you."

And he held out his right hand. Hunt stepped back a few paces, shaking his head with the air of a man who did not want so many compliments for a thing so simple, and quietly walked forward to join his shipmates, who were working vigorously under the orders of West.

Decidedly, this man was a hero in courage and self-devotion; but equally decidedly he was a being impervious to impressions, and not on that day either was the boatswain destined to know "the colour of his words!"

For three whole days, the 6th, 7th, and 8th of December, the tempest raged in these waters, accompanied by snow storms which perceptibly lowered the temperature. It is needless to say that Captain Len Guy proved himself a true seaman, that James West had an eye to everything, that the crew seconded them loyally, and that Hunt was always foremost when there was work to be done or danger to be incurred.

In truth, I do not know how to give an idea of this man! What a difference there was between him and most of the sailors recruited at the Falklands, and especially between him and Hearne, the sealing-master! They obeyed, no doubt, for such a master as James West gets himself obeyed, whether with good or ill will. But behind backs what complaints were made, what recriminations were exchanged! All this, I feared, was of evil presage for the future.

Martin Holt had been able to resume his duties very soon, and he fulfilled them with hearty good-will. He knew the business of a sailor right well, and was the only man on board who could compete with Hunt in handiness and zeal.

"Well, Holt," said I to him one day when he was talking with the boatswain, "what terms are you on with that queer fellow Hunt now? Since the salvage affair, is he a little more communicative?"

"No, Mr. Jeorling, and I think he even tries to avoid me."

"To avoid you?"

"Well, he did so before, for that matter."

"Yes, indeed, that is true," added Hurliguerly; "I have made the same remark more than once."

"Then he keeps aloof from you, Holt, as from the others?"

"From me more than from the others."

"What is the meaning of that?"

"I don't know, Mr. Jeorling."

I was surprised at what the two men had said, but a little observation convinced me that Hunt actually did avoid every occasion of coming in contact with Martin Holt. Did he not think that he had a right to Holt's gratitude although the latter owed his life to him? This man's conduct was certainly very strange.

In the early morning of the 9th the wind showed a

tendency to change in the direction of the east, which would mean more manageable weather for us. And, in fact, although the sea still remained rough, at about two in the morning it became feasible to put on more sail without risk, and thus the *Halbrane* regained the course from which she had been driven by the prolonged tempest.

In that portion of the Antarctic sea the ice-packs were more numerous, and there was reason to believe that the tempest, by hastening the smash-up, had broken the barrier of the iceberg wall towards the east.

CHAPTER XIII.

ALONG THE FRONT OF THE ICEBERGS.

ALTHOUGH the seas beyond the Polar Circle were wildly tumultuous, it is but just to acknowledge that our navigation had been accomplished so far under exceptional conditions. And what good luck it would be if the *Halbrane*, in this first fortnight of December, were to find the Weddell route open!

There! I am talking of the Weddell route as though it were a macadamized road, well kept, with mile-stones and "This way to the South Pole" on a signpost!

The numerous wandering masses of ice gave our men no trouble; they were easily avoided. It seemed likely that no real difficulties would arise until the schooner should have to try to make a passage for herself through the icebergs.

Besides, there was no surprise to be feared. The presence of ice was indicated by a yellowish tint in the atmosphere, which the whalers called "blink." This is a phenomenon peculiar to the glacial zones which never deceives the observer.

For five successive days the *Halbrane* sailed without sustaining any damage, without having, even for a moment, had to fear a collision. It is true that in proportion as she advanced towards the south the number of ice-packs increased and the channels became narrower. On the 14th an observation gave us 72′37′ for latitude, our longitude remaining the same, between the forty-second and the forty-third meridian. This was already a point beyond the Antarctic Circle that few navigators had been able to reach. We were at only two degrees lower than Weddell.

The navigation of the schooner naturally became a more delicate matter in the midst of those dim, wan masses soiled with the excreta of birds. Many of them had a leprous look: compared with their already considerable volume, how small our little ship, over whose mast some of the icebergs already towered, must have appeared!

Captain Len Guy admirably combined boldness and prudence in his command of his ship. He never passed to leeward of an iceberg, if the distance did not guarantee the success of any manœuvre whatsoever that might suddenly become necessary. He was familiar with all the contingencies of ice-navigation, and was not afraid to venture into the midst of these flotillas of drifts and packs. That day he said to me,—

"Mr. Jeorling, this is not the first time that I have tried to penetrate into the Polar Sea, and without success. Well, if I made the attempt to do this when I had nothing but presumption as to the fate of the *Jane* to go upon, what shall I not do now that presumption is changed into certainty?"

"I understand that, captain, and of course your experience of navigation in these waters must increase our chances of success."

"Undoubtedly. Nevertheless, all that lies beyond the

fixed icebergs is still the Unknown for me, as it is for other navigators."

"The Unknown! No, not absolutely, captain, since we possess the important reports of Weddell, and, I must add, of Arthur Pym also."

"Yes, I know; they have spoken of the open sea."

"Do you not believe that such a sea exists?"

"Yes, I do believe that it exists, and for valid reasons. In fact, it is perfectly manifest that these masses, called icebergs and icefields, could not be formed in the ocean itself. It is the tremendous and irresistible action of the surge which detaches them from the continents or islands of the high latitudes. Then the currents carry them into less cold waters, where their edges are worn by the waves, while the temperature disintegrates their bases and their sides, which are subjected to thermometric influences."

"That seems very plain," I replied. "Then these masses have come from the icebergs.[1] They clash with them in drifting, sometimes break into the main body, and clear their passage through. Again, we must not judge the southern by the northern zone. The conditions are not identical. Cook has recorded that he never met the equivalent of the Antarctic ice mountains in the Greenland seas, even at a higher latitude."

"What is the reason?" I asked.

"No doubt that the influence of the south winds is predominant in the northern regions. Now, those winds do not reach the northern regions until they have been heated in their passage over America, Asia, and Europe, and they

[1] The French word is *banquise*, which means the vast stretch of icebergs farther south than the *barrière* or ice-wall.

contribute to raise the temperature of the atmosphere. The nearest land, ending in the points of the Cape of Good Hope, Patagonia, and Tasmania, does not modify the atmospheric currents."

"That is an important observation, captain, and it justifies your opinion with regard to an open sea."

"Yes, open—at least, for ten degrees behind the icebergs. Let us then only get through that obstacle, and our greatest difficulty will have been conquered. You were right in saying that the existence of that open sea has been formally recognized by Weddell."

"And by Arthur Pym, captain."

"And by Arthur Pym."

From the 15th of December the difficulties of navigation increased with the number of the drifting masses. The wind, however, continued to be uniformly favourable, showing no tendency to veer to the south. The breeze freshened now and then, and we had to take in sail. When this occurred we saw the sea foaming along the sides of the ice packs, covering them with spray like the rocks on the coast of a floating island, but without hindering their onward march.

Our crew could not fail to be impressed by the sight of the schooner making her way through these moving masses; the new men among them, at least, for the old hands had seen such manœuvres before. But they soon became accustomed to it, and took it all for granted.

It was necessary to organize the look-out ahead with the greatest care. West had a cask fixed at the head of the foremast—what is called a crow's-nest—and from thence an unremitting watch was kept.

The 16th was a day of excessive fatigue to the men. The packs and drifts were so close that only very narrow and winding passage-way between them was to be found, so that the working of the ship was more than commonly laborious.

Under these circumstances, none of the men grumbled, but Hunt distinguished himself by his activity. Indeed, he was admitted by Captain Len Guy and the crew to be an incomparable seaman. But there was something mysterious about him that excited the curiosity of them all.

At this date the *Halbrane* could not be very far from the icebergs. If she held on in her course in that direction she would certainly reach them before long, and would then have only to seek for a passage. Hitherto, however, the look-out had not been able to make out between the icebergs an unbroken crest of ice beyond the ice-fields.

Constant and minute precautions were indispensable all day on the 16th, for the helm, which was loosened by merciless blows and bumps, was in danger of being unshipped.

The sea mammals had not forsaken these seas. Whales were seen in great numbers, and it was a fairy-like spectacle when several of them spouted simultaneously. With fin-backs and hump-backs, porpoises of colossal size appeared, and these Hearne harpooned cleverly when they came within range. The flesh of these creatures was much relished on board, after Endicott had cooked it in his best manner.

As for the usual Antarctic birds, petrels, pigeons, and cormorants, they passed in screaming flocks, and legions of penguins, ranged along the edges of the icefields, watched the evolutions of the schooner. These penguins are the real inhabitants of these dismal solitudes, and nature could not have created a type more suited to the desolation of the glacial zone.

On the morning of the 17th the man in the crow's-nest at last signalled the icebergs.

Five or six miles to the south a long dentated crest upreared itself, plainly standing out against the fairly clear sky, and all along it drifted thousands of ice-packs. This motionless barrier stretched before us from the north-west to the south-east, and by merely sailing along it the schooner would still gain some degrees southwards.

When the *Halbrane* was within three miles of the icebergs, she lay-to in the middle of a wide basin which allowed her complete freedom of movement.

A boat was lowered, and Captain Len Guy got into it, with the boatswain, four sailors at the oars, and one at the helm. The boat was pulled in the direction of the enormous rampart, vain search was made for a channel through which the schooner could have slipped, and after three hours of this fatiguing reconnoitring, the men returned to the ship. Then came a squall of rain and snow which caused the temperature to fall to thirty-six degrees (2·22 C. above zero), and shut out the view of the ice-rampart from us.

During the next twenty-four hours the schooner lay within four miles of the icebergs. To bring her nearer would have been to get among winding channels from which it might not have been possible to extricate her. Not that Captain Len Guy did not long to do this, in his fear of passing some opening unperceived.

"If I had a consort," he said, "I would sail closer along the icebergs, and it is a great advantage to be two, when

Four sailors at the oars, and one at the helm.

one is on such an enterprise as this! But the *Halbrane* is alone, and if she were to fail us—"

Even though we approached no nearer to the icebergs than prudence permitted, our ship was exposed to great risk, and West was constantly obliged to change his trim in order to avoid the shock of an icefield.

Fortunately, the wind blew from east to north-nor'-east without variation, and it did not freshen. Had a tempest arisen I know not what would have become of the schooner—yes, though, I do know too well: she would have been lost and all on board of her. In such a case the *Halbrane* could not have escaped; we must have been flung on the base of the barrier.

After a long examination Captain Len Guy had to renounce the hope of finding a passage through the terrible wall of ice. It remained only to endeavour to reach the south-east point of it. At any rate, by following that course we lost nothing in latitude; and, in fact, on the 18th the observation taken made the seventy-third parallel the position of the *Halbrane*.

I must repeat, however, that navigation in the Antarctic seas will probably never be accomplished under more felicitous circumstances—the precocity of the summer season, the permanence of the north wind, the temperature forty-nine degrees at the lowest; all this was the best of good-fortune. I need not add that we enjoyed perpetual light, and the whole twenty-four hours round the sun's rays reached us from every point of the horizon.

Two or three times the captain approached within two miles of the icebergs. It was impossible but that the vast mass must have been subjected to climateric influences; ruptures must surely have taken place at some points.

But his search had no result, and we had to fall back into the current from west to east.

I must observe at this point that during all our search we never descried land or the appearance of land out at sea, as indicated on the charts of preceding navigators. These maps are incomplete, no doubt, but sufficiently exact in their main lines. I am aware that ships have often passed over the indicated bearings of land. This, however, was not admissible in the case of Tsalal. If the *Jane* had been able to reach the islands, it was because that portion of the Antarctic sea was free, and in so "early" a year, we need not fear any obstacle in that direction.

At last, on the 19th, between two and three o'clock in the afternoon, a shout from the crow's-nest was heard.

"What is it?" roared West.

"The iceberg wall is split on the south-east."

"What is beyond?"

"Nothing in sight.'

It took West very little time to reach the point of observation, and we all waited below, how impatiently may be imagined. What if the look-out were mistaken, if some optical delusion?—— But West, at all events, would make no mistake.

After ten interminable minutes his clear voice reached us on the deck.

"Open sea!" he cried.

Unanimous cheers made answer.

The schooner's head was put to the south-east, hugging the wind as much as possible.

Two hours later we had doubled the extremity of the ice-barrier, and there lay before our eyes a sparkling sea, entirely open.

CHAPTER XIV.

A VOICE IN A DREAM.

ENTIRELY free from ice? No. It would have been premature to affirm this as a fact. A few icebergs were visible in the distance, while some drifts and packs were still going east. Nevertheless, the break-up had been very thorough on that side, and the sea was in reality open, since a ship could sail freely.

"God has come to our aid," said Captain Len Guy. "May He be pleased to guide us to the end."

"In a week," I remarked, "our schooner might come in sight of Tsalal Island."

"Provided that the east wind lasts, Mr. Jeorling. Don't forget that in sailing along the icebergs to their eastern extremity, the *Halbrane* went out of her course, and she must be brought back towards the west."

"The breeze is for us, captain."

"And we shall profit by it, for my intention is to make for Bennet Islet. It was there that my brother first landed, and so soon as we shall have sighted that island we shall be certain that we are on the right route. To-day, when I have ascertained our position exactly, we shall steer for Bennet Islet."

"Who knows but that we may come upon some fresh sign?"

"It is not impossible, Mr. Jeorling."

I need not say that recourse was had to the surest guide within our reach, that veracious narrative of Arthur Gordon Pym, which I read and re-read with intense attention, fascinated as I was by the idea that I might be permitted to behold with my own eyes those strange phenomena of nature in the Antarctic world which I, in common with all Edgar Poe's readers, had hitherto regarded as creations of the most imaginative writer who ever gave voice by his pen to the phantasies of a unique brain. No doubt a great part of the wonders of Arthur Gordon Pym's narrative would prove pure fiction, but if even a little of the marvellous story were found to be true, how great a privilege would be mine!

The picturesque and wonderful side of the story we were studying as gospel truth had little charm and but slight interest for Captain Len Guy; he was indifferent to everything in Pym's narrative that did not relate directly to the castaways of Tsalal Island: his mind was solely and constantly set upon their rescue.

According to the narrative of Arthur Pym, the *Jane* experienced serious difficulties, due to bad weather, from the 1st to the 4th of January, 1828. It was not until the morning of the 5th, in latitude 73° 15′, that she found a free passage through the last iceberg that barred her way. The final difference between our position and the *Jane* in a parallel case, was that the *Jane* took fifteen days to accomplish the distance of ten degrees, or six hundred miles, which separated her on the 5th of January from Tsalal Island, while on the 19th of December the *Halbrane* was only about seven degrees, or four hundred miles, off the island. Bennet Islet, where Captain Guy intended to put in for twenty-four hours, was fifty miles nearer. Our voyage was progressing under prosperous conditions; we were no longer visited by sudden hail and snow storms, or those rapid falls of temperature which tried the crew of the *Jane* so sorely. A few ice-floes drifted by us, occasionally peopled, as tourists throng a pleasure yacht, by penguins, and also by dusky seals, lying flat upon the white surfaces like enormous leeches. Above this strange flotilla we traced the incessant flight of petrels, pigeons, black puffins, divers, grebe, sterns, cormorants, and the sooty-black albatross of the high latitudes. Huge medusæ, exquisitely tinted, floated on the water like spread parasols. Among the denizens of the deep, captured by the crew of the schooner with line and net, I noted more particularly a sort of giant John Dory [1] (*dorade*) three feet in length, with firm and savoury flesh.

During the night, or rather what ought to have been the night of the 19th-20th, my sleep was disturbed by a strange dream. Yes! there could be no doubt but that it was only a dream! Nevertheless, I think it well to record it here, because it is an additional testimony to the haunting influence under which my brain was beginning to labour.

I was sleeping—at two hours after midnight—and was awakened by a plaintive and continuous murmuring sound. I opened—or I imagined I opened my eyes. My cabin was in profound darkness. The murmur began again; I listened,

[1] The legendary etymology of this piscatorial designation is *Janitore*, the "door-keeper," in allusion to St. Peter, who brought a fish, said to be of that species, to our Lord at His command.

and it seemed to me that a voice—a voice which I did not know—whispered these words :—

"Pym . . . Pym . . . poor Pym!"

Evidently this could only be a delusion; unless, indeed, some one had got into my cabin: the door was not locked.

"Pym!" the voice repeated. "Poor Pym never must be forgotten."

This time the words were spoken close to my ear. What was the meaning of the injunction, and why was it addressed to me? And besides, had not Pym, after his return to America, met with a sudden and deplorable death, the circumstances or the details being unknown?

I began to doubt whether I was in my right mind, and shook myself into complete wakefulness, recognizing that I had been disturbed by an extremely vivid dream due to some cerebral cause.

I turned out of my berth, and, pushing back the shutter, looked out of my cabin. No one aft on the deck, except Hunt, who was at the helm.

I had nothing to do but to lie down again, and this I did. It seemed to me that the name of Arthur Pym was repeated in my hearing several times; nevertheless, I fell asleep and did not wake until morning, when I retained only a vague impression of this occurrence, which soon faded away. No other incident at that period of our voyage calls for notice. Nothing particular occurred on board our schooner. The breeze from the north, which had forsaken us, did not recur, and only the current carried the *Halbrane* towards the south. This caused a delay unbearable to our impatience.

At last, on the 21st, the usual observation gave 82° 50′ of

latitude, and 42° 20′ of west longitude. Bennet Islet, if it had any existence, could not be far off now.

Yes! the islet did exist, and its bearings were those indicated by Arthur Pym.

At six o'clock in the evening one of the crew cried out that there was land ahead on the port side.

CHAPTER XV.

BENNET ISLET.

THE *Halbrane* was then within sight of Bennet Islet! The crew urgently needed rest, so the disembarkation was deferred until the following day, and I went back to my cabin.

The night passed without disturbance, and when day came not a craft of any kind was visible on the waters, not a native on the beach. There were no huts upon the coast, no smoke arose in the distance to indicate that Bennet Islet was inhabited. But William Guy had not found any trace of human beings there, and what I saw of the islet answered to the description given by Arthur Pym. It rose upon a rocky base of about a league in circumference, and was so arid that no vegetation existed on its surface.

"Mr. Jeorling," said Captain Len Guy, "do you observe a promontory in the direction of the north-east?"

"I observe it, captain."

"Is it not formed of heaped-up rocks which look like giant bales of cotton?"

"That is so, and just what the narrative describes."

"Then all we have to do is to land on the promontory, Mr. Jeorling. Who knows but we may come across some vestige of the crew of the *Jane*, supposing them to have succeeded in escaping from Tsalal Island."

The speaker was devouring the islet with his eyes. What must his thoughts, his desires, his impatience have been! But there was a man whose gaze was set upon the same point even more fixedly; that man was Hunt.

Before we left the *Halbrane* Len Guy enjoined the most minute and careful watchfulness upon his lieutenant. This was a charge which West did not need. Our exploration would take only half a day at most. If the boat had not returned in the afternoon a second was to be sent in search of us.

"Look sharp also after our recruits," added the captain.

"Don't be uneasy, captain," replied the lieutenant. "Indeed, since you want four men at the oars you had better take them from among the new ones. That will leave four less troublesome fellows on board."

This was a good idea, for, under the deplorable influence of Hearne, the discontent of his shipmates from the Falklands was on the increase. The boat being ready, four of the new crew took their places forward, while Hunt, at his own request, was steersman. Captain Len Guy, the boatswain and myself, all well armed, seated ourselves aft, and we started for the northern point of the islet. In the course of an hour we had doubled the promontory, and come in sight of the little bay whose shores the boats of the *Jane* had touched.

Hunt steered for this bay, gliding with remarkable skill between the rocky points which stuck up here and there. One would have thought he knew his way among them.

We disembarked on a stony coast. The stones were covered with sparse lichen. The tide was already ebbing, leaving uncovered the sandy bottom of a sort of beach strewn with black blocks, resembling big nail-heads.

Two men were left in charge of the boat while we landed amid the rocks, and, accompanied by the other two, Captain Len Guy, the boatswain, Hunt and I proceeded towards the centre, where we found some rising ground, from whence we could see the whole extent of the islet. But there was nothing to be seen on any side, absolutely nothing. On coming down from the slight eminence Hunt went on in front, as it had been agreed that he was to be our guide. We followed him therefore, as he led us towards the southern extremity of the islet. Having reached the point, Hunt looked carefully on all sides of him, then stooped and showed us a piece of half rotten wood lying among the scattered stones.

"I remember!" I exclaimed; "Arthur Pym speaks of a piece of wood with traces of carving on it which appeared to have belonged to the bow of a ship."

"Among the carving my brother fancied he could trace the design of a tortoise," added Captain Len Guy.

"Just so," I replied, "but Arthur Pym pronounced that resemblance doubtful. No matter; the piece of wood is still in the same place that is indicated in the narrative, so we may conclude that since the *Jane* cast anchor here no other crew has ever set foot upon Bennet Islet. It follows that we should only lose time in looking out for any tokens of another landing. We shall know nothing until we reach Tsalal Island."

"Yes, Tsalal Island," replied the captain.

We then retraced our steps in the direction of the bay. In various places we observed fragments of coral reef, and bêche-de-mer was so abundant that our schooner might have taken a full cargo of it.

Hunt walked on in silence with downcast eyes, until

as we were close upon the beach to the east, he, being about ten paces ahead, stopped abruptly, and summoned us to him by a hurried gesture.

In an instant we were by his side. Hunt had evinced no surprise on the subject of the piece of wood first found, but his attitude changed when he knelt down in front of a worm-eaten plank lying on the sand. He felt it all over with his huge hands, as though he were seeking some tracery on its rough surface whose signification might be intelligible to him. The black paint was hidden under the thick dirt that had accumulated upon it. The plank had probably formed part of a ship's stern, as the boatswain requested us to observe.

"Yes, yes," repeated Captain Len Guy, "it made part of a stern."

Hunt, who still remained kneeling, nodded his big head in assent.

"But," I remarked, "this plank must have been cast upon Bennet Islet from a wreck! The cross-currents must have found it in the open sea, and—"

"If that were so—" cried the captain.

The same thought had occurred to both of us. What was our surprise, indeed our amazement, our unspeakable emotion, when Hunt showed us eight letters cut in the plank, not painted, but hollow and distinctly traceable with the finger.

It was only too easy to recognize the letters of two names, arranged in two lines, thus:

AN
LI.E.PO.L.

The Jane of Liverpool! The schooner commanded by Captain William Guy! What did it matter that time had blurred the other letters? Did not those suffice to tell the name of the ship and the port she belonged to? *The Jane of Liverpool!*

Captain Len Guy had taken the plank in his hands, and now he pressed his lips to it, while tears fell from his eyes.

It was a fragment of the *Jane!* I did not utter a word until the captain's emotion had subsided. As for Hunt, I had never seen such a lightning glance from his brilliant hawk-like eyes as he now cast towards the southern horizon.

Captain Len Guy rose.

Hunt, without a word, placed the plank upon his shoulder, and we continued our route.

When we had made the tour of the island, we halted at the place where the boat had been left under the charge of two sailors, and about half-past two in the afternoon we were again on board.

Early on the morning of the 23rd of December the *Halbrane* put off from Bennet Islet, and we carried away with us new and convincing testimony to the catastrophe which Tsalal Island had witnessed.

During that day, I observed the sea water very attentively, and it seemed to me less deeply blue than Arthur Pym describes it. Nor had we met a single specimen of his monster of the austral fauna, an animal three feet long, six inches high, with four short legs, long coral claws, a silky body, a rat's tail, a cat's head, the hanging ears, blood-red lips and white teeth of a dog. The truth is that I regarded several of these details as "suspect," and entirely due to an over-imaginative temperament.

Seated far aft in the ship, I read Edgar Poe's book with

sedulous attention, but I was not unaware of the fact that Hunt, whenever his duties furnished him with an opportunity, observed me pertinaciously, and with looks of singular meaning.

And, in fact, I was re-perusing the end of Chapter XVII., in which Arthur Pym acknowledged his responsibility for the sad and tragic events which were the results of his advice. It was, in fact, he who over-persuaded Captain William Guy, urging him "to profit by so tempting an opportunity of solving the great problem relating to the Antarctic Continent." And, besides, while accepting that responsibility, did he not congratulate himself on having been the instrument of a great discovery, and having aided in some degree to reveal to science one of the most marvellous secrets which had ever claimed its attention?

At six o'clock the sun disappeared behind a thick curtain of mist. After midnight the breeze freshened, and the *Halbrane's* progress marked a dozen additional miles.

On the morrow the good ship was less than the third of a degree, that is to say less than twenty miles, from Tsalal Island.

Unfortunately, just after mid-day, the wind fell. Nevertheless, thanks to the current, the Island of Tsalal was signalled at forty-five minutes past six in the evening.

The anchor was cast, a watch was set, with loaded firearms within hand-reach, and boarding-nets ready.

The *Halbrane* ran no risk of being surprised. Too many eyes were watching on board—especially those of Hunt, whose gaze never quitted the horizon of that southern zone for an instant.

CHAPTER XVI.

TSALAL ISLAND.

THE night passed without alarm. No boat had put off from the island, nor had a native shown himself upon the beach. The *Halbrane*, then, had not been observed on her arrival; this was all the better.

We had cast anchor in ten fathoms, at three miles from the coast.

When the *Jane* appeared in these waters, the people of Tsalal beheld a ship for the first time, and they took it for an enormous animal, regarding its masts as limbs, and its sails as garments. Now, they ought to be better informed on this subject, and if they did not attempt to visit us, to what motive were we to assign such conduct?

Captain Len Guy gave orders for the lowering of the ship's largest boat, in a voice which betrayed his impatience.

The order was executed, and the captain, addressing West, said,—

"Send eight men down with Martin Holt; send Hunt to the helm. Remain yourself at the moorings, and keep a look-out landwards as well as to sea."

"Aye, aye, sir; don't be uneasy."

"We are going ashore, and we shall try to gain the

village of Klock-Klock. If any difficulty should arise on sea, give us warning by firing three shots."

"All right," replied West—"at a minute's interval."

"If we should not return before evening, send the second boat with ten armed men under the boatswain's orders, and let them station themselves within a cable's length of the shore, so as to escort us back. You understand?"

"Perfectly, captain."

"If we are not to be found, after you have done all in your power, you will take command of the schooner, and bring her back to the Falklands."

"I will do so."

The large boat was rapidly got ready. Eight men embarked in it, including Martin Holt and Hunt, all armed with rifles, pistols, and knives; the latter weapons were slung in their belts. They also carried cartridge-pouches.

I stepped forward and said,—

"Will you not allow me to accompany you, captain?"

"If you wish to do so, Mr. Jeorling."

I went to my cabin, took my gun—a repeating rifle—with ball and powder, and rejoined Captain Len Guy, who had kept a place in the stern of the boat for me. Our object was to discover the passage through which Arthur Pym and Dirk Peters had crossed the reef on the 19th of January, 1828, in the *Jane's* boat. For twenty minutes we rowed along the reef, and then Hunt discovered the pass, which was through a narrow cut in the rocks. Leaving two men in the boat, we landed, and having gone through the winding gorge which gave access to the crest of the coast, our little force, headed by Hunt, pushed on towards the centre of the island. Captain Len Guy and myself exchanged observations, as we walked, on the subject of this country, which, as Arthur Pym declared, differed essentially from every other land hitherto visited by human beings. We soon found that Pym's description was trustworthy. The general colour of the plains was black, as though the clay were made of lava-dust; nowhere was anything white to be seen. At a hundred paces' distance Hunt began to run towards an enormous mass of rock, climbed on it with great agility, and looked out over a wide extent of space like a man who ought to recognize the place he is in, but does not.

"What is the matter with him?" asked Captain Len Guy, who was observing Hunt attentively.

"I don't know what is the matter with him, captain. But, as you are aware, everything about this man is odd: his ways are inexplicable, and on certain sides of him he seems to belong to those strange beings whom Arthur Pym asserts that he found on this island. One would even say that—"

"That—" repeated the captain.

And then, without finishing my sentence, I said,—

"Captain, are you sure that you made a good observation when you took the altitude yesterday?"

"Certainly."

"So that your point—"

"Gave 83° 20′ of latitude and 43° 5 of longitude."

"Exactly?"

"Exactly."

"There is, then, no doubt that we are on Tsalal Island?"

"None, Mr. Jeorling, if Tsalal Island lies where Arthur Pym places it."

This was quite true, there could be no doubt on the point, and yet of all that Arthur Pym described nothing existed, or rather, nothing was any longer to be seen. Not a tree, not a shrub, not a plant was visible in the landscape. There was no sign of the wooded hills between which the village of Klock-Klock ought to lie, or of the streams from which the crew of the *Jane* had not ventured to drink. There was no water anywhere; but everywhere absolute, awful drought.

Nevertheless, Hunt walked on rapidly, without showing any hesitation. It seemed as though he was led by a natural instinct, "a bee's flight," as we say in America. I know not what presentiment induced us to follow him as the best of guides, a Chingachgook, a Renard-Subtil. And why not? Was not he the fellow-countryman of Fenimore Cooper's heroes?

But, I must repeat that we had not before our eyes that fabulous land which Arthur Pym described. The soil we were treading had been ravaged, wrecked, torn by convulsion. It was black, a cindery black, as though it had been vomited from the earth under the action of Plutonian forces; it suggested that some appalling and irresistible cataclysm had overturned the whole of its surface.

Not one of the animals mentioned in the narrative was to be seen, and even the penguins which abound in the Antarctic regions had fled from this uninhabitable land. Its stern silence and solitude made it a hideous desert. No human being was to be seen either on the coast or in the interior. Did any chance of finding William Guy and the survivors of the *Jane* exist in the midst of this scene of desolation?

I looked at Captain Len Guy. His pale face dim eyes,

and knit brow told too plainly that hope was beginning to die within his breast.

And then the population of Tsalal Island, the almost naked men, armed with clubs and lances, the tall, well-made, upstanding women, endowed with grace and freedom of bearing not to be found in a civilized society—those are the expressions of Arthur Pym—and the crowd of children accompanying them, what had become of all these? Where were the multitude of natives, with black skins, black hair, black teeth, who regarded white colour with deadly terror?

All of a sudden a light flashed upon me. "An earthquake!" I exclaimed. "Yes, two or three of those terrible shocks, so common in these regions where the sea penetrates by infiltration, and a day comes when the quantity of accumulated vapour makes its way out and destroys everything on the surface."

"Could an earthquake have changed Tsalal Island to such an extent?" asked Len Guy, musingly.

"Yes, captain, an earthquake has done this thing; it has destroyed every trace of all that Arthur Pym saw here."

Hunt, who had drawn nigh to us, and was listening, nodded his head in approval of my words.

"Are not these countries of the southern seas volcanic?" I resumed. "If the *Halbrane* were to transport us to Victoria Land, we might find the *Erebus* and the *Terror* in the midst of an eruption."

"And yet," observed Martin Holt, "if there had been an eruption here, we should find lava beds."

"I do not say that there has been an eruption," I replied, "but I do say the soil has been convulsed by an earthquake."

On reflection it will be seen that the explanation given by me deserved to be admitted. And then it came to my remembrance that according to Arthur Pym's narrative, Tsalal belonged to a group of islands which extended towards the west. Unless the people of Tsalal had been destroyed, it was possible that they might have fled into one of the neighbouring islands. We should do well, then, to go and reconnoitre that archipelago, for Tsalal clearly had no resources whatever to offer after the cataclysm.

I spoke of this to the captain.

"Yes," he replied, and tears stood in his eyes, "yes, it may be so. And yet, how could my brother and his unfortunate companions have found the means of escaping? Is it not far more probable that they all perished in the earthquake?"

Here Hunt made us a signal to follow him, and we did so.

After he had pushed across the valley for a considerable distance, he stopped.

What a spectacle was before our eyes!

There, lying in heaps, were human bones, all the fragments of that framework of humanity which we call the skeleton, hundreds of them, without a particle of flesh, clusters of skulls still bearing some tufts of hair—a vast bone heap, dried and whitened in this place! We were struck dumb and motionless by this spectacle. When Captain Len Guy could speak, he murmured,—

"My brother, my poor brother!"

On a little reflection, however, my mind refused to admit certain things. How was this catastrophe to be reconciled with Patterson's memoranda? The entries in his note-book stated explicitly that the mate of the *Jane* had left his companions on Tsalal Island seven months previously. They could not then have perished in this earthquake, for the state of the bones proved that it had taken place several years earlier, and must have occurred after the departure of Arthur Pym and Dirk Peters, since no mention of it was made in the narrative of the former.

These facts were, then, irreconcilable. If the earthquake was of recent date, the presence of those time-bleached skeletons could not be attributed to its action. In any case, the survivors of the *Jane* were not among them. But then, where were they?

The valley of Klock-Klock extended no farther; we had to retrace our steps in order to regain the coast.

We had hardly gone half a mile on the cliff's edge when Hunt again stopped, on perceiving some fragments of bones which were turning to dust, and did not seem to be those of a human being.

Were these the remains of one of the strange animals described by Walter Pym, of which we had not hitherto seen any specimens?

Hunt suddenly uttered a cry, or rather a sort of savage growl, and held out his enormous hand, holding a metal collar. Yes! a brass collar, a collar eaten by rust, but bearing letters which might still be deciphered. These letters formed the three following words:—

"*Tiger*—Arthur Pym."

Tiger!—the name of the dog which had saved Arthur Pym's life in the hold of the *Grampus*, and, during the revolt of the crew, had sprung at the throat of Jones, the sailor, who was immediately "finished" by Dirk Peters.

So, then, that faithful animal had not perished in the

Hunt extended his enormous hand, holding a metal collar.

shipwreck of the *Grampus*. He had been taken on board the *Jane* at the same time as Arthur Pym and the half-breed. And yet the narrative did not allude to this, and after the meeting with the schooner there was no longer any mention of the dog. All these contradictions occurred to me. I could not reconcile the facts. Nevertheless, there could be no doubt that Tiger had been saved from the shipwreck like Arthur Pym, had escaped the landslip of the Klock-Klock hill, and had come to his death at last in the catastrophe which had destroyed a portion of the population of Tsalal.

But, again, William Guy and his five sailors could not be among those skeletons which were strewn upon the earth, since they were living at the time of Patterson's departure, seven months ago, and the catastrophe already dated several years back!

Three hours later we had returned on board the *Halbrane*, without having made any other discovery. Captain Len Guy went direct to his cabin, shut himself up there, and did not reappear even at dinner hour.

The following day, as I wished to return to the island in order to resume its exploration from one coast to the other, I requested West to have me rowed ashore.

He consented, after he had been authorized by Captain Len Guy, who did not come with us.

Hunt, the boatswain, Martin Holt, four men, and myself took our places in the boat, without arms; for there was no longer anything to fear.

We disembarked at our yesterday's landing-place, and Hunt again led the way towards the hill of Klock-Klock. Nothing remained of the eminence that had been carried away in the artificial landslip, from which the captain of the

Jane, Patterson, his second officer, and five of his men had happily escaped. The village of Klock-Klock had thus disappeared; and doubtless the mystery of the strange discoveries narrated in Edgar Poe's work was now and ever would remain beyond solution.

We had only to regain our ship, returning by the east side of the coast. Hunt brought us through the space where sheds had been erected for the preparation of the *bêche-de-mer*, and we saw the remains of them. On all sides silence and abandonment reigned.

We made a brief pause at the place where Arthur Pym and Dirk Peters seized upon the boat which bore them towards higher latitudes, even to that horizon of dark vapour whose rents permitted them to discern the huge human figure, the white giant.

Hunt stood with crossed arms, his eyes devouring the vast extent of the sea.

"Well, Hunt?" said I, tentatively.

Hunt did not appear to hear me; he did not turn his head in my direction.

"What are we doing here?" I asked him, and touched him on the shoulder.

He started, and cast a glance upon me which went to my heart.

"Come along, Hunt," cried Hurliguerly. "Are you going to take root on this rock? Don't you see the *Halbrane* waiting for us at her moorings? Come along. We shall be off to-morrow. There is nothing more to do here."

It seemed to me that Hunt's trembling lips repeated the word "nothing," while his whole bearing protested against what the boatswain said.

The boat brought us back to the ship. Captain Len Guy had not left his cabin. West, having received no orders, was pacing the deck aft. I seated myself at the foot of the mainmast, observing the sea which lay open and free before us.

At this moment the captain came on deck ; he was very pale, and his features looked pinched and weary.

"Mr. Jeorling," said he, "I can affirm conscientiously that I have done all it was possible to do. Can I hope henceforth that my brother William and his companions—No! No! We must go away—before winter—"

He drew himself up, and cast a last glance towards Tsalal Island.

"To-morrow, Jim," he said to West, "to morrow we will make sail as early as possible."

At this moment a rough voice uttered the words:

"And Pym—poor Pym!"

I recognized this voice.

It was the voice I had heard in my dream.

CHAPTER XVII.

AND PYM?

"AND Pym—poor Pym?"

I turned round quickly.

Hunt had spoken. This strange person was standing motionless at a little distance, gazing fixedly at the horizon.

It was so unusual to hear Hunt's voice on board the schooner, that the men, whom the unaccustomed sound reached, drew near, moved by curiosity. Did not his unexpected intervention point to—I had a presentiment that it did—some wonderful revelation?

A movement of West's hand sent the men forward, leaving only the mate, the boatswain, Martin Holt, the sailing-master, and Hardy, with the captain and myself in the vicinity of Hunt. The captain approached and addressed him:

"What did you say?"

"I said, 'And Pym—poor Pym.'"

"Well, then, what do you mean by repeating the name of the man whose pernicious advice led my brother to the island on which the *Jane* was lost, the greater part of her crew was massacred, and where we have not found even one left of those who were still here seven months ago?"

Hunt did not speak.

"Answer, I say—answer!" cried the captain.

Hunt hesitated, not because he did not know what to say, but from a certain difficulty in expressing his ideas. The latter were quite clear, but his speech was confused, his words were unconnected. He had a certain language of his own which sometimes was picturesque, and his pronunciation was strongly marked by the hoarse accent of the Indians of the Far West.

"You see," he said, "I do not know how to tell things. My tongue stops. Understand me, I spoke of Pym, poor Pym, did I not?"

"Yes," answered West, sternly; "and what have you to say about Arthur Pym?"

"I have to say that he must not be abandoned."

"Abandoned!" I exclaimed.

"No, never! It would be cruel—too cruel. We must go to seek him."

"To seek him?" repeated Captain Len Guy.

"Understand me; it is for this that I have embarked on the *Halbrane*—yes, to find poor Pym!"

"And where is he," I asked, "if not deep in a grave, in the cemetery of his natal city?"

"No, he is in the place where he remained, alone, all alone," continued Hunt, pointing towards the south; "and since then the sun has risen on that horizon seven times."

It was evident that Hunt intended to designate the Antarctic regions, but what did he mean by this?

"Do you not know that Arthur Pym is dead?" said the captain.

"Dead!" replied Hunt, emphasizing the word with an

expressive gesture. "No! listen to me: I know things; understand me, he is not dead."

"Come now, Hunt," said I, "remember what you do know. In the last chapter of the adventures of Arthur Pym, does not Edgar Poe relate his sudden and deplorable end?"

"Explain yourself, Hunt," said the captain, in a tone of command. "Reflect, take your time, and say plainly whatever you have to say."

And, while Hunt passed his hand over his brow, as though to collect his memory of far-off things, I observed to Captain Len Guy,—

"There is something very singular in the intervention of this man, if indeed he be not mad."

At my words the boatswain shook his head, for he did not believe Hunt to be in his right mind.

The latter understood this shake of the boatswain's head, and cried out in a harsh tone,—

"No, not mad. And madmen are respected on the prairies, even if they are not believed. And I—I must be believed. No, no, no! Pym is not dead!"

"Edgar Poe asserts that he is," I replied.

"Yes, I know, Edgar Poe of Baltimore. But—he never saw poor Pym, never, never."

"What!" exclaimed Captain Len Guy; "the two men were not acquainted?"

"No!"

"And it was not Arthur Pym himself who related his adventures to Edgar Poe?"

"No, captain, no! He, below there, at Baltimore, had only the notes written by Pym from the day when he hid himself on board the *Grampus* to the very last hour—the last—understand me the last."

"Who, then, brought back that journal?" asked Captain Len Guy, as he seized Hunt's hand.

"It was Pym's companion, he who loved him, his poor Pym, like a son. It was Dirk Peters, the half-breed, who came back alone from there—beyond."

"The half-breed, Dirk Peters!" I exclaimed.

"Yes."

"Alone?"

"Alone."

"And Arthur Pym may be—"

"There," answered Hunt, in a loud voice, bending towards the southern line, from which he had not diverted his gaze for a moment.

Could such an assertion prevail against the general incredulity? No, assuredly not! Martin Holt nudged Hurliguerly with his elbow, and both regarded Hunt with pity, while West observed him without speaking. Captain Len Guy made me a sign, meaning that nothing serious was to be got out of this poor fellow, whose mental faculties must have been out of gear for a long time.

And nevertheless, when I looked keenly at Hunt, it seemed to me that a sort of radiance of truth shone out of his eyes.

Then I set to work to interrogate the man, putting to him precise and pressing questions which he tried to answer categorically, as we shall see, and not once did he contradict himself.

"Tell me," I asked, "did Arthur Pym really come to Tsalal Island on board the *Grampus?*"

"Yes."

"Did Arthur Pym separate himself, with the half-breed and one of the sailors, from his companions while

Captain William Guy had gone to the village of Klock-Klock?"

"Yes. The sailor was one Allen, and he was almost immediately stifled under the stones."

"Then the two others saw the attack, and the destruction of the schooner, from the top of the hill?"

"Yes."

"Then, some time later, the two left the island, after they had got possession of one of the boats which the natives could not take from them?"

"Yes."

"And, after twenty days, having reached the front of the curtain of vapour, they were both carried down into the gulf of the cataract?"

This time Hunt did not reply in the affirmative; he hesitated, he stammered out some vague words; he seemed to be trying to rekindle the half-extinguished flame of his memory. At length, looking at me and shaking his head, he answered,—

"No, not both. Understand me—Dirk never told me—"

"Dirk Peters," interposed Captain Len Guy, quickly. "You knew Dirk Peters?"

"Yes."

"Where?"

"At Vandalia, State of Illinois."

"And it is from him that you have all this information concerning the voyage?"

"From him."

"And he came back alone—alone—from that voyage, having left Arthur Pym."

"Alone!"

"Speak, man—do speak!" I cried, impatiently. Then, in broken, but intelligible sentences, Hunt spoke,—

"Yes—there—a curtain of vapour—so the half-breed often said—understand me. The two, Arthur Pym and he, were in the Tsalal boat. Then an enormous block of ice came full upon them. At the shock Dirk Peters was thrown into the sea, but he clung to the ice block, and—understand me, he saw the boat drift with the current, far, very far, too far! In vain did Pym try to rejoin his companion, he could not; the boat drifted on and on, and Pym, that poor dear Pym, was carried away. It is he who has never come back, and he is there, still there!"

If Hunt had been the half-breed in person he could not have spoken with more heartfelt emotion of "poor Pym."

It was then, in front of the "curtain of vapour," that Arthur Pym and the half-breed had been separated from each other. Dirk Peters had succeeded in returning from the ice-world to America, whither he had conveyed the notes that were communicated to Edgar Poe.

Hunt was minutely questioned upon all these points and he replied, conformably, he declared, to what the half-breed had told him many times. According to this statement, Dirk Peters had Arthur Pym's note-book in his pocket at the moment when the ice-block struck them, and thus the journal which the half-breed placed at the disposal of the American romance-writer was saved.

"Understand me," Hunt repeated, "for I tell you things as I have them from Dirk Peters. While the drift was carrying him away, he cried out with all his strength. Pym, poor Pym, had already disappeared in the midst of the vapour. The half-breed, feeding upon raw fish, which he contrived to catch, was carried back by a cross current to Tsalal Island, where he landed half dead from hunger."

"To Tsalal Island!" exclaimed Captain Len Guy. "And how long was it since they had left it?"

"Three weeks—yes, three weeks at the farthest, so Dirk Peters told me."

"Then he must have found all that remained of the crew of the *Jane*—my brother William and those who had survived with him?"

"No," replied Hunt; "and Dirk Peters always believed that they had perished—yes, to the very last man. There was no one upon the island."

"No one?"

"Not a living soul."

"But the population?"

"No one! No one, I tell you. The island was a desert—yes, a desert!"

This statement contradicted certain facts of which we were absolutely certain. After all, though, it was possible that when Dirk Peters returned to Tsalal Island, the population, seized by who can tell what terror, had already taken refuge upon the south-western group, and that William Guy and his companions were still hidden in the gorges of Klock-Klock. That would explain why the half-breed had not come across them, and also why the survivors of the *Jane* had had nothing to fear during the eleven years of their sojourn in the island. On the other hand, since Patterson had left them there seven months previously, if we did not find them, that must have been because they had been obliged to leave Tsalal, the place being rendered uninhabitable by the earthquake.

"So that," resumed Captain Len Guy, "on the return

of Dirk Peters, there was no longer an inhabitant on the island?"

"No one," repeated Hunt, "no one. The half-breed did not meet a single native."

"And what did Dirk Peters do?"

"Understand me. A forsaken boat lay there, at the back of the bay, containing some dried meat and several casks of water. The half-breed got into it, and a south wind—yes, south, very strong, the same that had driven the ice block, with the cross current, towards Tsalal Island—carried him on for weeks and weeks—to the iceberg barrier, through a passage in it—you may believe me, I am telling you only what Dirk Peters told me—and he cleared the polar circle."

"And beyond it?" I inquired.

"Beyond it. He was picked up by an American whaler, the *Sandy Hook*, and taken back to America."

Now, one thing at all events was clear. Edgar Poe had never known Arthur Pym. This was the reason why, wishing to leave his readers in exciting uncertainty, he had brought Pym to an end "as sudden as it was deplorable," but without indicating the manner or the cause of his death.

"And yet, although Arthur Pym did not return, could it be reasonably admitted that he had survived his companion for any length of time, that he was still living, eleven years having elapsed since his disappearance?"

"Yes, yes," replied Hunt.

And this he affirmed with the strong conviction that Dirk Peters had infused into his mind while the two were living together at Vandalia, in Illinois.

Now the question arose, was Hunt sane? Was it not

he who had stolen into my cabin in a fit of insanity—of this I had no doubt—and murmured in my ear the words: "And Pym—poor Pym"?

Yes, and I had not been dreaming! In short, if all that Hunt had just said was true, if he was but the faithful reporter of secrets which had been entrusted to him by Dirk Peters, ought he to be believed when he repeated in a tone of mingled command and entreaty,—

"Pym is not dead. Pym is there. Poor Pym must not be forsaken!"

When I had made an end of questioning Hunt, Captain Len Guy came out of his meditative mood, profoundly troubled, and gave the word, "All hands forward!"

When the men were assembled around him, he said,—

"Listen to me, Hunt, and seriously consider the gravity of the questions I am about to put to you."

Hunt held his head up, and ran his eyes over the crew of the *Halbrane*.

"You assert, Hunt, that all you have told us concerning Arthur Pym is true?"

"Yes."

"You knew Dirk Peters?"

"Yes."

"You lived some years with him in Illinois?"

"Nine years."

"And he often related these things to you?"

"Yes."

"And, for your own part, you have no doubt that he told you the exact truth?"

"None."

"Well, then, did it never occur to him that some of the

crew of the *Jane* might have remained on Tsalal Island?"

"No."

"He believed that William Guy and his companions must all have perished in the landslip of the hill of Klock-Klock?"

"Yes, and from what he often repeated to me, Pym believed it also."

"Where did you see Dirk Peters for the last time?"

"At Vandalia."

"How long ago?"

"Over two years."

"And which of you two was the first to leave Vandalia?"

I thought I detected a slight hesitation in Hunt before he answered,—

"We left the place together."

"You, to go to?"

"The Falklands."

"And he?"

"He?" repeated Hunt.

And then his wandering gaze fixed itself on Martin Holt, our sailing-master, whose life he had saved at the risk of his own during the tempest.

"Well!" resumed the captain, "do you not understand what I am asking you?"

"Yes."

"Then answer me. When Dirk Peters left Illinois, did he finally give up America?"

"Yes."

"To go whither? Speak!"

"To the Falklands."

"And where is he now?"

"He stands before you."

Dirk Peters! Hunt was the half-breed Dirk Peters, the devoted companion of Arthur Pym, he whom Captain Guy had so long sought for in the United States, and whose presence was probably to furnish us with a fresh reason for pursuing our daring campaign.

I shall not be at all surprised if my readers have already recognized Dirk Peters in Hunt; indeed, I shall be astonished if they have failed to do so. The extraordinary thing is that Captain Len Guy and myself, who had read Edgar Poe's book over and over again, did not see at once, when Hunt came on the ship at the Falklands, that he and the half-breed were identical! I can only admit that we were both blindfolded by some hidden action of Fate, just when certain pages of that book ought to have effectually cleared our vision.

There was no doubt whatever that Hunt really was Dirk Peters. Although he was eleven years older, he answered in every particular to the description of him given by Arthur Pym, except that he was no longer "of fierce aspect." In fact, the half-breed had changed with age and the experience of terrible scenes through which he had passed; nevertheless, he was still the faithful companion to whom Arthur Pym had often owed his safety, that same Dirk Peters who loved him as his own son, and who had never—no, never—lost the hope of finding him again one day amid the awful Antarctic wastes.

Now, why had Dirk Peters hidden himself in the Falklands under the name of Hunt? Why, since his embarkation on the *Halbrane*, had he kept up that *incognito?* Why had he not told who he was, since he was aware of the intentions of the captain, who was about to make every effort to save his countrymen by following the course of the *Jane?*

Why? No doubt because he feared that his name would inspire horror. Was it not the name of one who had shared in the horrible scenes of the *Grampus*, who had killed Parker, the sailor, who had fed upon the man's flesh, and quenched his thirst in the man's blood? To induce him to reveal his name he must needs be assured that the *Halbrane* would attempt to discover and rescue Arthur Pym!

And as to the existence of Arthur Pym? I confess that my reason did not rebel against the admission of it as a possibility. The imploring cry of the half-breed, "Pym, poor Pym! he must not be forsaken!" troubled me profoundly.

Assuredly, since I had resolved to take part in the expedition of the *Halbrane*, I was no longer the same man!

A long silence had followed the astounding declaration of the half-breed. None dreamed of doubting his veracity. He had said, "I am Dirk Peters." He was Dirk Peters.

At length, moved by irresistible impulse, I said:

"My friends, before any decision is made, let us carefully consider the situation. Should we not lay up everlasting regret for ourselves if we were to abandon our expedition at the very moment when it promises to succeed? Reflect upon this, captain, and you, my companions. It is less than seven months since Patterson left your countrymen alive on Tsalal Island. If they were there then, the fact proves that for eleven years they had been enabled to exist on the resources provided by the island, having nothing to fear from the islanders, some of whom had fallen victims to circumstances unknown to us, and others had probably transferred themselves to some neighbouring island. This is quite plain, and I do not see how any objection can be raised to my reasoning."

No one made answer: there was none to be made.

"If we have not come across the captain of the *Jane* and his people," I resumed, "it is because they have been obliged to abandon Tsalal Island since Patterson's departure. Why? In my belief, it was because the earthquake had rendered the island uninhabitable. Now, they would only have required a native boat to gain either another island or some point of the Antarctic continent by the aid of the southern current. I hardly hesitate to assert that all this has occurred; but in any case, I know, and I repeat, that we shall have done nothing if we do not persevere in the search on which the safety of your countrymen depends."

I questioned my audience by a searching look. No answer.

Captain Len Guy, whose emotion was unrestrained, bowed his head, for he felt that I was right, that by invoking the duties of humanity I was prescribing the only course open to men with feeling hearts.

"And what is in question?" I continued, after the silent pause. "To accomplish a few degrees of latitude, and that while the sea is open, while we have two months of good weather to look for, and nothing to fear from the southern winter. I certainly should not ask you to brave its severity. And shall we hesitate, when the *Halbrane*

Dirk Peters shows the way.

is abundantly furnished, her crew complete and in good health? Shall we take fright at imaginary dangers? Shall we not have courage to go on, on, thither?"

And I pointed to the southern horizon. Dirk Peters pointed to it also, with an imperative gesture which spoke for him.

Still, the eyes of all were fixed upon us, but there was no response. I continued to urge every argument, and to quote every example in favour of the safety of pursuing our voyage, but the silence was unbroken, and now the men stood with eyes cast down.

And yet I had not once pronounced the name of Dirk Peters, nor alluded to Dirk Peters' proposal.

I was asking myself whether I had or had not succeeded in inspiring my companions with my own belief, when Captain Len Guy spoke:

"Dirk Peters," he said, "do you assert that Arthur Pym and you after your departure from Tsalal Island saw land in the direction of the south?"

"Yes, land," answered the half-breed. "Islands or continent—understand me—and I believe that Pym, poor Pym, is waiting there until aid comes to him."

"There, where perhaps William Guy and his companions are also waiting," said I, to bring back the discussion to more practical points.

Captain Len Guy reflected for a little while, and then spoke:

"Is it true, Dirk Peters," he asked, "that beyond the eighty-fourth parallel the horizon is shut in by that curtain of vapour which is described in the narrative? Have you seen—seen with your own eyes—those cataracts in the air, that gulf in which Arthur Pym's boat was lost?"

The half-breed looked from one to the other of us, and shook his big head.

"I don't know," he said. "What are you asking me about, captain? A curtain of vapour? Yes, perhaps, and also appearances of land towards the south."

Evidently Dirk Peters had never read Edgar Poe's book, and very likely did not know how to read. After having handed over Pym's journal, he had not troubled himself about its publication. Having retired to Illinois at first and to the Falklands afterwards, he had no notion of the stir that the work had made, or of the fantastic and baseless climax to which our great poet had brought those strange adventures.

And, besides, might not Arthur Pym himself, with his tendency to the supernatural, have fancied that he saw these wondrous things, due solely to his imaginative brain?

Then, for the first time in the course of this discussion, West's voice made itself heard. I had no idea which side he would take. The first words he uttered were:

"Captain, your orders?"

Captain Len Guy turned towards his crew, who surrounded him, both the old and the new. Hearne remained in the background, ready to intervene if he should think it necessary.

The captain questioned the boatswain and his comrades, whose devotion was unreservedly his, by a long and anxious look, and I heard him mutter between his teeth,—

"Ah! if it depended only on me! if I were sure of the assent and the help of them all!"

Then Hearne spoke roughly:

"Captain," said he, "it's two months since we left the

Falklands. Now, my companions were engaged for a voyage which was not to take them farther beyond the icebergs than Tsalal Island."

"That is not so," exclaimed Captain Len Guy. "No! That is not so. I recruited you all for an enterprise which I have a right to pursue, so far as I please."

"Beg pardon," said Hearne, coolly, "but we have come to a point which no navigator has ever yet reached, in a sea, no ship except the *Jane* has ever ventured into before us, and therefore my comrades and I mean to return to the Falklands before the bad season. From there *you* can return to Tsalal Island, and even go on to the Pole, if you so please."

A murmur of approbation greeted his words; no doubt the sealing-master justly interpreted the sentiments of the majority, composed of the new recruits. To go against their opinion, to exact the obedience of these ill-disposed men, and under such conditions to risk the unknown Antarctic waters, would have been an act of temerity—or, rather, an act of madness—that would have brought about some catastrophe.

Nevertheless, West, advancing upon Hearne, said to him in a threatening tone, "Who gave you leave to speak?"

"The captain questioned us," replied Hearne. "I had a right to reply."

The man uttered these words with such insolence that West, who was generally so self-restrained, was about to give free vent to his wrath, when Captain Len Guy, stopping him by a motion of his hand, said quietly,—

"Be calm, Jem. Nothing can be done unless we are all agreed. What is your opinion, Hurliguerly?"

"It is very clear, captain," replied the boatswain. "I

will obey your orders, whatever they may be! It is our duty not to forsake William Guy and the others so long as any chance of saving them remains."

The boatswain paused for a moment, while several of the sailors gave unequivocal signs of approbation.

"As for what concerns Arthur Pym—"

"There is no question of Arthur Pym," struck in the captain, "but only of my brother William and his companions."

I saw at this moment that Dirk Peters was about to protest, and caught hold of his arm. He shook with anger, but kept silence.

The captain continued his questioning of the men, desiring to know by name all those upon whom he might reckon. The old crew to a man acquiesced in his proposals, and pledged themselves to obey his orders implicitly and follow him whithersoever he chose to go.

Three only of the recruits joined those faithful seamen; these were English sailors. The others were of Hearne's opinion, holding that for them the campaign was ended at Tsalal Island. They therefore refused to go beyond that point, and formally demanded that the ship should be steered northward so as to clear the icebergs at the most favourable period of the season.

Twenty men were on their side, and to constrain them to lend a hand to the working of the ship if she were to be diverted to the south would have been to provoke them to rebel. There was but one resource: to arouse their covetousness, to strike the chord of self-interest.

I intervened, therefore, and addressed them in a tone which placed the seriousness of my proposal beyond a doubt.

"Men of the *Halbrane*, listen to me! Just as various

States have done for voyages of discovery in the Polar Regions, I offer a reward to the crew of this schooner. Two thousand dollars shall be shared among you for every degree we make beyond the eighty-fourth parallel."

Nearly seventy dollars to each man; this was a strong temptation.

I felt that I had hit the mark.

"I will sign an agreement to that effect," I continued, "with Captain Len Guy as your representative, and the sums gained shall be handed to you on your return, no matter under what conditions that return be accomplished."

I waited for the effect of this promise, and, to tell the truth, I had not to wait long.

"Hurrah!" cried the boatswain, acting as fugleman to his comrades, who almost unanimously added their cheers to his. Hearne offered no farther opposition; it would always be in his power to put in his word when the circumstances should be more propitious.

Thus the bargain was made, and, to gain my ends, I would have made a heavier sacrifice.

It is true we were within seven degrees of the South Pole, and, if the *Halbrane* should indeed reach that spot, it would never cost me more than fourteen thousand dollars.

Early in the morning of the 27th of December the *Halbrane* put out to sea, heading south-west.

After the scene of the preceding evening Captain Len Guy had taken a few hours' rest. I met him next day on deck while West was going about fore and aft, and he called us both to him.

"Mr. Jeorling," he said, "it was with a terrible pang

that I came to the resolution to bring our schooner back to the north! I felt I had not done all I ought to do for our unhappy fellow-countrymen; but I knew that the majority of the crew would be against me if I insisted on going beyond Tsalal Island."

"That is true, captain; there was a beginning of indiscipline on board, and perhaps it might have ended in a revolt."

"A revolt we should have speedily put down," said West, coolly, "were it only by knocking Hearne, who is always exciting the mutinous men, on the head."

"And you would have done well, Jem," said the captain. "Only, justice being satisfied, what would have become of the agreement together, which we must have in order to do anything?"

"Of course, captain, it is better that things passed off without violence! But for the future Hearne will have to look out for himself."

"His companions," observed the captain, "are now greedy for the prizes that have been promised them. The greed of gain will make them more willing and persevering. The generosity of Mr. Jeorling has succeeded where our entreaties would undoubtedly have failed. I thank him for it."

Captain Len Guy held out a hand to me, which I grasped cordially.

After some general conversation relating to our purpose, the ship's course, and the proposed verification of the bearings of the group of islands on the west of Tsalal which is described by Arthur Pym, the captain said,—

"As it is possible that the ravages of the earthquake

did not extend to this group, and that it may still be inhabited, we must be on our guard in approaching the bearings."

"Which cannot be very far off," I added. "And then, captain, who knows but that your brother and his sailors might have taken refuge on one of these islands!"

This was admissible, but not a consoling eventuality, for in that case the poor fellows would have fallen into the hands of those savages of whom they were rid while they remained at Tsalal.

"Jem," resumed Captain Len Guy, "we are making good way, and no doubt land will be signalled in a few hours. Give orders for the watch to be careful."

"It's done, captain."

"There is a man in the crow's-nest?"

"Dirk Peters himself, at his own request."

"All right, Jem; we may trust his vigilance."

"And also his eyes," I added, "for he is gifted with amazing sight."

For two hours of very quick sailing not the smallest indication of the group of eight islands was visible.

"It is incomprehensible that we have not come in sight of them," said the captain. "I reckon that the *Halbrane* has made sixty miles since this morning, and the islands in question are tolerably close together."

"Then, captain, we must conclude—and it is not unlikely—that the group to which Tsalal belonged has entirely disappeared in the earthquake."

"Land ahead!" cried Dirk Peters.

We looked, but could discern nothing on the sea, nor was it until a quarter of an hour had elapsed that our glasses enabled us to recognize the tops of a few scattered islets shining in the oblique rays of the sun, two or three miles to the westward.

What a change! How had it come about? Arthur Pym described spacious islands, but only a small number of tiny islets, half a dozen at most, protruded from the waters.

At this moment the half-breed came sliding down from his lofty perch and jumped to the deck.

"Well, Dirk Peters! Have you recognized the group?" asked the captain.

"The group?" replied the half-breed, shaking his head. "No, I have only seen the tops of five or six islets. There is nothing but stone heaps there—not a single island!"

As the schooner approached we easily recognized these fragments of the group, which had been almost entirely destroyed on its western side. The scattered remains formed dangerous reefs which might seriously injure the keel or the sides of the *Halbrane*, and there was no intention of risking the ship's safety among them. We accordingly cast anchor at a safe distance, and a boat was lowered for the reception of Captain Len Guy, the boatswain, Dirk Peters, Holt, two men and myself. The still, transparent water, as Peters steered us skilfully between the projecting edges of the little reefs, allowed us to see, not a bed of sand strewn with shells, but blackish heaps which were overgrown by land vegetation, tufts of plants not belonging to the marine flora that floated on the surface of the sea. Presently we landed on one of the larger islets which rose to about thirty feet above the sea.

"Do the tides rise sometimes to that height?" I inquired of the captain.

The half-breed in the crow's-nest.

"Never," he replied, "and perhaps we shall discover some remains of the vegetable kingdom, of habitations, or of an encampment."

"The best thing we can do," said the boatswain, "is to follow Dirk Peters, who has already distanced us. The half-breed's lynx eyes will see what we can't."

Peters had indeed scaled the eminence in a moment, and we presently joined him on the top.

The islet was strewn with remains (probably of those domestic animals mentioned in Arthur Pym's journal), but these bones differed from the bones on Tsalal Island by the fact that the heaps dated from a few months only. This then agreed with the recent period at which we placed the earthquake. Besides, plants and tufts of flowers were growing here and there.

"And these are this year's," I cried, "no southern winter has passed over them."

These facts having been ascertained, no doubt could remain respecting the date of the cataclysm after the departure of Patterson. The destruction of the population of Tsalal whose bones lay about the village was not attributable to that catastrophe. William Guy and the five sailors of the *Jane* had been able to fly in time, since no bones that could be theirs had been found on the island.

Where had they taken refuge? This was the ever-pressing question. What answer were we to obtain? Must we conclude that having reached one of these islets they had perished in the swallowing-up of the archipelago? We debated this point, as may be supposed, at a length and with detail which I can only indicate here. Suffice it to say that a decision was arrived at to the following effect. Our sole chance of discovering the unfortunate castaways was to continue our voyage for two or three parallels farther; the goal was there, and which of us would not sacrifice even his life to attain it?

"God is guiding us, Mr. Jeorling," said Captain Len Guy.

CHAPTER XVIII.

A REVELATION.

THE following day, the 29th of December, at six in the morning, the schooner set sail with a north-east wind, and this time her course was due south. The two succeeding days passed wholly without incident; neither land nor any sign of land was observed. The men on the *Halbrane* took great hauls of fish, to their own satisfaction and ours. It was New Year's Day, 1840, four months and seventeen days since I had left the Kerguelens and two months and five days since the *Halbrane* had sailed from the Falklands. The half-breed, between whom and myself an odd kind of tacit understanding subsisted, approached the bench on which I was sitting—the captain was in his cabin, and West was not in sight—with a plain intention of conversing with me. The subject may easily be guessed.

"Dirk Peters," said I, taking up the subject at once, "do you wish that we should talk of *him?*"

"Him!" he murmured.

"You have remained faithful to his memory, Dirk Peters."

"Forget him, sir! Never!"

"He is always there—before you?"

"Always! So many dangers shared! That makes brothers! No, it makes a father and his son! Yes! And I have seen America again, but Pym—poor Pym—he is still beyond there!"

"Dirk Peters," I asked, "have you any idea of the route which you and Arthur Pym followed in the boat after your departure from Tsalal Island?"

"None, sir! Poor Pym had no longer any instrument—you know—sea machines—for looking at the sun. We could not know, except that for the eight days the current pushed us towards the south, and the wind also. A fine breeze and a fair sea, and our shirts for a sail."

"Yes, white linen shirts, which frightened your prisoner Nu Nu—"

"Perhaps so—I did not notice. But if Pym has said so, Pym must be believed."

"And during those eight days you were able to supply yourselves with food?"

"Yes, sir, and the days after—we and the savage. You know—the three turtles that were in the boat. These animals contain a store of fresh water—and their flesh is sweet, even raw. Oh, raw flesh, sir!"

He lowered his voice, and threw a furtive glance around him. It would be impossible to describe the frightful expression of the half-breed's face as he thus recalled the terrible scenes of the *Grampus*. And it was not the expression of a cannibal of Australia or the New Hebrides, but that of a man who is pervaded by an insurmountable horror of himself.

"Was it not on the 1st of March, Dirk Peters," I asked, "that you perceived for the first time the veil of grey vapour shot with luminous and moving rays?"

"I do not remember, sir, but if Pym says it was so, Pym must be believed."

"Did he never speak to you of fiery rays which fell from the sky?" I did not use the term "polar aurora," lest the half-breed should not understand it.

"Never, sir," said Dirk Peters, after some reflection.

"Did you not remark that the colour of the sea changed, grew white like milk, and that its surface became ruffled around your boat?"

"It may have been so, sir; I did not observe. The boat went on and on, and my head went with it."

"And then, the fine powder, as fine as ashes, that fell—"

"I don't remember it."

"Was it not snow?"

"Snow? Yes! No! The weather was warm. What did Pym say? Pym must be believed." He lowered his voice and continued: "But Pym will tell you all that, sir. He knows. I do not know. He saw, and you will believe him."

"Yes, Dirk Peters, I shall believe him."

"We are to go in search of him, are we not?"

"I hope so."

"After we shall have found William Guy and the sailors of the *Jane?*"

"Yes, after."

"And even if we do not find them?"

"Yes, even in that case. I think I shall induce our captain. I think he will not refuse—"

"No, he will not refuse to bring help to a man—a man like him!"

"And yet," I said, "if William Guy and his people are living, can we admit that Arthur Pym—"

"Living? Yes! Living!" cried the half-breed. "By the great spirit of my fathers, he is—he is waiting for me, my poor Pym! How joyful he will be when he clasps his old Dirk in his arms, and I—I, when I feel him, there, there."

And the huge chest of the man heaved like a stormy sea. Then he went away, leaving me inexpressibly affected by the revelation of the tenderness for his unfortunate companion that lay deep in the heart of this semi-savage.

In the meantime I said but little to Captain Len Guy, whose whole heart and soul were set on the rescue of his brother, of the possibility of our finding Arthur Gordon Pym. Time enough, if in the course of this strange enterprise of ours we succeeded in that object, to urge upon him one still more visionary.

At length, on the 7th of January—according to Dirk Peters, who had fixed it only by the time that had expired—we arrived at the place where Nu Nu the savage breathed his last, lying in the bottom of the boat. On that day an observation gave 86° 33′ for the latitude, the longitude remaining the same between the forty-second and the forty-third meridian. Here it was, according to the half-breed, that the two fugitives were parted after the collision between the boat and the floating mass of ice. But a question now arose. Since the mass of ice carrying away Dirk Peters had drifted towards the north, was this because it was subjected to the action of a counter-current?

Yes, that must have been so, for our schooner had not felt the influence of the current which had guided her on leaving the Falklands, for fully four days. And yet, there was nothing surprising in that, for everything is variable in the austral seas. Happily, the fresh breeze from the north-east continued to blow, and the *Halbrane* made progress toward higher waters, thirteen degrees in advance upon Weddell's ship and two degrees upon the *Jane.* As for the land—islands or continent—which Captain Len Guy was seeking on the surface of that vast ocean, it did not appear. I was well aware that he was gradually losing confidence in our enterprise.

As for me, I was possessed by the desire to rescue Arthur Pym as well as the survivors of the *Jane.* And yet, how could he have survived! But then, the half-breed's fixed idea! Supposing our captain were to give the order to go back, what would Dirk Peters do? Throw himself into the sea rather than return northwards? This it was which made me dread some act of violence on his part, when he heard the greater number of the sailors protesting against this insensate voyage, and talking of putting the ship about, especially towards Hearne, who was stealthily inciting his comrades of the Falklands to insubordination.

It was absolutely necessary not to allow discipline to decline, or discouragement to grow among the crew; so that, on the 7th of January, Captain Len Guy at my request assembled the men and addressed them in the following words:—

"Sailors of the *Halbrane*, since our departure from Tsalal Island, the schooner has gained two degrees southwards, and I now inform you, that, conformably with the engagement signed by Mr. Jeorling, four thousand dollars—that is two thousand dollars for each degree—are due to you, and will be paid at the end of the voyage."

These words were greeted with some murmurs of satisfaction, but not with cheers, except those of Hurliguerly the boatswain, and Endicott the cook, which found no echo.

On the 13th of January a conversation took place between the boatswain and myself of a nature to justify my anxiety concerning the temper of our crew.

The men were at breakfast, with the exception of Drap and Stern. The schooner was cutting the water under a stiff breeze. I was walking between the fore and main masts, watching the great flights of birds wheeling about the ship with deafening clangour, and the petrels occasionally perching on our yards. No effort was made to catch or shoot them; it would have been useless cruelty, since their oily and stringy flesh is not eatable.

At this moment Hurliguerly approached me, looked attentively at the birds, and said,—

"I remark one thing, Mr. Jeorling."

"What is it, boatswain?"

"That these birds do not fly so directly south as they did up to the present. Some of them are setting north."

"I have noticed the same fact."

"And I add, Mr. Jeorling, that those who are below there will come back without delay."

"And you conclude from this?"

"I conclude that they feel the approach of winter."

"Of winter?"

"Undoubtedly."

"No, no, boatswain; the temperature is so high that the birds can't want to get to less cold regions so prematurely."

"Oh! prematurely, Mr. Jeorling."

"Yes, boatswain; do we not know that navigators have always been able to frequent the Antarctic waters until the month of March?"

"Not at such a latitude. Besides, there are precocious winters as well as precocious summers. The fine season this year was full two months in advance, and it is to be feared the bad season may come sooner than usual."

"That is very likely," I replied. "After all, it does not signify to us, since our campaign will certainly be over in three weeks."

"If some obstacle does not arise beforehand, Mr. Jeorling."

"And what obstacle?"

"For instance, a continent stretching to the south and barring our way."

"A continent, Hurliguerly!"

"I should not be at all surprised."

"And, in fact, there would be nothing surprising in it."

"As for the lands seen by Dirk Peters," said the boatswain, "where the men of the *Jane* might have landed on one or another of them, I don't believe in them."

"Why?"

"Because William Guy, who can only have had a small craft at his disposal, could not have got so far into these seas."

"I do not feel quite so sure of that."

"Nevertheless, Mr. Jeorling—"

"What would there be so surprising in William Guy's being carried to land somewhere by the action of the currents? He did not remain on board his boat for eight months, I suppose. His companions and he may have been able to land on an island, or even on a continent, and that is a sufficient motive for us to pursue our search."

"No doubt—but all are not of your opinion," replied Hurliguerly, shaking his head.

"I know," said I, "and that is what makes me most anxious. Is the ill-feeling increasing?"

"I fear so, Mr. Jeorling. The satisfaction of having gained several hundreds of dollars is already lessened, and the prospect of gaining a few more hundreds does not put a stop to disputes. And yet the prize is tempting! From Tsalal Island to the pole, admitting that we might get there, is six degrees. Now six degrees at two thousand dollars each makes twelve thousand dollars for thirty men, that is four hundred dollars a head A nice little sum to slip into one's pocket on the return of the *Halbrane*, but, notwithstanding, that fellow Hearne works so wickedly upon his comrades that I believe they are ready to 'bout ship in spite of anybody."

"I can believe that of the recruits, boatswain, but the old crew—"

"H—m! there are three or four of those who are beginning to reflect, and they are not easy in their minds about the prolongation of the voyage."

"I fancy Captain Len Guy and his lieutenant will know how to get themselves obeyed."

"We shall see, Mr. Jeorling. But may it not happen that our captain himself will get disheartened; that the sense of his responsibility will prevail, and that he will renounce his enterprise?"

Yes! this was what I feared, and there was no remedy on that side.

"As for my friend Endicott, Mr. Jeorling, I answer

for him as for myself. We would go to the end of the world—if the world has an end—did the captain want to go there. True, we two, Dirk Peters and yourself, are but a few to be a law to the others."

"And what do you think of the half-breed?" I asked.

"Well, our men appear to accuse him chiefly of the prolongation of the voyage. You see, Mr. Jeorling, though you have a good deal to do with it, you pay, and pay well, while this crazy fellow, Dirk Peters, persists in asserting that his poor Pym is still living—his poor Pym who was drowned, or frozen, or crushed—killed, anyhow, one way or another, eleven years ago!"

So completely was this my own belief that I never discussed the subject with the half-breed.

"You see, Mr. Jeorling," resumed the boatswain, "at the first some curiosity was felt about Dirk Peters. Then, after he saved Martin Holt, it was interest. Certainly, he was no more talkative than before, and the bear came no oftener out of his den! But now we know what he is, and no one likes him the better for that. At all events it was he who induced our captain, by talking of land to the south of Tsalal Island, to make this voyage, and it is owing to him that he has reached the eighty-sixth degree of latitude."

"That is quite true, boatswain."

"And so, Mr. Jeorling, I am always afraid that one of these days somebody will do Peters an ill turn."

"Dirk Peters would defend himself, and I should pity the man who laid a finger on him."

"Quite so. It would not be good for anybody to be in his hands, for they could bend iron! But then, all being against him, he would be forced into the hold."

"Well, well, we have not yet come to that, I hope, and I count on you, Hurliguerly, to prevent any attempt against Dirk Peters. Reason with your men. Make them understand that we have time to return to the Falklands before the end of the fine season. Their reproaches must not be allowed to provide the captain with an excuse for turning back before the object is attained."

"Count on me, Mr. Jeorling. I will serve you to the best of my ability."

"You will not repent of doing so, Hurliguerly. Nothing is easier than to add a round 0 to the four hundred dollars which each man is to have, if that man be something more than a sailor—even were his functions simply those of boatswain on board the *Halbrane.*

Nothing important occurred on the 13th and 14th, but a fresh fall in the temperature took place. Captain Len Guy called my attention to this, pointing out the flocks of birds continuously flying north.

While he was speaking to me I felt that his last hopes were fading. And who could wonder? Of the land indicated by the half-breed nothing was seen, and we were already more than one hundred and eighty miles from Tsalal Island. At every point of the compass was the sea, nothing but the vast sea with its desert horizon which the sun's disk had been nearing since the 21st of December, and would touch on the 21st March, prior to disappearing during the six months of the austral night. Honestly, was it possible to admit that William Guy and his five companions could have accomplished such a distance on a frail craft, and was there one chance in a hundred that they could ever be recovered?

On the 15th of January an observation most carefully taken gave 43° 13′ longitude and 88° 17′ latitude. The *Halbrane* was less than two degrees from the pole.

Captain Len Guy did not seek to conceal the result of this observation, and the sailors knew enough of nautical calculation to understand it. Besides, if the consequences had to be explained to them, were not Holt and Hardy there to do this, and Hearne, to exaggerate them to the utmost ?

During the afternoon I had indubitable proof that the sealing-master had been working on the minds of the crew. The men, emerging at the foot of the mainmast, talked in whispers and cast evil glances at us. Two or three sailors made threatening gestures undisguisedly; then arose such angry mutterings that West could not feign to be deaf to them.

He strode forward and called out: 'Silence, there! The first man who speaks will have to reckon with me!"

Captain Len Guy was shut up in his cabin, but every moment I expected to see him come out, give one last long look around the waste of waters, and then order the ship's course to be reversed. Nevertheless, on the next day the schooner was sailing in the same direction. Unfortunately —for the circumstance had some gravity—a mist was beginning to come down on us. I could not keep still, I confess. My apprehensions were redoubled. It was evident that West was only awaiting the order to change the helm. What mortal anguish soever the captain's must be, I understood too well that he would not give that order without hesitation.

For several days past I had not seen the half-breed, or, at least, I had not exchanged a word with him. He was boycotted by the whole crew, with the exception of the boatswain, who was careful to address him, although he rarely got a word in return. Dirk Peters took not the faintest notice of this state of things. He remained completely absorbed in his own thoughts, yet, had he heard West give the word to steer north, I know not to what acts of violence he might have been driven. He seemed to avoid me; was this from a desire not to compromise me?

On the 17th, in the afternoon, however, Dirk Peters manifested an intention of speaking to me, and never, no, never, could I have imagined what I was to learn in that interview.

It was about half-past two, and, not feeling well, I had gone to my cabin, where the side window was open, while that at the back was closed. I heard a knock at the door, and asked who was there.

"Dirk Peters," was the reply.

"You want to speak to me?"

"Yes."

"I am coming out."

"If you please—I should prefer—may I come into your cabin?"

"Come in."

"He entered, and shut the door behind him.

Without rising I signed to him to seat himself in the arm-chair, but he remained standing.

"What do you want of me, Dirk Peters?" I asked at length, as he seemed unable to make up his mind to speak.

"I want to tell you something—because it seems well that you should know it, and you only. In the crew—they must never know it."

"If it is a grave matter, and you fear any indiscretion, Dirk Peters, why do you speak to me?"

"If!—I must! Ah, yes! I must! It is impossible to keep it there! It weighs on me like a stone."

And Dirk Peters struck his breast violently.

Then he resumed:

"Yes! I am always afraid it may escape me during my sleep, and that someone will hear it, for I dream of it, and in dreaming—"

"You dream," I replied, "and of what?"

"Of him, of him. Therefore it is that I sleep in corners, all alone, for fear that his true name should be discovered."

Then it struck me that the half-breed was perhaps about to respond to an inquiry which I had not yet made —why he had gone to live at the Falklands under the name of Hunt after leaving Illinois?

I put the question to him, and he replied,—

"It is not that; no, it is not that I wish—"

"I insist, Dirk Peters, and I desire to know in the first place for what reason you did not remain in America, for what reason you chose the Falklands—"

"For what reason, sir? Because I wanted to get near Pym, my poor Pym—because I hoped to find an opportunity at the Falklands of embarking on a whaling ship bound for the southern sea."

"But that name of Hunt?"

"I would not bear my own name any longer—on account of the affair of the *Grampus*."

The half-breed was alluding to the scene of the "short straw" (or lot-drawing) on board the American brig, when it was decided between Augustus Barnard, Arthur Pym,

Dirk Peters, and Parker, the sailor, that one of the four should be sacrificed—as food for the three others. I remembered the obstinate resistance of Arthur Pym, and how it was impossible for him to refuse to take his part in the tragedy about to be performed—he says this himself—and the horrible act whose remembrance must poison the existence of all those who had survived it.

Oh, that lot-drawing! The "short straws" were little splinters of wood of uneven length which Arthur Pym held in his hand. The shortest was to designate him who should be immolated. And he speaks of the sort of involuntary fierce desire to deceive his companions that he felt—"to cheat" is the word he uses—but he did not "cheat," and he asks pardon for having had the idea! Let us try to put ourselves in his place!

He made up his mind, and held out his hand, closed on the four slips. Dirk Peters drew the first. Fate had favoured him. He had nothing more to fear. Arthur Pym calculated that one more chance was against him. Arthur Barnard drew in his turn. Saved, too, he! And now Arthur Pym reckoned up the exact chances between Parker and himself. At that moment all the ferocity of the tiger entered into his soul. He conceived an intense and devilish hatred of his poor comrade, his fellow-man.

Five minutes elapsed before Parker dared to draw. At length Arthur Pym, standing with closed eyes, not knowing whether the lot was for or against him, felt a hand seize his own. It was the hand of Dirk Peters. Arthur Pym had escaped death. And then the half-breed rushed upon Parker and stabbed him in the back. The frightful repast followed—immediately—and words are not sufficient to convey to the mind the horror of the reality.

Yes! I knew that hideous story, not a fable, as I had long believed. This was what had happened on board the *Grampus*, on the 16th of July, 1827, and vainly did I try to understand Dirk Peters' reason for recalling it to my recollection.

"Well, Dirk Peters," I said, "I will ask you, since you were anxious to hide your name, what it was that induced you to reveal it, when the *Halbrane* was moored off Tsalal Island; why you did not keep to the name of Hunt?"

"Sir—understand me—there was hesitation about going farther—they wanted to turn back. This was decided, and then I thought that by telling who I was—Dirk Peters—of the *Grampus*—poor Pym's companion—I should be heard; they would believe with me that he was still living, they would go in search of him! And yet, it was a serious thing to do—to acknowledge that I was Dirk Peters, he who had killed Parker! But hunger, devouring hunger!"

"Come, come, Dirk Peters," said I, "you exaggerate! If the lot had fallen to you, you would have incurred the fate of Parker. You cannot be charged with a crime."

"Sir, would Parker's family speak of it as you do?"

"His family! Had he then relations?"

"Yes—and that is why Pym changed his name in the narrative. Parker's name was not Parker—it was—"

"Arthur Pym was right," I said, interrupting him quickly, "and as for me, I do not wish to know Parker's real name. Keep this secret."

"No, I will tell it to you. It weighs too heavily on me, and I shall be relieved, perhaps, when I have told you, Mr. Jeorling."

"No, Dirk Peters, no!"

" His name was Holt—Ned Holt."

" Holt!" I exclaimed, "the same name as our sailing-master's."

" Who is his own brother, sir."

" Martin Holt?"

" Yes—understand me—his brother."

" But he believes that Ned Holt perished in the wreck of the *Grampus* with the rest."

" It was not so, and if he learned that I—'

Just at that instant a violent shock flung me out of my bunk.

The schooner had made such a lurch to the port side that she was near foundering.

I heard an angry voice cry out:

" What dog is that at the helm?"

It was the voice of West, and the person he addressed was Hearne.

I rushed out of my cabin.

" Have you let the wheel go?" repeated West, who had seized Hearne by the collar of his jersey.

" Lieutenant—I don't know—"

" Yes, I tell you, you have let it go. A little more and the schooner would have capsized under full sail."

" Gratian," cried West, calling one of the sailors, " take the helm; and you, Hearne, go down into the hold."

On a sudden the cry of "Land!" resounded, and every eye was turned southwards.

CHAPTER XIX

LAND?

"LAND" is the only word to be found at the beginning of the nineteenth chapter of Edgar Poe's book. I thought it would be a good idea—placing after it a note of interrogation—to put it as a heading to this portion of our narrative.

Did that word, dropped from our fore-masthead, indicate an island or a continent? And, whether a continent or an island, did not a disappointment await us? Could they be there whom we had come to seek? And Arthur Pym, who was dead, unquestionably dead, in spite of Dirk Peters' assertions, had he ever set foot on this land?

When the welcome word resounded on board the *Jane* on the 17th January, 1828—(a day full of incidents according to Arthur Pym's diary)—it was succeeded by "Land on the starboard bow!" Such might have been the signal from the masthead of the *Halbrane.*

The outlines of land lightly drawn above the sky line were visible on this side.

The land announced to the sailors of the *Jane* was the wild and barren Bennet Islet. Less than one degree south of it lay Tsalal Island, then fertile, habitable and inhabited, and on which Captain Len Guy had hoped to meet his fellow-countrymen. But what would this unknown island, five degrees farther off in the depths of the southern sea, be for our schooner? Was it the goal so ardently desired and so earnestly sought for? Were the two brothers, William and Len Guy, to meet at this place? Would the *Halbrane* come there to the end of a voyage whose success would be definitely secured by the restoration of the survivors of the *Jane* to their country?

I repeat that I was just like the half-breed. Our aim was not merely to discover the survivors, nor was success in this matter the only success we looked for. However, since land was before our eyes, we must get nearer to it first.

That cry of "Land" caused an immediate diversion of our thoughts. I no longer dwelt upon the secret Dirk Peters had just told me—and perhaps the half-breed forgot it also, for he rushed to the bow and fixed his eyes immovably on the horizon. As for West, whom nothing could divert from his duty, he repeated his commands. Gratian came to take the helm, and Hearne was shut up in the hold.

On the whole this was a just punishment, and none of the old crew protested against it, for Hearne's inattention or awkwardness had really endangered the schooner, though for a short time only.

Five or six of the Falklands sailors did, however, murmur a little.

A sign from the mate silenced them, and they returned at once to their posts.

Needless to say, Captain Len Guy, upon hearing the cry of the look-out man, had tumbled up from his cabin and eagerly examined this land at ten or twelve miles distance.

As I have said, I was no longer thinking about the secret Dirk Peters had confided to me. Besides, so long as the secret remained between us two—and neither would betray it—there would be nothing to fear. But if ever an unlucky accident were to reveal to Martin Holt that his brother's name had been changed to Parker, that the unfortunate man had not perished in the shipwreck of the *Grampus*, but had been sacrificed to save his companions from perishing of hunger; that Dirk Peters, to whom Martin Holt himself owed his life, had killed him with his own hand, what might not happen then? This was the reason why the half-breed shrank from any expression of thanks from Martin Holt—why he avoided Martin Holt, the victim's brother.

The boatswain had just struck six bells. The schooner was sailing with the caution demanded by navigation in unknown seas. There might be shoals or reefs barely hidden under the surface on which she might run aground or be wrecked. As things stood with the *Halbrane*, and even admitting that she could be floated again, an accident would have rendered her return impossible before the winter set in. We had urgent need that every chance should be in our favour and not one against us.

West had given orders to shorten sail. When the boatswain had furled the top-gallant-sail, the top-sail and royal, the *Halbrane* remained under her mainsail, her fore-sail and her jib: sufficient canvas to cover the distance that separated her from land in a few hours. Captain Len Guy immediately heaved the lead, which showed a depth of twenty fathoms. Several other soundings showed that the coast, which was very steep, was probably prolonged like a wall under the water. Nevertheless, as the bottom might happen to rise sharply instead of following the slope of the coast, we did not venture to proceed without the sounding line in hand.

The weather was still beautiful, although the sky was overcast by a mist from south-east to south-west. Owing to this there was some difficulty in identifying the vague outlines which stood out like floating vapour in the sky, disappearing and then reappearing between the breaks of the mist.

However, we all agreed to regard this land as being from twenty-five to thirty fathoms in height, at least at its highest part.

No! we would not admit that we were the victims of a delusion, and yet our uneasy minds feared that it might be so!

Is it not natural, after all, for the heart to be assailed by a thousand apprehensions as we near the end of any enterprise? At this thought my mind became confused and dreamy. The *Halbrane* seemed to be reduced to the dimensions of a small boat lost in this boundless space—the contrary of that limitless sea of which Edgar Poe speaks, where, like a living body, the ship grows larger.

When we have charts, or even sailing directions to instruct us concerning the hydrography of the coasts, the nature of the landfalls, the bays and the creeks, we may sail along boldly. In every other region, the master of a ship must not defer the order to cast anchor near the shore until the morrow. But, where we were, what an amount of prudence was necessary! And yet, no manifest obstacle was before us. Moreover, we had no cause to fear that the light would fail us during the sunny hours of the night. At this season the sun did not set so soon under the western horizon, and its rays bathed the vast Antarctic zone in unabated light.

From that day forward the ship's log recorded that the temperature fell continuously. The thermometer in the air and in the shade did not mark more than 32°·(0° C.), and when plunged into water it only indicated 26° (3° 33′ C. below 0°). What could be the cause of this fall, since we were at the height of the southern summer? The crew were obliged to resume their woollen clothing, which they had left off a month previously. The schooner, however, was sailing before the wind, and these first cold blasts were less keenly felt. Yet we recognized the necessity of reaching our goal as soon as possible. To linger in this region or to expose ourselves to the danger of wintering out would be to tempt Providence!

Captain Len Guy tested the direction of the current repeatedly by heavy lead lines, and discovered that it was beginning to deviate from its former course.

"Whether it is a continent," said he, "that lies before us, or whether it is an island, we have at present no means of determining. If it be a continent, we must conclude that the current has an issue towards the south-east."

"And it is quite possible," I replied, "that the solid part of the Antarctic region may be reduced to a mere polar mound. In any case, it is well to note any of those observations which are likely to be accurate."

"That is just what I am doing, Mr. Jeorling, and we shall bring back a mass of information about this portion of the southern sea which will prove useful to navigators."

"If ever any venture to come so far south, captain! We have penetrated so far, thanks to the help of particular circumstances. the earliness of the summer season, an abnormal temperature and a rapid thaw. Such conditions may only occur once in twenty or fifty years!'

"Wherefore, Mr. Jeorling, I thank Providence for this, and hope revives in me to some extent. As the weather has been constantly fine, what is there to make it impossible for my brother and my fellow-countrymen to have landed on this coast, whither the wind and the tide bore them? What our schooner has done, their boat may have done! They surely did not start on a voyage which might be prolonged to an indefinite time without a proper supply of provisions! Why should they not have found the same resources as those afforded to them by the island of Tsalal during many long years? They had ammunition and arms elsewhere. Fish abound in these waters, water-fowl also. Oh yes! my heart is full of hope, and I wish I were a few hours older!"

Without being quite so sanguine as Len Guy, I was glad to see he had regained his hopeful mood. Perhaps, if his investigations were successful, I might be able to have them continued in Arthur Pym's interest—even into the heart of this strange land which we were approaching.

The *Halbrane* was going along slowly on these clear waters, which swarmed with fish belonging to the same species as we had already met. The sea-birds were more numerous, and were evidently not frightened; for they kept flying round the mast, or perching in the yards. Several whitish ropes about five or six feet long were brought on board. They were chaplets formed of millions of pearly shell-fish.

Whales, spouting jets of feathery water from their blow-holes, appeared at a distance, and I remarked that all of them took a southerly direction. There was therefore reason to believe that the sea extended far and wide in that direction.

The schooner covered two or three miles of her course without any increase of speed. This coast evidently stretched from north-west to south-east. Nevertheless, the telescopes revealed no distinctive features—even after three hours' navigation.

The crew, gathered together on the forecastle, were looking on without revealing their impressions. West, after going aloft to the fore-cross-trees, where he had remained ten minutes, had reported nothing precise. Stationed at the port side, leaning my elbows on the bulwarks, I closely watched the sky line, broken only towards the east.

At this moment the boatswain rejoined me, and without further preface said:

"Will you allow me to give you my opinion, Mr. Jeorling?"

"Give it, boatswain," I replied, "at the risk of my not adopting it if I don't agree with it."

"It is correct, and according as we get nearer one must really be blind not to adopt it!"

"And what idea have you got?"

"That it is not land which lies before us, Mr. Jeorling!"

"What is it you are saying?"

"Look attentively, putting one finger before your eyes—look there—out a—starboard."

I did as Hurliguerly directed.

"Do you see?" he began again. "May I lose my liking for my grog if these heights do not change place, not with regard to the schooner, but with regard to themselves!"

"And what do you conclude from this?"

"That they are moving icebergs."

"Icebergs?"

"Sure enough, Mr. Jeorling."

Was not the boatswain mistaken? Were we in for a disappointment? Were there only drifting ice-mountains in the distance instead of a shore?

Presently, there was no doubt on the subject; for some time past the crew had no longer believed in the existence of land in that direction.

Ten minutes afterwards, the man in the crow's-nest announced that several icebergs were coming from the north-west, in an oblique direction, into the course of the *Halbrane.*

This news produced a great sensation on board. Our last hope was suddenly extinguished. And what a blow to Captain Len Guy! We should have to seek this land of the austral zone under higher latitudes without being sure of ever coming across it!"

And then the cry, "Back ship! back ship!" resounded almost unanimously on board the *Halbrane.*

Yes, indeed, the recruits from the Falklands were demanding that we should turn back, although Hearne was not there to fan the flame of insubordination, and I must acknowledge that the greater part of the old tars seemed to agree with them.

West awaited his chief's orders, not daring to impose silence.

Gratian was at the helm, ready to give a turn to the wheel, whilst his comrades with their hands on the cleats were preparing to ease off the sheets.

Dirk Peters remained immovable, leaning against the

fore-mast, his head down, his body bent, and his mouth set firm. Not a word passed his lips.

But now he turned towards me, and what a look of mingled wrath and entreaty he gave me!

I don't know what irresistible motive induced me to interfere personally, and once again to protest! A final argument had just crossed my mind—an argument whose weight could not be disputed.

So I began to speak, and I did so with such conviction that none tried to interrupt me.

The substance of what I said was as follows:—

"No! all hope must not be abandoned. Land cannot be far off. The icebergs which are formed in the open sea by the accumulation of ice are not before us. These icebergs must have broken off from the solid base of a continent or an island. Now, since the thaw begins at this season of the year, the drift will last for only a short time. Behind them we must meet the coast on which they were formed. In another twenty-four hours, or forty-eight at the most, if the land does not appear, Captain Len Guy will steer to the north again!

Had I convinced the crew, or ought I to take advantage of Hearne's absence and of the fact that he could not communicate with them to make them understand that they were being deceived, and to repeat to them that it would endanger the schooner if our course were now to be reversed.

The boatswain came to my help, and in a good-humoured voice exclaimed,—

"Very well reasoned, and for my part I accept Mr. Jeorling's opinion. Assuredly, land is near! If we seek it beyond those icebergs, we shall discover it without much hard work, or great danger! What is one degree farther south, when it is a question of putting a hundred additional dollars into one's pocket? And let us not forget that if they are acceptable when they go in, they are none the less so when they come out!"

Upon this, Endicott, the cook, came to the aid of his friend the boatswain.

"Yes, very good things indeed are dollars!" cried he, showing two rows of shining white teeth.

Did the crew intend to yield to Hurliguerly's argument, or would they try to resist if the *Halbrane* went on in the direction of the icebergs?

Captain Len Guy took up his telescope again, and turned it upon these moving masses; he observed them with much attention, and cried out in a loud voice,—

"Steer south-sou'-west!"

West gave orders to execute the manœuvres. The sailors hesitated an instant. Then, recalled to obedience, they began to brace the yards and slack the sheets, and the schooner increased her speed.

When the operation was over, I went up to Hurliguerly, and drawing him aside, I said,—

"Thank you, boatswain."

"Ah, Mr. Jeorling," he replied, shaking his head, "it is all very fine for this time, but you must not do it again! Everyone would turn against me, even Endicott, perhaps."

"I have urged nothing which is not at least probable," I answered sharply.

"I don't deny that fact, Mr. Jeorling."

"Yes, Hurliguerly, yes—I believe what I have said, and I have no doubt but that we shall really see the land beyond the icebergs."

"Just possible, Mr. Jeorling, quite possible. But it must appear before two days, or, on the word of a boatswain, nothing can prevent us from putting about!"

During the next twenty-four hours the *Halbrane* took a south-south-westerly course. Nevertheless, her direction must have been frequently changed and her speed decreased in avoiding the ice. The navigation became very difficult so soon as the schooner headed towards the line of the bergs, which it had to cut obliquely. However, there were none of the packs which blocked up all access to the iceberg on the 67th parallel. The enormous heaps were melting away with majestic slowness. The ice-blocks appeared "quite new" (to employ a perfectly accurate expression), and perhaps they had only been formed some days. However, with a height of one hundred and fifty feet, their bulk must have been calculated by millions of tons. West was watching closely in order to avoid collisions, and did not leave the deck even for an instant.

Until now, Captain Len Guy had always been able to rely upon the indications of the compass. The magnetic pole, still hundreds of miles off, had no influence on the compass, its direction being east. The needle remained steady, and might be trusted.

So, in spite of my conviction, founded, however, on very serious arguments, there was no sign of land, and I was wondering whether it would not be better to steer more to the west, at the risk of removing the *Halbrane* from that extreme point where the meridians of the globe cross each other.

Thus, as the hours went by—and I was only allowed forty-eight—it was only too plain that lack of courage prevailed, and that everyone was inclined to be insubordinate.

After another day and a half, I could no longer contend with the general discontent. The schooner must ultimately retrace her course towards the north.

The crew were working in silence, whilst West was giving sharp short orders for manœuvring through the channels, sometimes luffing in order to avoid a collision, now bearing away almost square before the wind. Nevertheless, in spite of a close watch, in spite of the skill of the sailors, in spite of the prompt execution of the manœuvres, dangerous friction against the hull, which left long traces of the ridge of the icebergs, occurred. And, in truth, the bravest could not repress a feeling of terror when thinking that the planking might have given way and the sea have invaded us.

The base of these floating ice-mountains was very steep, so that it would have been impossible for us to land upon one. Moreover, we saw no seals—these were usually very numerous where the ice-fields abounded—nor even a flock of the screeching penguins which, on other occasions, the *Halbrane* sent diving by myriads as she passed through them; the birds themselves seemed rarer and wilder. Dread, from which none of us could escape, seemed to come upon us from these desolate and deserted regions. How could we still entertain a hope that the survivors of the *Jane* had found shelter, and obtained means of existence in those awful solitudes?

And if the *Halbrane* were also shipwrecked, would there remain any evidence of her fate?

Since the previous day, from the moment our southern course had been abandoned, to cut the line of the icebergs, a change had taken place in the demeanour of the half-breed. Nearly always crouched down at the foot of the fore-mast.

looking afar into the boundless space, he only got up in order to lend a hand to some manœuvre, and without any of his former vigilance or zeal. Not that he had ceased to believe that his comrade of the *Jane* was still living—that thought never even came into his mind! But he felt by instinct that the traces of poor Pym were not to be recovered by following this course.

"Sir," he would have said to me, "this is not the way! No, this is not the way!" And how could I have answered him?

Towards seven o'clock in the evening a rather thick mist arose; this would tend to make the navigation of the schooner difficult and dangerous.

The day, with its emotions of anxiety and alternatives, had worn me out. So I returned to my cabin, where I threw myself on my bunk in my clothes.

But sleep did not come to me, owing to my besetting thoughts. I willingly admit that the constant reading of Edgar Poe's works, and reading them in this place in which his heroes delighted, had exercised an influence on me which I did not fully recognize.

To-morrow, the forty-eight hours would be up, the last concession which the crew had made to my entreaties.

"Things are not going as you wish?" the boatswain said to me just as I was leaving the deck.

No, certainly not, since land was not to be seen behind the fleet of icebergs. If no sign of a coast appeared between these moving masses, Captain Len Guy would steer north to-morrow.

Ah! were I only master of the schooner! If I could have bought it even at the price of all my fortune, if these men had been my slaves to drive by the lash, the *Halbrane* should never have given up this voyage, even if it led her so far as the point above which flames the Southern Cross.

My mind was quite upset, and teemed with a thousand thoughts, a thousand regrets, a thousand desires! I wanted to get up, but a heavy hand held me down in my bunk! And I longed to leave this cabin where I was struggling against nightmare in my half-sleep, to launch one of the boats of the *Halbrane*, to jump into it with Dirk Peters, who would not hesitate about following me, and so abandon both of us to the current running south.

And lo! I was doing this in a dream. It is to-morrow! Captain Len Guy has given orders to reverse our course, after a last glance at the horizon. One of the boats is in tow. I warn the half-breed. We creep along without being seen. We cut the painter. Whilst the schooner sails on ahead, we stay astern and the current carries us off.

Thus we drift on the sea without hindrance! At length our boat stops. Land is there. I see a sort of sphinx surmounting the southern peak—the sea-sphinx. I go to him. I question him. He discloses the secrets of these mysterious regions to me. And then, the phenomena whose reality Arthur Pym asserted appear around the mythic monster. The curtain of flickering vapours, striped with luminous rays, is rent asunder. And it is not a face of superhuman grandeur which arises before my astonished eyes: it is Arthur Pym, fierce guardian of the south pole, flaunting the ensign of the United States in those high latitudes!

Was this dream suddenly interrupted, or was it changed by a freak of my brain? I cannot tell, but I felt as though I had been suddenly awakened. It seemed as though a change had taken place in the motion of the schooner, which was sliding along on the surface of the quiet sea, with a slight list to starboard. And yet, there was neither rolling nor pitching. Yes, I felt myself carried off as though my bunk were the car of an air-balloon. I was not mistaken, and I had fallen from dreamland into reality.

Crash succeeded crash overhead. I could not account for them. Inside my cabin the partitions deviated from the vertical in such a way as to make one believe that the *Halbrane* had fallen over on her beam ends. Almost immediately, I was thrown out of my bunk and barely escaped splitting my skull against the corner of the table. However, I got up again, and, clinging on to the edge of the door frame, I propped myself against the door.

At this instant the bulwarks began to crack and the port side of the ship was torn open.

Could there have been a collision between the schooner and one of those gigantic floating masses which West was unable to avoid in the mist?

Suddenly loud shouts came from the after-deck, and then screams of terror, in which the maddened voices of the crew joined.

At length there came a final crash, and the *Halbrane* remained motionless.

I had to crawl along the floor to reach the door and gain the deck. Captain Len Guy having already left his cabin, dragged himself on his knees, so great was the list to port, and caught on as best he could.

In the fore part of the ship, between the forecastle and the fore-mast, many heads appeared.

Dirk Peters, Hardy, Martin Holt and Endicott, the latter with his black face quite vacant, were clinging to the starboard shrouds.

A man came creeping up to me, because the slope of the deck prevented him from holding himself upright: it was Hurliguerly, working himself along with his hands like a top-man on a yard.

Stretched out at full length, my feet propped up against the jamb of the door, I held out my hand to the boatswain, and helped him, not without difficulty, to hoist himself up near me.

"What is wrong?" I asked.

"A stranding, Mr. Jeorling."

"We are ashore!"

"A shore presupposes land," replied the boatswain ironically, "and so far as land goes there was never any except in that rascal Dirk Peters' imagination."

"But tell me—what has happened?"

"We came upon an iceberg in the middle of the fog, and were unable to keep clear of it."

"An iceberg, boatswain?"

"Yes, an iceberg, which has chosen just now to turn head over heels. In turning, it struck the *Halbrane* and carried it off just as a battledore catches a shuttlecock, and now here we are, stranded at certainly one hundred feet above the level of the Antarctic Sea."

Could one have imagined a more terrible conclusion to the adventurous voyage of the *Halbrane*?

In the middle of these remote regions our only means of transport had just been snatched from its natural element, and carried off by the turn of an iceberg to a height of more than one hundred feet! What a conclusion! To be swallowed up in a polar tempest, to be destroyed in a fight with savages, to be crushed in the ice, such are the dangers to which any ship engaged in the polar seas is exposed! But to think that the *Halbrane* had been lifted by a floating mountain just as that mountain was turning over, was stranded and almost at its summit—no! such a thing seemed quite impossible.

I did not know whether we could succeed in letting down the schooner from this height with the means we had at our disposal. But I did know that Captain Len Guy, the mate and the older members of the crew, when they had recovered from their first fright, would not give up in despair, no matter how terrible the situation might be; of that I had no doubt whatsoever! They would all look to the general safety; as for the measures to be taken, no one yet knew anything. A foggy veil, a sort of greyish mist still hung over the iceberg. Nothing could be seen of its enormous mass except the narrow craggy cleft in which the schooner was wedged, nor even what place it occupied in the middle of the ice-fleet drifting towards the south-east.

Common prudence demanded that we should quit the *Halbrane*, which might slide down at a sharp shake of the iceberg. Were we even certain that the latter had regained its position on the surface of the sea? Was her stability secure? Should we not be on the look-out for a fresh upheaval? And if the schooner were to fall into the abyss, which of us could extricate himself safe and sound from such a fall, and then from the final plunge into the depths of the ocean?

In a few minutes the crew had abandoned the *Halbrane*. Each man sought for refuge on the ice-slopes, awaiting the time when the iceberg should be freed from mist. The oblique rays from the sun did not succeed in piercing it, and the red disk could hardly be perceived through the opaque mass.

However, we could distinguish each other at about twelve feet apart. As for the *Halbrane*, she looked like a confused blackish mass standing out sharply against the whiteness of the ice.

We had now to ascertain whether any of those who were on the deck at the time of the catastrophe had been thrown over the bulwarks and precipitated into the sea?

By Captain Len Guy's orders all the sailors then present joined the group in which I stood with the mate, the boatswain, Hardy and Martin Holt.

So far, this catastrophe had cost us five men—these were the first since our departure from Kerguelen, but were they to be the last?

There was no doubt that these unfortunate fellows had perished, because we called them in vain, and in vain we sought for them, when the fog abated, along the sides of the iceberg, at every place where they might have been able to catch on to a projection.

When the disappearance of the five men had been ascertained, we fell into despair. Then we felt more keenly than before the dangers which threaten every expedition to the Antarctic zone.

"What about Hearne?" said a voice.

Martin Holt pronounced the name at a moment when there was general silence. Had the sealing-master been crushed to death in the narrow part of the hold where he was shut up?

The *Halbrane* fast in the iceberg.

West rushed towards the schooner, hoisted himself on board by means of a rope hanging over the bows, and gained the hatch which gives access to that part of the hold.

We waited silent and motionless to learn the fate of Hearne, although the evil spirit of the crew was but little worthy of our pity.

And yet, how many of us were then thinking that if we had heeded his advice, and if the schooner had taken the northern course, a whole crew would not have been reduced to take refuge on a drifting ice-mountain! I scarcely dared to calculate my own share of the vast responsibility, I who had so vehemently insisted on the prolongation of the voyage.

At length the mate reappeared on deck and Hearne followed him! By a miracle, neither the bulkheads, nor the ribs, nor the planking had yielded at the place where the sealing-master was confined.

Hearne rejoined his comrades without opening his lips, and we had no further trouble about him.

Towards six o'clock in the morning the fog cleared off, owing to a marked fall in the temperature. We had no longer to do with completely frozen vapour, but had to deal with the phenomenon called frost-rime, which often occurs in these high latitudes. Captain Len Guy recognized it by the quantity of prismatic threads, the point following the wind which roughened the light ice-crust deposited on the sides of the iceberg. Navigators know better than to confound this frost-rime with the hoar frost of the temperate zones, which only freezes when it has been deposited on the surface of the soil.

We were now enabled to estimate the size of the solid mass on which we clustered like flies on a sugar-loaf, and the schooner, seen from below, looked no bigger than the yawl of a trading vessel.

This iceberg of between three and four hundred fathoms in circumference measured from 130 to 140 feet high. According to all calculations, therefore, its depth would be four or five times greater, and it would consequently weigh millions of tons.

This is what had happened:

The iceberg, having been melted away at its base by contact with warmer waters, had risen little by little; its centre of gravity had become displaced, andits equilibrium could only be re-established by a sudden capsize, which had lifted up the part that had been underneath above the sea-level. The *Halbrane*, caught in this movement, was hoisted as by an enormous lever. Numbers of icebergs capsize thus on the polar seas, and form one of the greatest dangers to which approaching vessels are exposed.

Our schooner was caught in a hollow on the west side of the iceberg. She listed to starboard with her stern raised and her bow lowered. We could not help thinking that the slightest shake would cause her to slide along the slope of the iceberg into the sea. The collision had been so violent as to stave in some of the planks of her hull. After the first collision, the galley situated before the fore-mast had broken its fastenings. The door between Captain Len Guy's and the mate's cabins was torn away from the hinges. The topmast and the top-gallant-mast had come down after the back-stays parted, and fresh fractures could plainly be seen as high as the cap of the masthead.

Fragments of all kinds, yards, spars, a part of the sails,

breakers, cases, hen-coops, were probably floating at the foot of the mass and drifting with it.

The most alarming part of our situation was the fact that of the two boats belonging to the *Halbrane*, one had been stove in when we grounded, and the other, the larger of the two, was still hanging on by its tackles to the starboard davits. Before anything else was done this boat had to be put in a safe place, because it might prove our only means of escape.

As a result of the first examination, we found that the lower masts had remained in their places, and might be of use if ever we succeeded in releasing the schooner. But how were we to release her from her bed in the ice and restore her to her natural element ?

When I found myself with Captain Len Guy, the mate, and the boatswain, I questioned them on this subject.

"I agree with you," replied West, "that the operation involves great risks, but since it is indispensable, we will accomplish it. I think it will be necessary to dig out a sort of slide down to the base of the iceberg."

"And without the delay of a single day," added Captain Len Guy.

"Do you hear, boatswain ?" said Jem West. "Work begins to-day."

"I hear, and everyone will set himself to the task," replied Hurliguerly. "If you allow me, I shall just make one observation, captain."

"What is it ?"

"Before beginning the work, let us examine the hull and see what the damage is, and whether it can be repaired. For what use would it be to launch a ship stripped of her planks, which would go to the bottom at once?"

We complied with the boatswain's just demand.

The fog having cleared off, a bright sun then illumined the eastern side of the iceberg, whence the sea was visible round a large part of the horizon. Here the sides of the iceberg showed rugged projections, ledges, shoulders, and even flat instead of smooth surfaces, giving no foothold. However, caution would be necessary in order to avoid the falling of those unbalanced blocks, which a single shock might set loose. And, as a matter of fact, during the morning, several of these blocks did roll into the sea with a frightful noise just like an avalanche.

On the whole, the iceberg seemed to be very steady on its new base. So long as the centre of gravity was below the level of the water-line, there was no fear of a fresh capsize.

I had not yet had an opportunity of speaking to Dirk Peters since the catastrophe. As he had answered to his name, I knew he was not numbered among the victims. At this moment, I perceived him standing on a narrow projection; needless to specify the direction in which his eyes were turned.

Captain Len Guy, the mate, the boatswain, Hardy, and Martin Holt, whom I accompanied, went up again towards the schooner in order to make a minute investigation of the hull. On the starboard side the operation would be easy enough, because the *Halbrane* had a list to the opposite side. On the port side we would have to slide along to the keel as well as we could by scooping out the ice, in order to insure the inspection of every part of the planking.

After an examination which lasted two hours, it was discovered that the damage was of little importance, and could be repaired in a short time. Two or three planks only were wrenched away by the collision. In the inside the skin was intact, the ribs not having given way. Our vessel, constructed for the polar seas, had resisted where many others less solidly built would have been dashed to pieces. The rudder had indeed been unshipped, but that could easily be set right.

Having finished our inspection inside and outside, we agreed that the damage was less considerable than we feared, and on that subject we became reassured. Reassured! Yes, if we could only succeed in getting the schooner afloat again.

CHAPTER XX.

"UNMERCIFUL DISASTER."

In the morning, after breakfast, it was decided that the men should begin to dig a sloping bed which would allow the *Halbrane* to slide to the foot of the iceberg. Would that Heaven might grant success to the operation, for who could contemplate without terror having to brave the severity of the austral winter, and to pass six months under such conditions as ours on a vast iceberg, dragged none could tell whither? Once the winter had set in, none of us could have escaped from that most terrible of fates—dying of cold.

At this moment, Dirk Peters, who was observing the horizon from south to east at about one hundred paces off, cried out in a rough voice: "Lying to!"

Lying to? What could the half-breed mean by that, except that the floating mass had suddenly ceased to drift? As for the cause of this stoppage, it was neither the moment to investigate it, nor to ask ourselves what the consequences were likely to be.

"It is true, however," cried the boatswain. "The iceberg is not stirring, and perhaps has not stirred since it capsized!"

"How?" said I, "it no longer changes its place."

"No," replied the mate, "and the proof is that the others, drifting on, are leaving it behind!"

And, in fact, whilst five or six icebergs were descending towards the south, ours was as motionless as though it had been stranded on a shoal.

The simplest explanation was that the new base had encountered ground at the bottom of the sea to which it now adhered, and would continue to adhere, unless the submerged part rose in the water so as to cause a second capsize.

This complicated matters seriously, because the dangers of positive immobility were such that the chances of drifting were preferable. At least, in the latter case there was some hope of coming across a continent or an island, or even (if the currents did not change) of crossing the boundaries of the austral region.

Here we were, then, after three months of this terrible voyage! Was there now any question of trying to save William Guy, his comrades on the *Jane*, and Arthur Pym? Was it not for our own safety that any means at our disposal should be employed? And could it be wondered at were the sailors of the *Halbrane* to rebel, were they to listen to Hearne's suggestions, and make their officers, or myself especially, responsible for the disasters of this expedition?

Moreover, what was likely to take place, since, notwithstanding their losses, the followers of the sealing-master were still a majority of the ship's company?

This question I could clearly see was occupying the thoughts of Captain Len Guy and West.

Again, although the recruits from the Falklands formed only a total of fourteen men, as against the twelve of the old crew, was it not to be feared that some of the latter would take Hearne's side? What if Hearne's people, urged by despair, were already thinking of seizing the only boat we now possessed, setting off towards the north, and leaving us on this iceberg? It was, then, of great importance that our boat should be put in safety and closely watched.

A marked change had taken place in Captain Len Guy since the recent occurrences. He seemed to be transformed upon finding himself face to face with the dangers which menaced us. Up to that time he had been solely occupied in searching for his fellow-countrymen; he had handed over the command of the schooner to West, and he could not have given it to anyone more zealous and more capable. But from this date he resumed his position as master of the ship, and used it with the energy required by the circumstances; in a word, he again became sole master on board, after God.

At his command the crew were drawn up around him on a flat spot a little to the left of the *Halbrane*. In that place the following were assembled:—on the seniors' side: Martin Holt and Hardy, Rogers, Francis, Gratian, Bury, Stern, the cook (Endicott), and I may add Dirk Peters; on the side of the new-comers, Hearne and the thirteen other Falkland sailors. The latter composed a distinct group; the sealing-master was their spokesman and exercised a baneful influence over them.

Captain Len Guy cast a stern glance upon the men and said in a sharp tone:

"Sailors of the *Halbrane*, I must first speak to you of our lost companions. Five of us have just perished in this catastrophe."

"We are waiting to perish in our turn, in these seas, where we have been dragged in spite of—"

"Be silent, Hearne," cried West, pale with anger, "or if not—"

"Hearne has said what he had to say," Captain Len Guy continued, coldly. "Now it is said, and I advise him not to interrupt me a second time!"

The sealing-master might possibly have ventured on an answer, for he felt that he was backed by the majority of the crew; but Martin Holt held him back, and he was silent.

Captain Len Guy then took off his hat and pronounced the following words with an emotion that affected us to the bottom of our hearts:—

"We must pray for those who have died in this dangerous voyage, which was undertaken in the name of humanity. May God be pleased to take into consideration the fact that they devoted their lives to their fellow-creatures, and may He not be insensible to our prayers! Kneel down, sailors of the *Halbrane!*"

They all knelt down on the icy surface, and the murmurs of prayer ascended towards heaven.

We waited for Captain Len Guy to rise before we did so.

"Now," he resumed, "after those who are dead come those who have survived. To them I say that they must obey me, whatever my orders may be, and even in our present situation I shall not tolerate any hesitation or opposition. The responsibility for the general safety is mine, and I will not yield any of it to anyone. I am master here, as on board—"

"On board—when there is no longer a ship," muttered the sealing-master.

"You are mistaken, Hearne, the vessel is there, and we will put it back into the sea. Besides, if we had only a boat, I am the captain of it. Let him beware who forgets this!"

That day, Captain Len Guy, having taken the height of the sun by the sextant and fixed the hour by the chronometer (both of these instruments had escaped destruction in the collision), obtained the following position of his ship:—

South latitude: 88° 55′.

West longitude: 39° 12′.

The *Halbrane* was only at 1° 5′—about 65 miles—from the south pole.

"All hands to work," was the captain's order that afternoon, and every one obeyed it with a will. There was not a moment to lose, as the question of time was more important than any other. So far as provisions were concerned, there was enough in the schooner for eighteen months on full rations, so we were not threatened with hunger, nor with thirst either, notwithstanding that owing to the water-casks having been burst in the collision, their contents had escaped through their staves. Luckily, the barrels of gin, whisky, beer, and wine, being placed in the least exposed part of the hold, were nearly all intact. Under this head we had experienced no loss, and the iceberg would supply us with good drinking-water. It is a well-known fact that ice, whether formed from fresh or salt water, contains no salt, owing to the chloride of sodium being eliminated in the change from the liquid to the solid state. The origin of the ice, therefore, is a matter of no importance. However, those blocks which are easily distinguished by their greenish colour and their perfect transparency are preferable. They are solidified rain, and therefore much more suitable for drinking-water.

Without doubt, our captain would have recognized any blocks of this description, but none were to be found on the glacier, owing to its being that part of the berg which was originally submerged, and came to the top after the fall.

The captain and West decided first to lighten the vessel, by conveying everything on board to land. The masts were to be cleared of rigging, taken out, and placed on the plateau. It was necessary to lighten the vessel as much as possible, even to clear out the ballast, owing to the difficult and dangerous operation of launching. It would be better to put off our departure for some days if this operation could be performed under more favourable circumstances. The loading might be afterwards accomplished without much difficulty.

Besides this, another reason by no means less serious presented itself to us. It would have been an act of unpardonable rashness to leave the provisions in the store-room of the *Halbrane*, her situation on the side of the iceberg being very precarious. One shake would suffice to detach the ship, and with her would have disappeared the supplies on which our lives depended.

On this account, we passed the day in removing casks of half-salted meat, dried vegetables, flour, biscuits, tea, coffee, barrels of gin, whisky, wine and beer from the hold and store-room and placing them in safety in the hammocks near the *Halbrane*.

We also had to insure our landing against any possible accident, and, I must add, against any plot on the part of Hearne and others to seize the boat in order to return to the ice-barrier.

We placed the long boat in a cavity which would be easy to watch, about thirty feet to the left of the schooner, along with its oars, rudder, compass, anchor, masts and sail.

By day there was nothing to fear, and at night, or rather during the hours of sleep, the boatswain and one of the superiors would keep guard near the cavity, and we might rest assured that no evil could befall.

The 19th, 20th, and 21st of January were passed in working extra hard in the unshipping of the cargo and the dismantling of the *Halbrane*. We slung the lower masts by means of yards forming props. Later on, West would see to replacing the main and mizzen masts ; in any case, we could do without them until we had reached the Falklands or some other winter port.

Needless to say, we had set up a camp on the plateau of which I have spoken, not far from the *Halbrane*. Sufficient shelter against the inclemency of the weather, not unfrequent at this time of the year, was to be found under tents, constructed of sails placed on spars and fastened down by pegs. The glass remained set fair ; the wind was nor'-east, the temperature having risen to 46 degrees (2° 78′ C.).

Endicott's kitchen was fitted up at the end of the plain, near a steep projection by which we could climb to the very top of the berg.

It is only fair to state that during these three days of hard work no fault was to be found with Hearne. The sealing-master knew he was being closely watched, and he was well aware that Captain Len Guy would not spare him if he tried to get up insubordination amongst his comrades. It was a pity that his bad instincts had induced him to play such a part, for his strength, skill, and cleverness made him a very valuable man, and he had never proved more useful than under these circumstances.

Was he changed for the better? Did he understand that general good feeling was necessary for the safety of all? I know not, but I had no confidence in him, neither had Hurliguerly!

I need not dwell on the ardour with which the half-breed did the rough work, always first to begin and the last to leave off, doing as much as four men, and scarcely sleeping, only resting during meals, which he took apart from the others. He had hardly spoken to me at all since the schooner had met with this terrible accident.

What indeed could he say to me? Did I not know as well as he that it would be necessary to renounce every hope of pursuing our intended voyage?

Now and again I noticed Martin Holt and the half-breed near each other while some difficult piece of work was in progress. Our sailing-master did not miss a chance of getting near Dirk Peters, who always tried his best to escape from him, for reasons well known to me. And whenever I thought of the secret of the fate of the so-called Parker, Martin Holt's brother, which had been entrusted to me, that dreadful scene of the *Grampus* filled me with horror. I was certain that if this secret were made known the half-breed would become an object of terror. He would no longer be looked upon as the rescuer of the sailing-master; and the latter, learning that his brother— Luckily, Dirk Peters and myself were the only two acquainted with the fact.

While the *Halbrane* was being unloaded, Captain Len Guy and the mate were considering how the vessel might be launched. They had to allow for a drop of one hundred feet between the cavity in which the ship lay and the sea; this to be effected by means of an inclined bed hollowed in an oblique line along the west side of the iceberg, and to measure two or three hundred perches in length. So, while the first lot of men, commanded by the boatswain, was unloading the schooner, a second batch under West's orders began to cut the trench between the blocks which covered the side of the floating mountain.

Floating? I know not why I use this expression, for the iceberg no longer floated, but remained as motionless as an island. There was nothing to indicate that it would ever move again. Other icebergs drifted along and passed us, going south-east, whilst ours, to use Dirk Peters' expression, was "lying to." Would its base be sufficiently undermined to allow it to detach itself? Perhaps some heavy mass of ice might strike it and set it free by the shock. No one could predict such an event, and we had only the *Halbrane* to rely upon for getting us out of these regions.

We were engaged in these various tasks until the 24th of January. The atmosphere was clear, the temperature was even, and the thermometer had indeed gone up to two or three degrees above freezing-point. The number of icebergs coming from the nor'-west was therefore increasing; there were now a hundred of them, and a collision with any of these might have a most disastrous result. Hardy, the caulker, hastened first of all to mend the hull; pegs had to be changed, bits of planking to be replaced, seams to be caulked. We had everything that was necessary for this work, and we might rest assured that it would be performed in the best possible manner. In the midst of the silence of these solitudes, the noise of the hammers striking nails into the side, and the sound of the mallet stuffing tow into the seams, had a startling effect. Sea-gulls, wild duck, albatross, and petrels flew in a circle round the top of the berg with a shrill screaming, and made a terrible uproar.

When I found myself with West and the captain, our conversation naturally turned on our situation and how to get out of it, and upon our chances of pulling through. The mate had good hopes that if no accident occurred the launching would be successfully accomplished. The captain was more reserved on the subject, but at the thought that he would have to renounce all hope of finding the survivors of the *Jane*, his heart was ready to break.

When the *Halbrane* should again be ready for the sea, and when West should inquire what course he was to steer, would Captain Len Guy dare to reply, "To the south"? No! for he would not be followed either by the new hands, or by the greater portion of the older members of the crew. To continue our search in this direction, to go beyond the pole, without being certain of reaching the Indian Ocean instead of the Atlantic, would have been rashness of which no navigator would be guilty. If a continent bound the sea on this side, the schooner would run the danger of being crushed by the mass of ice before it could escape the southern winter.

Under such circumstances, to attempt to persuade Captain Len Guy to pursue the voyage would only be to court a certain refusal. It could not even be proposed, now that necessity obliged us to return northwards, and not to delay a single day in this portion of the Antarctic regions. At any rate, though I resolved not again to speak of the matter to the captain, I lost no opportunity of sounding the boatswain. Often when he had finished his work, Hurliguerly would come and join me; we would chat, and we would compare our recollections of travel.

One day as we were seated on the summit of the iceberg, gazing fixedly on the deceptive horizon, he exclaimed,—

"Who could ever have imagined, Mr. Jeorling, when the *Halbrane* left Kerguelen, that six and a half months afterwards she would be stuck on the side of an ice-mountain?"

"A fact much more to be regretted," I replied, "because only for that accident we should have attained our object, and we should have begun our return journey."

"I don't mean to contradict," replied the boatswain, "but you say we should have attained our object. Do you mean by that, that we should have found our countrymen?"

"Perhaps."

"I can scarcely believe such would have been the case, Mr. Jeorling, although this was the principal and perhaps even the only object of our navigation in the polar-seas."

"The only one—yes—at the start," I insinuated. "But since the half-breed's revelations about Arthur Pym—"

"Ah! You are always harking back on that subject, like brave Dirk Peters."

"Always, Hurliguerly; and only that a deplorable and unforeseen accident made us run aground—"

"I leave you to your delusions, Mr. Jeorling, since you believe you have run aground—"

"Why? Is not this the case?"

"In any case it is a wonderful running aground," replied the boatswain. "Instead of a good solid bottom, we have run aground in the air."

"Then I am right, Hurliguerly, in saying it is an unfortunate adventure."

"Unfortunate, truly, but in my opinion we should take warning by it."

"What warning?"

"That it is not permitted to us to venture so far in these latitudes, and I believe that the Creator forbids His creatures to climb to the summit of the poles."

"Notwithstanding that the summit of one pole is only sixty miles away from us now."

"Granted, Mr. Jeorling, but these sixty miles are equal to thousands when we have no means of making them! And if the launch of the schooner is not successful, here are we condemned to winter quarters which the polar bears themselves would hardly relish!"

I replied only by a shake of my head, which Hurliguerly could not fail to understand.

"Do you know, Mr. Jeorling, of what I think oftenest?"

"What do you think of, boatswain?"

"Of the Kerguelens, whither we are certainly not travelling. Truly, in a bad season it was cold enough there! There is not much difference between this archipelago and the islands situated on the edge of the Antarctic Sea! But there one is not far from the Cape, and if we want to warm our shins, no iceberg bars the way. Whereas here it is the devil to weigh anchor, and one never knows if one shall find a clear course."

"I repeat it, boatswain. If this last accident had not

occurred, everything would have been over by this time, one way or another. We should still have had more than six weeks to get out of these southern seas. It is seldom that a ship is so roughly treated as ours has been, and I consider it real bad luck, after our having profited by such fortunate circumstances—"

"These circumstances are all over, Mr. Jeorling," exclaimed Hurliguerly, "and I fear indeed—"

"What—you also, boatswain—you whom I believed to be so confident!"

"Confidence, Mr. Jeorling, wears out like the ends of one's trousers. What would you have me do? When I compare my lot to old Atkins, installed in his cosy inn; when I think of the Green Cormorant, of the big parlours downstairs with the little tables round which friends sip whisky and gin, discussing the news of the day, while the stove makes more noise than the weathercock on the roof—oh, then the comparison is not in our favour, and in my opinion Mr. Atkins enjoys life better than I do."

"You shall see them all again, boatswain—Atkins, the Green Cormorant, and Kerguelen! For God's sake do not let yourself grow downhearted! And if you, a sensible and courageous man, despair already—"

"Oh, if I were the only one it would not be half so bad as it is!"

"The whole crew does not despair, surely?"

"Yes—and no," replied Hurliguerly, "for I know some who are not at all satisfied!"

"Has Hearne begun his mischief again? Is he exciting his companions?"

"Not openly at least, Mr. Jeorling, and since I have kept him under my eye I have neither seen nor heard anything. Besides, he knows what awaits him if he budges. I believe I am not mistaken, the sly dog has changed his tactics. But what does not astonish me in him, astonishes me in Martin Holt."

"What do you mean, boatswain?"

"That they seem to be on good terms with each other. See how Hearne seeks out Martin Holt, talks to him frequently, and Holt does not treat his overtures unfavourably."

"Martin Holt is not one of those who would listen to Hearne's advice, or follow it if he tried to provoke rebellion amongst the crew."

"No doubt, Mr. Jeorling. However, I don't fancy seeing them so much together. Hearne is a dangerous and unscrupulous individual, and most likely Martin Holt does not distrust him sufficiently."

"He is wrong, boatswain."

"And—wait a moment—do you know what they were talking about the other day when I overheard a few scraps of their conversation?"

"I could not possibly guess until you tell me, Hurliguerly."

"Well, while they were conversing on the bridge of the *Halbrane*, I heard them talking about Dirk Peters, and Hearne was saying: 'You must not owe a grudge to the half-breed, Master Holt, because he refused to respond to your advances and accept your thanks! If he be only a sort of brute, he possesses plenty of courage, and has showed it in getting you out of a bad corner at the risk of his life. And besides, do not forget that he formed part of the crew of the *Grampus*, and your brother Ned, if I don't mistake—'

"He said that, boatswain; he spoke of the *Grampus?*" I exclaimed.

"Yes—of the *Grampus!*"

"And of Ned Holt?"

"Precisely, Mr. Jeorling!"

"And what answer did Martin Holt make?"

"He replied: 'I don't even know under what circumstances my unfortunate brother perished. Was it during a revolt on board? Brave man that he was, he would not betray his captain, and perhaps he was massacred."

"Did Hearne dwell on this, boatswain?"

"Yes, but he added: 'It is very sad for you, Master Holt! The captain of the *Grampus*, according to what I have been told, was abandoned, being placed in a small boat with one or two of his men—and who knows if your brother was not along with him?'"

"And what next?"

"Then, Mr. Jeorling, he added: 'Did it never occur to you to ask Dirk Peters to enlighten you on the subject?' 'Yes, once,' replied Martin Holt, 'I questioned the half-breed about it, and never did I see a man so overcome. He replied in so low a voice that I could scarcely understand him, 'I know not—I know not—' and he ran away with his face buried in his hands."

"Was that all you heard of the conversation, boatswain?"

"That was all, Mr. Jeorling, and I thought it so strange that I wished to inform you of it."

And what conclusion did you draw from it?"

"Nothing, except that I look upon the sealing-master as a scoundrel of the deepest dye, perfectly capable of working in secret for some evil purpose with which he would like to associate Martin Holt!"

What did Hearne's new attitude mean? Why did he strive to gain Martin Holt, one of the best of the crew, as an ally? Why did he recall the scenes of the *Grampus?* Did Hearne know more of this matter of Dirk Peters and Ned Holt than the others; this secret of which the half-breed and I believed ourselves to be the sole possessors?

The doubt caused me serious uneasiness. However, I took good care not to say anything of it to Dirk Peters. If he had for a moment suspected that Hearne spoke of what happened on board the *Grampus*, if he had heard that the rascal (as Hurliguerly called him, and not without reason) constantly talked to Martin Holt about his brother, I really do not know what would have happened.

In short, whatever the intentions of Hearne might be, it was dreadful to think that our sailing-master, on whose fidelity Captain Len Guy ought to be able to count, was in conspiracy with him.

The sealing-master must have a strong motive for acting in this way. What it was I could not imagine. Although the crew seemed to have abandoned every thought of mutiny, a strict watch was kept, especially on Hearne.

Besides, the situation must soon change, at least so far as the schooner was concerned. Two days afterwards the work was finished. The caulking operations were completed, and also the slide for lowering the vessel to the base of our floating mountain.

Just now the upper portion of the ice had been slightly

softened, so that this last work did not entail much labour for pickaxe or spade. The course ran obliquely round the west side of the berg, so that the incline should not be too great at any point. With cables properly fixed, the launch, it seemed, might be effected without any mishap. I rather feared lest the melting of the ice should make the gliding less smooth at the lower part of the berg.

Needless to say, the cargo, masting, anchors, chains, &c., had not been put on board. The hull was quite heavy enough, and not easily moved, so it was necessary to lighten it as much as possible. When the schooner was again in its element, the loading could be effected in a few days.

On the afternoon of the 28th, the finishing touches were given. It was necessary to put supports for the sides of the slide in some places where the ice had melted quickly. Then everyone was allowed to rest from 4 o'clock p.m. The captain had double rations served out to all hands, and well they merited this extra supply of spirits; they had indeed worked hard during the week. I repeat that every sign of mutiny had disappeared. The crew thought of nothing except this great operation of the launching. The *Halbrane* in the sea would mean departure, it would also mean return! For Dirk Peters and me it would be the definite abandonment of Arthur Pym.

That night the temperature was the highest we had so far experienced. The thermometer registered 53° (11° 67′ C. below zero). So, although the sun was nearing the horizon, the ice was melting, and thousands of small streams flowed in every direction. The early birds awoke at four o'clock, and I was one of their number. I had scarcely slept, and I fancy that Dirk Peters did not sleep much, haunted as he was by the sad thought of having to turn back!

The launch was to take place at ten o'clock. Taking every possible difficulty into account, and allowing for the minutest precautions, the captain hoped that it would be completed before the close of the day. Everyone believed that by evening the schooner would be at the foot of the berg.

Of course we had all to lend a hand to this difficult task. To each man a special duty was assigned; some were employed to facilitate the sliding with wooden rollers, if necessary; others to moderate the speed of the hull, in case it became too great, by means of hawsers and cables.

We breakfasted at nine o'clock in the tents. Our sailors were perfectly confident, and could not refrain from drinking "success to the event"; and although this was a little premature, we added our hurrahs to theirs. Success seemed very nearly assured, as the captain and the mate had worked out the matter so carefully and skilfully. At last we were about to leave our encampment and take up our stations (some of the sailors were there already), when cries of amazement and fear were raised. What a frightful scene, and, short as it may have been, what an impression of terror it left on our minds!

One of the enormous blocks which formed the bank of the mud-bed where the *Halbrane* lay, having become loose owing to the melting of its base, had slipped and was bounding over the others down the incline.

In another moment, the schooner, being no longer retained in position, was swinging on this declivity.

On board, on deck, in front, there were two sailors, Rogers and Gratian. In vain did the unfortunate men try to jump over the bulwarks, they had not time, and they were dragged away in this dreadful fall.

Yes! I saw it! I saw the schooner topple over, slide down first on its left side, crush one of the men who delayed too long about jumping to one side, then bound from block to block, and finally fling itself into space.

In another moment the *Halbrane*, staved in, broken up, with gaping planks and shattered ribs, had sunk, causing a tremendous jet of water to spout up at the foot of the iceberg.

Horrified! yes, indeed, we were horrified when the schooner, carried off as though by an avalanche, had disappeared in the abyss! Not a particle of our *Halbrane* remained, not even a wreck!

A minute ago she was one hundred feet in the air, now she was five hundred in the depths of the sea! Yes, we were so stupefied that we were unable to think of the dangers to come—our amazement was that of people who "cannot believe their eyes."

Prostration succeeded as a natural consequence. There was not a word spoken. We stood motionless, with our feet rooted to the icy soil. No words could express the horror of our situation!

As for West, when the schooner had disappeared in the abyss, I saw big tears fall from his eyes. The *Halbrane* that he loved so much was now an unknown quantity! Yes, our stout-hearted mate wept.

Three of our men had perished, and in what frightful fashion! I had seen Rogers and Gratian, two of our most faithful sailors, stretch out their hands in despair as they were knocked about by the rebounding of the schooner, and finally sink with her! The other man from the

The *Halbrane*, staved in, broken up.

Falklands, an American, was crushed in its rush; his shapeless form lay in a pool of blood. Three new victims within the last ten days had to be inscribed on the register of those who died during this fatal voyage! Ah! fortune had favoured us up to the hour when the *Halbrane* was snatched from her own element, but her hand was now against us. And was not this last the worst blow—must it not prove the stroke of death?

The silence was broken by a tumult of despairing voices, whose despair was justified indeed by this irreparable misfortune!

And I am sure that more than one thought it would have been better to have been on the *Halbrane* as she rebounded off the side of the iceberg!

Everything would have been over then, as all was over with Rogers and Gratian! This foolish expedition would thus have come to a conclusion worthy of such rashness and imprudence!

At last, the instinct of self-preservation triumphed, and except Hearne, who stood some distance off and affected silence, all the men shouted: "To the boat! to the boat!"

These unfortunate fellows were out of their mind. Terror led them astray. They rushed towards the crag where our one boat (which could not hold them all) had been sheltered during the unloading of the schooner.

Captain Len Guy and Jem West rushed after them. I joined them immediately, followed by the boatswain. We were armed, and resolved to make use of our arms. We had to prevent these furious men from seizing the boat, which did not belong to a few, but to all!

"Hallo, sailors!" cried the captain.

"Hallo!" repeated West, "stop there, or we fire on the first who goes a step farther!"

Both threatened the men with their pistols. The boatswain pointed his gun at them. I held my rifle, ready to fire.

It was in vain! The frenzied men heard nothing, would not hear anything, and one of them fell, struck by the mate's bullet, just as he was crossing the last block. He was unable to catch on to the bank with his hands, and slipping on the frozen slope, he disappeared in the abyss.

Was this the beginning of a massacre? Would others let themselves be killed at this place? Would the old hands side with the new-comers?

At that moment I remarked that Hardy, Martin Holt, Francis Bury, and Stern hesitated about coming over to our side, while Hearne, still standing motionless at some distance, gave no encouragement to the rebels.

However, we could not allow them to become masters of the boat, to bring it down, to embark ten or twelve men, and to abandon us to our certain fate on this iceberg. They had almost reached the boat, heedless of danger and deaf to threats, when a second report was heard, and one of the sailors fell, by a bullet from the boatswain's gun.

One American and one Fuegian less to be numbered amongst the sealing-master's partisans!

Then, in front of the boat, a man appeared. It was Dirk Peters, who had climbed the opposite slope.

The half-breed put one of his enormous hands on the stern and with the other made a sign to the furious men to clear off. Dirk Peters being there, we no longer needed our arms, as he alone would suffice to protect the boat.

And indeed, as five or six of the sailors were advancing,

he went up to them, caught hold of the nearest by the belt, lifted him up, and sent him flying ten paces off. The wretched man not being able to catch hold of anything, would have rebounded into the sea had not Hearne seized him.

Owing to the half-breed's intervention the revolt was instantly quelled. Besides, we were coming up to the boat, and with us those of our men whose hesitation had not lasted long.

No matter. The others were still thirteen to our ten.

Captain Len Guy made his appearance; anger shone in his eyes, and with him was West, quite unmoved. Words failed the captain for some moments, but his looks said what his tongue could not utter. At length, in a terrible voice, he said,—

"I ought to treat you as evil-doers; however, I will only consider you as madmen! The boat belongs to everybody. It is now our only means of salvation, and you wanted to steal it—to steal it like cowards! Listen attentively to what I say for the last time! This boat, belonging to the *Halbrane*, is now the *Halbrane* herself! I am the captain of it, and let him who disobeys me, beware!"

With these last words Captain Len Guy looked at Hearne, for whom this warning was expressly meant. The sealing-master had not appeared in the last scene, not openly at least, but nobody doubted that he had urged his comrades to make off with the boat, and that he had every intention of doing the same again.

"Now to the camp," said the captain, "and you, Dirk Peters, remain here!"

The half-breed's only reply was to nod his big head and betake himself to his post.

The crew returned to the camp without the least hesitation. Some lay down in their sleeping-places, others wandered about. Hearne neither tried to join them nor to go near Martin Holt.

Now that the sailors were reduced to idleness, there was nothing to do except to ponder on our critical situation, and invent some means of getting out of it.

The captain, the mate, and the boatswain formed a council, and I took part in their deliberations.

Captain Len Guy began by saying,—

"We have protected our boat, and we shall continue to protect it."

"Until death," declared West.

"Who knows," said I, "whether we shall not soon be forced to embark?"

"In that case," replied the captain, "as all cannot fit into it, it will be necessary to make a selection. Lots shall determine which of us are to go, and I shall not ask to be treated differently from the others."

"We have not come to that, luckily," replied the boatswain. "The iceberg is solid, and there is no fear of its melting before winter."

"No," assented West, "that is not to be feared. What it behoves us to do is, while watching the boat, to keep an eye on the provisions."

"We are lucky," added Hurliguerly, "to have put our cargo in safety. Poor, dear *Halbrane*. She will remain in these seas, like the *Jane*, her elder sister!"

Yes, without doubt, and I thought so for many reasons, the one destroyed by the savages of Tsalal, the other by one of these catastrophes that no human power can prevent.

"You are right," replied the captain, "and we must prevent our men from plundering. We are sure of enough provisions for one year, without counting what we may get by fishing."

"And it is so much the more necessary, captain, to keep a close watch, because I have seen some hovering about the spirit casks."

"I will see to that," replied West.

"But," I then asked, "had we not better prepare ourselves for the fact that we may be compelled to winter on this iceberg."

"May Heaven avert such a terrible probability," replied the captain.

"After all, if it were necessary, we could get through it, Mr. Jeorling," said the boatswain. "We could hollow out sheltering-places in the ice, so as to be able to bear the extreme cold of the pole, and so long as we had sufficient to appease our hunger—"

At this moment the horrid recollection of the *Grampus* came to my mind—the scenes in which Dirk Peters killed Ned Holt, the brother of our sailing-master. Should we ever be in such extremity?

Would it not, before we proceed to set up winter quarters for seven or eight months, be better to leave the iceberg altogether, if such a thing were possible?

I called the attention of Captain Len Guy and West to this point.

This was a difficult question to answer, and a long silence preceded the reply.

At last the captain said,—

"Yes, that would be the best resolution to come to; and if our boat could hold us all, with the provisions necessary for a voyage that might last three or four weeks, I would not hesitate to put to sea now and return towards the north."

But I made them observe that we should be obliged to direct our course contrary to wind and current; our schooner herself could hardly have succeeded in doing this. Whilst to continue towards the south—

"Towards the south?" repeated the captain, who looked at me as though he sought to read my thoughts.

"Why not?" I answered. "If the iceberg had not been stopped in its passage, perhaps it would have drifted to some land in that direction, and might not our boat accomplish what it would have done?"

The captain, shaking his head, answered nothing. West also was silent.

"Eh! our iceberg will end by raising its anchor," replied Hurliguerly. "It does not hold to the bottom, like the Falklands or the Kerguelens! So the safest course is to wait, as the boat cannot carry twenty-three, the number of our party."

I dwelt upon the fact that it was not necessary for all twenty-three to embark. It would be sufficient, I said, for five or six of us to reconnoitre further south for twelve or fifteen miles.

"South?" repeated Captain Len Guy.

"Undoubtedly, captain," I added. "You probably know what the geographers frankly admit, that the antarctic regions are formed by a capped continent."

"Geographers know nothing, and can know nothing about it," replied West, coldly.

"It is a pity," said I, "that as we are so near, we should not attempt to solve this question of a polar continent."

I thought it better not to insist just at present.

Moreover there would be danger in sending out our only boat on a voyage of discovery, as the current might carry it too far, or it might not find us again in the same place. And, indeed, if the iceberg happened to get loose at the bottom, and to resume its interrupted drift, what would become of the men in the boat?

The drawback was that the boat was too small to carry us all, with the necessary provisions. Now, of the seniors, there remained ten men, counting Dirk Peters; of the new men there were thirteen; twenty-three in all. The largest number our boat could hold was from eleven to twelve persons. Then eleven of us, indicated by lot, would have to remain on this island of ice. And what would become of them?

With regard to this Hurliguerly made a sound observation.

"After all," he said, "I don't know that those who would embark would be better off than those who remained! I am so doubtful of the result, that I would willingly give up my place to anyone who wanted it."

Perhaps the boatswain was right. But in my own mind, when I asked that the boat might be utilized, it was only for the purpose of reconnoitring the iceberg.

We finally decided to arrange everything with a view to wintering out, even were our ice-mountain again to drift.

"We may be sure that will be agreed to by our men," declared Hurliguerly.

"What is necessary must be done," replied the mate, "and to-day we must set to work."

That was a sad day on which we began our preparations.

Endicott, the cook, was the only man who submitted without murmuring. As a negro, who cares little about the future, shallow and frivolous like all his race, he resigned himself easily to his fate ; and this is, perhaps, true philosophy. Besides, when it came to the question of cooking, it mattered very little to him whether it was here or there, so long as his stoves were set up somewhere.

So he said to his friend the mate, with his broad negro smile,—

"Luckily my kitchen did not go off with the schooner, and you shall see, Hurliguerly, if I do not make up dishes just as good as on board the *Halbrane,* so long as provisions don't grow scarce, of course—"

"Well! they will not be wanting for some time to come," replied the boatswain. "We need not fear hunger, but cold, such cold as would reduce you to an icicle the minute you cease to warm your feet—cold that makes your skin crack and your skull split! Even if we had some hundreds of tons of coal—But, all things being well calculated, there is only just what will do to boil this large kettle."

"And that is sacred," cried Endicott; "touching is forbidden! The kitchen before all."

"And that is the reason why it never strikes you to pity yourself, you old nigger! You can always make sure of keeping your feet warm at your oven!"

"What would you have, boatswain? You are a first-rate cook, or you are not. When you are, you take advantage of it; but I will remember to keep you a little place before my stove."

"That's good! that's good, Endicott! Each one shall have his turn! There is no privilege, even for a boatswain! On the whole, it is better not to have to fear famine! One can fight against the cold. We shall dig holes in the iceberg, and cuddle ourselves up there. And why should we not have a general dwelling-room? We could make a cave for ourselves with pickaxes! I have heard tell that ice preserves heat. Well, let it preserve ours, and that is all I ask of it!"

The hour had come for us to return to the camp and to seek our sleeping-places.

Dirk Peters alone refused to be relieved of his duty as watchman of the boat, and nobody thought of disputing the post with him.

Captain Len Guy and West did not enter the tents until they had made certain that Hearne and his companions had gone to their usual place of rest.

I came back likewise and went to bed.

I could not tell how long I had been sleeping, nor what time it was, when I found myself rolling on the ground after a violent shock.

What could be happening? Was it another capsize of the iceberg?

We were all up in a second, then outside the tents in the full light of a night in the polar regions.

A second floating mass of enormous size had just struck our iceberg, which had "hoisted the anchor" (as the sailors say) and was drifting towards the south.

An unhoped-for change in the situation had taken place. What were to be the consequences of our being no longer cast away at that place? The current was now carrying us in the direction of the pole! The first feeling of joy inspired by this conviction was, however, succeeded by all the terrors of the unknown! and what an unknown!

Dirk Peters only was entirely rejoiced that we had resumed the route which, he believed, would lead us to the discovery of traces of his "poor Pym"—far other ideas occupied the minds of his companions.

Captain Len Guy no longer entertained any hope of rescuing his countrymen, and having reached the condition of despair, he was bound by his duty to take his crew back to the north, so as to clear the antarctic circle while the season rendered it possible to do so. And we were being carried away towards the south!

Naturally enough, we were all deeply impressed by the fearfulness of our position, which may be summed up in a few words. We were no longer cast away, with a possible ship, but the tenants of a floating iceberg, with no hope but that our monster tenement might encounter one of the whaling ships whose business in the deep waters lies between the Orkneys, New Georgia, and the Sandwich Islands. A quantity of things had been thrown into the ice by the collision which had set our iceberg afloat, but these were chiefly articles belonging to the *Halbrane*. Owing to the precaution that had been taken on the previous day, when the cargo was stowed away in the clefts, it had been only slightly damaged. What would have become of us, had all our reserves been swallowed up in that grim encounter?

Now, the two icebergs formed but one, which was travelling south at the rate of two miles an hour. At this rate, thirty hours would suffice to bring us to the point of the axis at which the terrestrial meridians unite. Did the current which was carrying us along pass on to the pole itself, or was there any land which might arrest our progress? This was another question, and I discussed it with the boatswain.

"Nobody knows, Mr. Jeorling," was Hurliguerly's reply. "If the current goes to the pole, we shall go there; and if it doesn't, we shan't. An iceberg isn't a ship, and as it has neither sails nor helm, it goes as the drift takes it."

"That's true, boatswain. And therefore I had the idea that if two or three of us were to embark in the boat—"

"Ah! you still hold to your notion of the boat—"

"Certainly, for, if there is land somewhere, is it not possible that the people of the *Jane*—"

"Have come upon it, Mr. Jeorling—at four thousand miles from Tsalal Island."

"Who knows, boatswain?"

"That may be, but allow me to say that your argument will be reasonable when the land comes in sight, if it ever does so. Our captain will see what ought to be done, and he will remember that time presses. We cannot delay in these waters, and, after all, the one thing of real importance to us is to get out of the polar circle before the winter makes it impassable."

There was good sense in Hurliguerly's words; I could not deny the fact.

During that day the greater part of the cargo was placed in the interior of a vast cave-like fissure in the side of the iceberg, where, even in case of a second collision, casks and barrels would be in safety. Our men then assisted Endicott to set up his cooking-stove between two blocks, so that it was firmly fixed, and they heaped up a great mass of coals close to it.

No murmurs, no recrimination disturbed these labours. It was evident that silence was deliberately maintained. The crew obeyed the captain and West because they gave no orders but such as were of urgent necessity. But, afterwards, would these men allow the authority of their leaders to be uncontested? How long would the recruits from the Falklands, who were already exasperated by the disasters of our enterprise, resist their desire to seize upon the boat and escape?

I did not think they would make the attempt, however, so long as our iceberg should continue to drift, for the boat could not outstrip its progress; but, if it were to run aground once more, to strike upon the coast of an island or a continent, what would not these unfortunate creatures do to escape the horrors of wintering under such conditions?

In the afternoon, during the hour of rest allowed to the crew, I had a second conversation with Dirk Peters. I had taken my customary seat at the top of the iceberg, and had occupied it for half an hour, being, as may be supposed, deep in thought, when I saw the half-breed coming quickly up the slope. We had exchanged hardly a dozen words since the iceberg had begun to move again. When Dirk Peters came up to me, he did not address me at first, and was so intent on his thoughts that I was not quite sure he saw me. At length, he leaned back against an ice-block, and spoke:

"Mr. Jeorling," he said, "you remember, in your cabin in the *Halbrane*, I told you the—the affair of the *Grampus?*"

I remembered well.

"I told you that Parker's name was not Parker, that it was Holt, and that he was Ned Holt's brother?"

"I was afraid; I got away from him."

"I know, Dirk Peters," I replied, "but why do you refer to that sad story again?"

"Why, Mr. Jeorling? Have not—have you never said anything about it to anybody?"

"Not to anybody," I protested. "How could you suppose I should be so ill-advised, so imprudent, as to divulge your secret, a secret which ought never to pass our lips—a dead secret?"

"Dead, yes, dead! And yet, understand me, it seems to me that, among the crew, something is known."

I instantly recalled to mind what the boatswain had told me concerning a certain conversation in which he had overheard Hearne prompting Martin Holt to ask the half-breed what were the circumstances of his brother's death on board the *Grampus*. Had a portion of the secret got out, or was this apprehension on the part of Dirk Peters purely imaginary?

"Explain yourself," I said.

"Understand me, Mr. Jeorling, I am a bad hand at explaining. Yes, yesterday—I have thought of nothing else since—Martin Holt took me aside, far from the others, and told me that he wished to speak to me—"

"Of the *Grampus*?"

"Of the *Grampus*—yes, and of his brother, Ned Holt. For the first time he uttered that name before me—and yet we have sailed together for nearly three months."

The half-breed's voice was so changed that I could hardly hear him.

"It seemed to me," he resumed, "that in Martin Holt's mind—no, I was not mistaken—there was something like a suspicion."

"But tell me what he said! Tell me exactly what he asked you. What is it?"

I felt sure that the question put by Martin Holt, whatsoever its bearing, had been inspired by Hearne. Nevertheless, as I considered it well that the half-breed should know nothing of the sealing-master's disquieting and inexplicable intervention in this tragic affair, I decided upon concealing it from him.

"He asked me," replied Dirk Peters, "did I not remember Ned Holt of the *Grampus*, and whether he had perished in the fight with the mutineers or in the shipwreck; whether he was one of the men who had been abandoned with Captain Barnard; in short, he asked me if I could tell him how his brother died. Ah! how!"

No idea could be conveyed of the horror with which the half-breed uttered words which revealed a profound loathing of himself.

"And what answer did you make to Martin Holt?"

"None, none!"

"You should have said that Ned Holt perished in the wreck of the brig."

"I could not—understand me—I could not. The two brothers are so like each other. In Martin Holt I seemed to see Ned Holt. I was afraid, I got away from him."

The half-breed drew himself up with a sudden movement, and I sat thinking, leaning my head on my hands. These tardy questions of Holt's respecting his brother were put, I had no doubt whatsoever, at the instigation of Hearne, but what was his motive, and was it at the Falklands that he had discovered the secret of Dirk Peters? I had not breathed a word on the subject to anyone. To the second question no answer suggested itself; the first involved a serious issue. Did the sealing-master merely desire to gratify his enmity against Dirk Peters, the only one of the Falkland sailors who had always taken the side of Captain Len Guy, and who had prevented the seizure of the boat by Hearne and his companions? Did he hope, by arousing the wrath and vengeance of Martin Holt, to detach the sailing-master from his allegiance and induce him to become an accomplice in Hearne's own designs? And, in fact, when it was a question of sailing the boat in these seas, had he not imperative need of Martin Holt, one of the best seamen of the *Halbrane?* A man who would succeed where Hearne and his companions would fail, if they had only themselves to depend on?

I became lost in this labyrinth of hypotheses, and it must be admitted that its complications added largely to the troubles of an already complicated position.

When I raised my eyes, Dirk Peters had disappeared; he had said what he came to say, and he now knew that I had not betrayed his confidence.

The customary precautions were taken for the night, no individual being allowed to remain outside the camp, with the exception of the half-breed, who was in charge of the boat.

The following day was the 31st of January. I pushed back the canvas of the tent, which I shared with Captain Len Guy and West respectively, as each succeeded the other on release from the alternate "watch," very early, and experienced a severe disappointment.

Mist, everywhere! Nay, more than mist, a thick yellow, mouldy-smelling fog. And more than this again; the temperature had fallen sensibly: this was probably a forewarning of the austral winter. The summit of our ice-mountain was lost in vapour, in a fog which would not resolve itself into rain, but would continue to muffle up the horizon.

"Bad luck!" said the boatswain, "for now if we were to pass by land we should not perceive it."

"And our drift?"

"More considerable than yesterday, Mr. Jeorling. The captain has sounded, and he makes the speed no less than between three and four miles."

"And what do you conclude from this?"

"I conclude that we must be within a narrower sea, since the current is so strong. I should not be surprised if we had land on both sides of us within ten or fifteen miles."

"This, then, would be a wide strait that cuts the antarctic continent?"

"Yes. Our captain is of that opinion."

"And, holding that opinion, is he not going to make an attempt to reach one or other of the coasts of this strait?"

"And how?"

"With the boat."

"Risk the boat in the midst of this fog!" exclaimed the boatswain, as he crossed his arms. "What are you thinking of, Mr. Jeorling? Can we cast anchor to wait for it? And all the chances would be that we should never see it again. Ah! if we only had the *Halbrane!*"

But there was no longer a *Halbrane!*

In spite of the difficulty of the ascent through the half-condensed vapour, I climbed up to the top of the iceberg, but when I had gained that eminence I strove in vain to pierce the impenetrable grey mantle in which the waters were wrapped.

I remained there, hustled by the north-east wind, which was beginning to blow freshly and might perhaps rend the fog asunder. But no, fresh vapours accumulated around our floating refuge, driven up by the immense ventilation of the open sea. Under the double action of the atmospheric and antarctic currents, we drifted more and more rapidly, and I perceived a sort of shudder pass throughout the vast bulk of the iceberg.

Then it was that I felt myself under the dominion of a sort of hallucination, one of those hallucinations which must have troubled the mind of Arthur Pym. It seemed to me that I was losing myself in his extraordinary personality; at last I was beholding all that he had seen! Was not that impenetrable mist the curtain of vapours which he had seen in his delirium? I peered into it, seeking for those luminous rays which had streaked the sky from east to west! I sought in its depths for that limitless cataract, rolling in silence from the height of some immense rampart lost in the vastness of the zenith! I sought for the awful white giant of the South Pole!

At length reason resumed her sway. This visionary madness, intoxicating while it lasted, passed off by degrees, and I descended the slope to our camp.

The whole day passed without a change. The fog never once lifted to give us a glimpse outside of its muffling folds, and if the iceberg, which had travelled forty miles since the previous day, had passed by the extremity of the axis of the earth, we should never know it.

CHAPTER XXI.

AMID THE MISTS.

So this was the sum of all our efforts, trials and disappointments! Not to speak of the destruction of the *Halbrane*, the expedition had already cost nine lives. From thirty-two men who had embarked on the schooner, our number was reduced to twenty-three: how low was that figure yet to fall?

Between the south pole and antarctic circle lay twenty degrees, and those would have to be cleared in a month or six weeks at the most; if not, the iceberg barrier would be re-formed and closed-up. As for wintering in that part of the antarctic circle, not a man of us could have survived it.

Besides, we had lost all hope of rescuing the survivors of the *Jane*, and the sole desire of the crew was to escape as quickly as possible from the awful solitudes of the south. Our drift, which had been south, down to the pole, was now north, and, if that direction should continue, perhaps we might be favoured with such good fortune as would make up for all the evil that had befallen us! In any case there was nothing for it but, in familiar phrase, "to let ourselves go."

The mist did not lift during the 2nd, 3rd, and 4th of February, and it would have been difficult to make out the rate of progress of our iceberg since it had passed the pole. Captain Len Guy, however, and West, considered themselves safe in reckoning it at two hundred and fifty miles.

The current did not seem to have diminished in speed or changed its course. It was now beyond a doubt that we were moving between the two halves of a continent, one on the east, the other on the west, which formed the vast antarctic region. And I thought it was matter of great regret that we could not get aground on one or the other side of this vast strait, whose surface would presently be solidified by the coming of winter.

When I expressed this sentiment to Captain Len Guy, he made me the only logical answer :

" What would you have, Mr. Jeorling ? We are powerless. There is nothing to be done, and the persistent fog is the worst part of our ill luck. I no longer know where we are. It is impossible to take an observation, and this befalls us just as the sun is about to disappear for long months."

"Let me come back to the question of the boat," said I, " for the last time. Could we not, with the boat—"

" Go on a discovery cruise? Can you think of such a thing? That would be an imprudence I would not commit, even though the crew would allow me."

I was on the point of exclaiming : " And what if your brother and your countrymen have found refuge on some spot of the land that undoubtedly lies about us ? "

But I restrained myself. Of what avail was it to reawaken our captain's grief? He, too, must have contemplated this eventuality, and he had not renounced his purpose of further search without being fully convinced of the folly of a last attempt.

During those three days of fog I had not caught sight of Dirk Peters, or rather he had made no attempt to approach, but had remained inflexibly at his post by the boat. Martin Holt's questions respecting his brother Ned seemed to indicate that his secret was known—at least in part, and the half-breed held himself more than ever aloof, sleeping while the others watched, and watching in their time of sleep. I even wondered whether he regretted having confided in me, and fancied that he had aroused my repugnance by his sad story. If so, he was mistaken; I deeply pitied the poor half-breed.

Nothing could exceed the melancholy monotony of the hours which we passed in the midst of a fog so thick that the wind could not lift its curtain. The position of the iceberg could not be ascertained. It went with the current at a like speed, and had it been motionless there would have been no appreciable difference for us, for the wind had fallen—at least, so we supposed—and not a breath was stirring. The flame of a torch held up in the air did not flicker. The silence of space was broken only by the clangour of the sea-birds, which came in muffled croaking tones through the stifling atmosphere of vapour. Petrels and albatross swept the top of the iceberg, where they kept a useless watch in their flight. In what direction were those swift-winged creatures—perhaps already driven towards the confines of the arctic region by the approach of winter—bound? We could not tell. One day, the boatswain, who was determined to solve this question if possible, having mounted to the extreme top, not without risk of breaking his neck, came into such violent contact with a *quebranta huesos*—a sort of gigantic petrel measuring twelve feet with spread wings—that he was flung on his back.

"Curse the bird!" he said on his return to the camp, addressing the observation to me. "I have had a narrow escape! A thump, and down I went, sprawling. I saved myself I don't know how, for I was all but over the side. Those ice ledges, you know, slip through one's fingers like water. I called out to the bird, 'Can't you even look before you, you fool?' But what was the good of that? The big blunderer did not even beg my pardon!"

In the afternoon of the same day our ears were assailed by a hideous braying from below. Hurliguerly remarked that as there were no asses to treat us to the concert, it must be given by penguins. Hitherto these countless dwellers in the polar regions had not thought proper to accompany us on our moving island; we had not seen even one, either at the foot of the iceberg or on the drifting packs. There could be no doubt that they were there in thousands, for the music was unmistakably that of a multitude of performers. Now those birds frequent by choice the edges of the coasts of islands and continents in high latitudes, or the ice-fields in their neighbourhood. Was not their presence an indication that land was near?

I asked Captain Len Guy what he thought of the presence of these birds.

"I think what you think, Mr. Jeorling," he replied. "Since we have been drifting, none of them have taken refuge on the iceberg, and here they are now in crowds, if we may judge by their deafening cries. From whence do they come? No doubt from land, which is probably near."

"Is this West's opinion?"

"Yes, Mr. Jeorling, and you know he is not given to vain imaginations."

"Certainly not."

"And then another thing has struck both him and me, which has apparently escaped your attention. It is that the braying of the penguins is mingled with a sound like the lowing of cattle. Listen and you will readily distinguish it."

I listened, and, sure enough, the orchestra was more full than I had supposed.

"I hear the lowing plainly," I said; "there are, then, seals and walrus also in the sea at the base."

"That is certain, Mr. Jeorling, and I conclude from the fact that those animals—both birds and mammals—very rare since we left Tsalal Island, frequent the waters into which the currents have carried us."

"Of course, captain, of course. Oh! what a misfortune it is that we should be surrounded by this impenetrable fog!"

"Which prevents us from even getting down to the base of the iceberg! There, no doubt, we should discover whether there are seaweed drifts around us; if that be so, it would be another sign."

"Why not try, captain?"

"No, no, Mr. Jeorling, that might lead to falls, and I will not permit anybody to leave the camp. If land be there, I imagine our iceberg will strike it before long."

"And if it does not?"

"If it does not, how are we to make it?"

I thought to myself that the boat might very well be used in the latter case. But Captain Len Guy preferred to wait, and perhaps this was the wiser course under our circumstances.

At eight o'clock that evening the half-condensed mist was so compact that it was difficult to walk through it. The composition of the air seemed to be changed, as though it were passing into a solid state. It was not possible to discern whether the fog had any effect upon the compass. I knew the matter had been studied by meteorologists, and that they believe they may safely affirm that the needle is not affected by this condition of the atmosphere. I will add here that since we had left the South Pole behind no confidence could be placed in the indications of the compass; it had gone wild at the approach to the magnetic pole, to which we were no doubt on the way. Nothing could be known, therefore, concerning the course of the iceberg.

The sun did not set quite below the horizon at this period, yet the waters were wrapped in tolerably deep darkness at nine o'clock in the evening, when the muster of the crew took place.

On this occasion each man as usual answered to his name except Dirk Peters.

The call was repeated in the loudest of Hurliguerly's stentorian tones. No reply.

"Has nobody seen Dirk Peters during the day?" inquired the captain.

"Nobody," answered the boatswain.

"Can anything have happened to him?"

"Don't be afraid," cried the boatswain. "Dirk Peters is in his element, and as much at his ease in the fog as a polar bear. He has got out of one bad scrape; he will get out of a second!"

I let Hurliguerly have his say, knowing well why the half-breed kept out of the way.

That night none of us, I am sure, could sleep. We were smothered in the tents, for lack of oxygen. And we were all more or less under the influence of a strange sort of presentiment, as though our fate were about to change, for better or worse, if indeed it could be worse.

The night wore on without any alarm, and at six o'clock in the morning each of us came out to breathe a more wholesome air.

The state of things was unchanged, the density of the fog was extraordinary. It was, however, found that the barometer had risen, too quickly, it is true, for the rise to be serious. Presently other signs of change became evident. The wind, which was growing colder—a south wind since we had passed beyond the south pole—began to blow a full gale, and the noises from below were heard more distinctly through the space swept by the atmospheric currents.

At nine o'clock the iceberg doffed its cap of vapour quite suddenly, producing an indescribable transformation scene which no fairy's wand could have accomplished in less time or with greater success.

In a few moments, the sky was clear to the extreme verge of the horizon, and the sea reappeared, illumined by the oblique rays of the sun, which now rose only a few degrees above it. A rolling swell of the waves bathed the base of our iceberg in white foam, as it drifted, together with a great multitude of floating mountains under the double action of wind and current, on a course inclining to the nor-'nor'-east.

"Land!"

This cry came from the summit of the moving mountain, and Dirk Peters was revealed to our sight, standing on the outermost block, his hand stretched towards the north.

The half-breed was not mistaken. The land this time—yes!—it was land! Its distant heights, of a blackish hue, rose within three or four miles of us.

86° 12′ south latitude.
114° 17′ east longitude.

The iceberg was nearly four degrees beyond the antarctic pole, and from the western longitudes that our schooner had followed tracing the course of the *Jane*, we had passed into the eastern longitudes.

CHAPTER XXII.

IN CAMP.

A LITTLE after noon, the iceberg was within a mile of the land.

After their dinner, the crew climbed up to the topmost block, on which Dirk Peters was stationed. On our approach the half-breed descended the opposite slope, and when I reached the top he was no longer to be seen.

The land on the north evidently formed a continent or island of considerable extent. On the west there was a sharply projecting cape, surmounted by a sloping height which resembled an enormous seal's head on the side view; then beyond that was a wide stretch of sea. On the east the land was prolonged out of sight.

Each one of us took in the position. It depended on the current whether it would carry the iceberg into an eddy which might drive it on the coast, or continue to drift it towards the north.

Which was the more admissible hypothesis?

Captain Len Guy, West, Hurliguerly, and I talked over the matter, while the crew discussed it among themselves. Finally, it was agreed that the current tended rather to carry the iceberg towards the northern point of land.

"After all," said Captain Len Guy, "if it is habitable

during the months of the summer season, it does not look like being inhabited, since we cannot descry a human being on the shore."

"Let us bear in mind, captain," said I, "that the iceberg is not calculated to attract attention as the *Halbrane* would have done."

"Evidently, Mr. Jeorling; and the natives, if there were any, would have been collected on the beach to see the *Halbrane* already."

"We must not conclude, captain, because we do not see any natives—"

"Certainly not, Mr. Jeorling; but you will agree with me that the aspect of this land is very unlike that of Tsalal Island when the *Jane* reached it; there is nothing here but desolation and barrenness."

"I acknowledge that—barrenness and desolation, that is all. Nevertheless, I want to ask you whether it is your intention to go ashore, captain?"

"With the boat?"

"With the boat, should the current carry our iceberg away from the land."

"We have not an hour to lose, Mr. Jeorling, and the delay of a few hours might condemn us to a cruel winter stay, if we arrived too late at the iceberg barrier."

"And, considering the distance, we are not too soon," observed West.

"I grant it," I replied, still persisting. "But, to leave this land behind us without ever having set foot on it, without having made sure that it does not preserve the traces of an encampment, if your brother, captain—his companions—"

Captain Len Guy shook his head. How could the

castaways have supported life in this desolate region for several months?

Besides, the British flag was hoisted on the summit of the iceberg, and William Guy would have recognized it and come down to the shore had he been living.

No one. No one.

At this moment, West, who had been observing certain points of approach, said,—

"Let us wait a little before we come to a decision. In less than an hour we shall be able to decide. Our speed is slackening, it seems to me, and it is possible that an eddy may bring us back obliquely to the coast."

"That is my opinion too," said the boatswain, "and if our floating machine is not stationary, it is nearly so. It seems to be turning round."

West and Hurliguerly were not mistaken. For some reason or other the iceberg was getting out of the course which it had followed continuously. A giratory movement had succeeded to that of drifting, owing to the action of an eddy which set towards the coast.

Besides, several ice-mountains, in front of us, had just run aground on the edge of the shore. It was, then, useless to discuss whether we should take to the boat or not. According as we approached, the desolation of the land became more and more apparent, and the prospect of enduring six months' wintering there would have appalled the stoutest hearts.

At five in the afternoon, the iceberg plunged into a deep rift in the coast ending in a long point on the right, and there stuck fast.

"On shore! On shore!" burst from every man, like a single exclamation, and the men were already hurrying down the slope of the iceberg, when West commanded:

"Wait for orders!"

Some hesitation was shown—especially on the part of Hearne and several of his comrades. Then the instinct of discipline prevailed, and finally the whole crew ranged themselves around Captain Len Guy. It was not necessary to lower the boat, the iceberg being in contact with the point.

The captain, the boatswain, and myself, preceding the others, were the first to quit the camp; ours were the first human feet to tread this virgin and volcanic soil.

We walked for twenty minutes on rough land, strewn with rocks of igneous origin, solidified lava, dusty slag, and grey ashes, but without enough clay to grow even the hardiest plants.

With some risk and difficulty, Captain Len Guy, the boatswain, and I succeeded in climbing the hill; this exploit occupied a whole hour. Although evening had now come, it brought no darkness in its train. From the top of the hill we could see over an extent of from thirty to forty miles, and this was what we saw.

Behind us lay the open sea, laden with floating masses; a great number of these had recently heaped themselves up against the beach and rendered it almost inaccessible.

On the west was a strip of hilly land, which extended beyond our sight, and was washed on its east side by a boundless sea. It was evident that we had been carried by the drift through a strait.

Ah! if we had only had our *Halbrane!* But our sole possession was a frail craft barely capable of containing a dozen men, and we were twenty-three!

There was nothing for it but to go down to the shore again, to carry the tents to the beach, and take measures in view of a winter sojourn under the terrible conditions imposed upon us by circumstances.

On our return to the coast the boatswain discovered several caverns in the granitic cliffs, sufficiently spacious to house us all and afford storage for the cargo of the *Halbrane*. Whatever might be our ultimate decision, we could not do better than place our material and instal ourselves in this opportune shelter.

After we had reascended the slopes of the iceberg and reached our camp, Captain Len Guy had the men mustered. The only missing man was Dirk Peters, who had decidedly isolated himself from the crew. There was nothing to fear from him, however ; he would be with the faithful against the mutinous, and under all circumstances we might count upon him. When the circle had been formed, Captain Len Guy spoke, without allowing any sign of discouragement to appear, and explained the position with the utmost frankness and lucidity, stating in the first place that it was absolutely necessary to lower the cargo to the coast and stow it away in one of the caverns. Concerning the vital question of food, he stated that the supply of flour, preserved meat, and dried vegetables would suffice for the winter, however prolonged, and on that of fuel he was satisfied that we should not want for coal, provided it was not wasted ; and it would be possible to economize it, as the hibernating waifs might brave the cold of the polar zone under a covering of snow and a roof of ice.

Was the captain's tone of security feigned? I did not think so, especially as West approved of what he said.

A third question raised by Hearne remained, and was well calculated to arouse jealousy and anger among the crew. It was the question of the use to be made of the only craft remaining to us. Ought the boat to be kept for the needs of our hibernation, or used to enable us to return to the iceberg barrier?

Captain Len Guy would not pronounce upon this; he desired to postpone the decision for twenty-four or forty-eight hours. The boat, carrying the provisions necessary for such a voyage, could not accommodate more than eleven or, at the outside, twelve men. If the departure of the boat were agreed to, then its passengers must be selected by lot. The captain proceeded to state that neither West, the boatswain, I, nor he would claim any privilege, but would submit to the fortune of the lot with all the others. Both Martin Holt and Hardy were perfectly capable of taking the boat to the fishing-grounds, where the whalers would still be found.

Then, those to whom the lot should fall were not to forget their comrades, left to winter on the eighty-sixth parallel, and were to send a ship to take them off at the return of summer.

All this was said in a tone as calm as it was firm. I must do Captain Len Guy the justice to say that he rose to the occasion.

When he had concluded—without any interruption even from Hearne—no one made a remark. There was, indeed, none to be made, since, in the given case, lots were to be drawn under conditions of perfect equality.

The hour of rest having arrived, each man entered the camp, partook of the supper prepared by Endicott, and went to sleep for the last time under the tents.

Dirk Peters had not reappeared, and I sought for him in vain.

On the following day, the 7th of February, everybody set to work early with a will. The boat was let down with all due precaution to the base of the iceberg, and drawn up by the men on a little sandy beach out of reach of the water. It was in perfectly good condition, and thoroughly serviceable.

The boatswain then set to work on the former contents of the *Halbrane*, furniture, bedding, sails, clothing, instruments, and utensils. Stowed away in a cabin, these things would no longer be exposed to the knocking about and damage of the iceberg. The cases containing preserved food and the casks of spirits were rapidly carried ashore.

I worked with the captain and West at this onerous task, and Dirk Peters also turned up and lent the valuable assistance of his great strength, but he did not utter a word to anyone.

Our occupation continued on the 8th, 9th, and 10th February, and our task was finished in the afternoon of the 10th. The cargo was safely stowed in the interior of a large grotto, with access to it by a narrow opening. We were to inhabit the adjoining grotto, and Endicott set up his kitchen in the latter, on the advice of the boatswain. Thus we should profit by the heat of the stove, which was to cook our food and warm the cavern during the long days, or rather the long nights of the austral winter.

During the process of housing and storing, I observed nothing to arouse suspicion in the bearing of Hearne and the Falklands men. Nevertheless, the half-breed was kept on guard at the boat, which might easily have been seized upon the beach.

Hurliguerly, who observed his comrades closely, appeared less anxious.

On that same evening Captain Len Guy, having re-assembled his people, stated that the question should be discussed on the morrow, adding that, if it were decided in the affirmative, lots should be drawn immediately. No reply was made.

It was late, and half dark outside, for at this date the sun was on the edge of the horizon, and would very soon disappear below it.

I had been asleep for some hours when I was awakened by a great shouting at a short distance. I sprang up instantly and darted out of the cavern, simultaneously with the captain and West, who had also been suddenly aroused from sleep.

"The boat! the boat!" cried West.

The boat was no longer in its place—that place so jealously guarded by Dirk Peters.

After they had pushed the boat into the sea, three men had got into it with bales and casks, while ten others strove to control the half-breed.

Hearne was there, and Martin Holt also; the latter, it seemed to me, was not interfering.

These wretches, then, intended to depart before the lots were drawn; they meant to forsake us. They had succeeded in surprising Dirk Peters, and they would have killed him, had he not fought hard for life.

In the face of this mutiny, knowing our inferiority of numbers, and not knowing whether he might count on all the old crew, Captain Len Guy re-entered the cavern with West in order to procure arms. Hearne and his accomplices were armed.

I was about to follow them when the following words arrested my steps.

The half-breed, overpowered by numbers, had been knocked down, and at this moment Martin Holt, in gratitude to the man who saved his life, was rushing to his aid, but Hearne called out to him,—

"Leave the fellow alone, and come with us!"

Martin Holt hesitated.

"Yes, leave him alone, I say; leave Dirk Peters, the assassin of your brother, alone."

"The assassin of my brother!"

"Your brother, killed on board the *Grampus*—"

"Killed! by Dirk Peters?"

"Yes! Killed and eaten—eaten—eaten!" repeated Hearne, who pronounced the hateful words with a kind of howl.

And then, at a sign from Hearne, two of his comrades seized Martin Holt and dragged him into the boat. Hearne was instantly followed by all those whom he had induced to join in this criminal deed.

At that moment Dirk Peters rose from the ground, and sprang upon one of the Falklands men as he was in the act of stepping on the platform of the boat, lifted him up bodily, hurled him round his head and dashed his brains out against a rock.

In an instant the half-breed fell, shot in the shoulder by a bullet from Hearne's pistol, and the boat was pushed off.

Then Captain Len Guy and West came out of the cavern—the whole scene had passed in less than a minute—and ran down to the point, which they reached together with the boatswain, Hardy, Francis, and Stern.

The boat, which was drawn by the current, was already some distance off, and the tide was falling rapidly.

West shouldered his gun and fired; a sailor dropped into the bottom of the boat. A second shot, fired by Captain Len Guy, grazed Hearne's breast, and the ball was lost among the ice-blocks at the moment when the boat disappeared behind the iceberg.

The only thing for us to do was to cross to the other side of the point. The current would carry the wretches thither, no doubt, before it bore them northward. If they passed within range, and if a second shot should hit Hearne, either killing or wounding him, his companions might perhaps decide on coming back to us.

A quarter of an hour elapsed. When the boat appeared at the other side of the point, it was so far off that our bullets could not reach it. Hearne had already had the sail set, and the boat, impelled by wind and current jointly, was soon no more than a white speck on the face of the waters, and speedily disappeared.

CHAPTER XXIII.

FOUND AT LAST.

THE question of our wintering on the land whereon we had been thrown was settled for us. But, after all, the situation was not changed for those among the nine (now only remaining of the twenty-three) who should not have drawn the lot of departure. Who could speculate upon the chances of the whole nine? Might not all of them have drawn the lot of "stay"? And, when every chance was fully weighed, was that of those who had left us the best? To this question there could be no answer.

When the boat had disappeared, Captain Len Guy and his companions retraced their steps towards the cavern in which we must live for all the time during which we could not go out, in the dread darkness of the antarctic winter. My first thought was of Dirk Peters, who, being wounded, could not follow us when we hurried to the other side of the point.

On reaching the cavern I failed to find the half-breed, Was he severely wounded? Should we have to mourn the death of this man who was as faithful to us as to his "poor Pym"?

"Let us search for him, Mr. Jeorling!" cried the boatswain.

"We will go together," said the captain. Dirk Peters would never have forsaken us, and we will not forsake him."

"Would he come back," said I, "now that what he thought was known to him and me only has come out?"

I informed my companions of the reason why the name of Ned Holt had been changed to that of Parker in Arthur Pym's narrative, and of the circumstances under which the half-breed had apprised me of the fact. At the same time I urged every consideration that might exculpate him, dwelling in particular upon the point that if the lot had fallen to Dirk Peters, he would have been the victim of the others' hunger.

"Dirk Peters confided this secret to you only?" inquired Captain Len Guy.

"To me only, captain."

"And you have kept it?"

"Absolutely."

"Then I cannot understand how it came to the knowledge of Hearne."

"At first," I replied, "I thought Hearne might have talked in his sleep, and that it was by chance Martin Holt learned the secret. After reflection, however, I recalled to mind that when the half-breed related the scene on the *Grampus* to me, he was in my cabin, and the side sash was raised. I have reason to think that the man at the wheel overheard our conversation. Now that man was Hearne, who, in order to hear it more clearly, let go the wheel, so that the *Halbrane* lurched—"

"I remember," said West. "I questioned the fellow sharply, and sent him down into the hold."

"Well, then, captain," I resumed, "it was from that day

that Hearne made up to Martin Holt. Hurliguerly called my attention to the fact."

"Of course he did," said the boatswain, "for Hearne, not being capable of managing the boat which he intended to seize, required a master-hand like Holt."

"And so," I said, "he kept on urging Holt to question the half-breed concerning his brother's fate, and you know how Holt came at last to learn the fearful truth. Martin Holt seemed to be stupefied by the revelation. The others dragged him away, and now he is with them!" We were all agreed that things had happened as I supposed, and now the question was, did Dirk Peters, in his present state of mind, mean to absent himself? Would he consent to resume his place among us?

We all left the cavern, and after an hour's search we came in sight of Dirk Peters, whose first impulse was to escape from us. At length, however, Hurliguerly and Francis came up with him. He stood still and made no resistance. I advanced and spoke to him, the others did the same. Captain Len Guy offered him his hand, which he took after a moment's hesitation. Then, without uttering a single word, he returned towards the beach.

From that day no allusion was ever made to the tragic story of the *Grampus*. Dirk Peters' wound proved to be slight; he merely wrapped a piece of sailcloth round the injured arm, and went off to his work with entire unconcern.

We made all the preparation in our power for a prolonged hibernation. Winter was threatening us. For some days past the sun hardly showed at all through the mists. The temperature fell to 36 degrees and would rise no more, while the solar rays, casting shadows of endless length upon the soil, gave hardly any heat. The captain made us put on warm woollen clothes without waiting for the cold to become more severe.

Icebergs, packs, streams, and drifts came in greater numbers from the south. Some of these struck and stayed upon the coast, which was already heaped up with ice, but the greater number disappeared in the direction of the north-east.

"All these pieces," said the boatswain, "will go to the closing up of the iceberg wall. If Hearne and his lot of scoundrels are not ahead of them, I imagine they will find the door shut, and as they have no key to open it with—"

"I suppose you think, boatswain, that our case is less desperate than theirs?"

"I do think so, Mr. Jeorling, and I have always thought so. If everything had been done as it was settled, and the lot had fallen to me to go with the boat, I would have given up my turn to one of the others. After all, there is something in feeling dry ground under your feet. I don't wish the death of anybody, but if Hearne and his friends do not succeed in clearing the iceberg barrier—if they are doomed to pass the winter on the ice, reduced for food to a supply that will only last a few weeks, you know the fate that awaits them!"

"Yes, a fate worse than ours!"

"And besides," said the boatswain, "even supposing they do reach the Antarctic Circle. If the whalers have already left the fishing-grounds, it is not a laden and overladen craft that will keep the sea until the Australian coasts are in sight."

This was my own opinion, and also that of the captain and West.

During the following four days, we completed the storage of the whole of our belongings, and made some excursions into the interior of the country, finding "all barren," and not a trace that any landing had ever been made there.

One day, Captain Len Guy proposed that we should give a geographical name to the region whither the iceberg had carried us. It was named Halbrane Land, in memory of our schooner, and we called the strait that separated the two parts of the polar continent the Jane Sound.

Then we took to shooting the penguins which swarmed upon the rocks, and to capturing some of the amphibious animals which frequented the beach. We began to feel the want of fresh meat, and Endicott's cooking rendered seal and walrus flesh quite palatable. Besides, the fat of these creatures would serve, at need, to warm the cavern and feed the cooking-stove. Our most formidable enemy would be the cold, and we must fight it by every means within our power. It remained to be seen whether the amphibia would not forsake Halbrane Land at the approach of winter, and seek a less rigorous climate in lower latitudes. Fortunately there were hundreds of other animals to secure our little company from hunger, and even from thirst, at need. The beach was the home of numbers of galapagos—a kind of turtle so called from an archipelago in the equinoctial sea, where also they abound, and mentioned by Arthur Pym as supplying food to the islanders. It will be remembered that Pym and Peters found three of these galapagos in the native boat which carried them away from Tsalal Island.

The movement of these huge creatures is slow, heavy, and waddling; they have thin necks two feet long, triangular snake-like heads, and can go without food for very long periods.

Arthur Pym has compared the antarctic turtles to dromedaries, because, like those ruminants, they have a pouch just where the neck begins, which contains from two to three gallons of cold fresh water. He relates, before the scene of the lot-drawing, that but for one of these turtles the shipwrecked crew of the *Grampus* must have died of hunger and thirst. If Pym is to be believed, some of the great turtles weigh from twelve to fifteen hundred pounds. Those of Halbrane Land did not go beyond seven or eight hundred pounds, but their flesh was none the less savoury.

On the 19th of February an incident occurred—an incident which those who acknowledge the intervention of Providence in human affairs will recognize as providential.

It was eight o'clock in the morning; the weather was calm; the sky was tolerably clear; the thermometer stood at thirty-two degrees Fahrenheit.

We were assembled in the cavern, with the exception of the boatswain, waiting for our breakfast, which Endicott was preparing, and were about to take our places at table, when we heard a call from outside.

The voice was Hurliguerly's, and we hurried out. On seeing us, he cried,—

"Come—come quickly!"

He was standing on a rock at the foot of the hillock above the beach in which Halbrane Land ended beyond the point, and his right hand was stretched out towards the sea.

"What is it?" asked Captain Len Guy.

"A boat."

"Is it the *Halbrane's* boat coming back?"

"No, captain—it is not."

Then we perceived a boat, not to be mistaken for that of our schooner in form or dimensions, drifting without oars or paddle, seemingly abandoned to the current.

We had but one idea in common—to seize at any cost upon this derelict craft, which would, perhaps, prove our salvation. But how were we to reach it? how were we to get it in to the point of Halbrane Land?

While we were looking distractedly at the boat and at each other, there came a sudden splash at the end of the hillock, as though a body had fallen into the sea.

It was Dirk Peters, who, having flung off his clothes, had sprung from the top of a rock, and was swimming rapidly towards the boat before we made him out.

We cheered him heartily. I never beheld anything like that swimming. He bounded through the waves like a porpoise, and indeed he possessed the strength and swiftness of one. What might not be expected of such a man!

In a few minutes the half-breed had swum several cables' lengths towards the boat in an oblique direction. We could only see his head like a black speck on the surface of the rolling waves. A period of suspense, of intense watching of the brave swimmer succeeded. Surely, surely he would reach the boat; but must he not be carried away with it? Was it to be believed that even his great strength would enable him, swimming, to tow it to the beach?

"After all, why should there not be oars in the boat?" said the boatswain.

"He has it! He has it! Hurrah, Dirk, hurrah!"

William Guy.

shouted Hurliguerly, and Endicott echoed his exultant cheer.

The half-breed had, in fact, reached the boat and raised himself alongside half out of the water. His big, strong hand grasped the side, and at the risk of causing the boat to capsize, he hoisted himself up to the side, stepped over it, and sat down to draw his breath.

Almost instantly a shout reached our ears. It was uttered by Dirk Peters. What had he found? Paddles! It must be so, for we saw him seat himself in the front of the boat, and paddle with all his strength in striving to get out of the current.

"Come along!" said the captain, and, turning the base of the hillock, we all ran along the edge of the beach between the blackish stones that bestrewed it.

After some time, West stopped us. The boat had reached the shelter of a small projection at that place, and it was evident that it would be run ashore there.

When it was within five or six cables' lengths, and the eddy was helping it on, Dirk Peters let go the paddles, stooped towards the after-part of the boat, and then raised himself, holding up an inert body.

An agonized cry from Captain Len Guy rent the air!

"My brother—my brother!"

"He is living! He is living!" shouted Dirk Peters.

A moment later, the boat had touched the beach, and Captain Len Guy held his brother in his arms.

Three of William Guy's companions lay apparently lifeless in the bottom of the boat.

And these four men were all that remained of the crew of the *Jane*.

CHAPTER XXIV.

ELEVEN YEARS IN A FEW PAGES.

THE heading of the following chapter indicates that the adventures of William Guy and his companions after the destruction of the English schooner, and the details of their history subsequent to the departure of Arthur Pym and Dirk Peters, are about to be narrated with all possible brevity.

We carried our treasure-trove to the cavern, and had the happiness of restoring all four men to life. In reality, it was hunger, nothing but hunger, which had reduced the poor fellows to the semblance of death.

. . . .

On the 8th of February, 1828, the crew of the *Jane*, having no reason to doubt the good faith of the population of Tsalal Island, or that of their chief, Too-Wit, disembarked, in order to visit the village of Klock-Klock, having previously put the schooner into a state of defence, leaving six men on board.

The crew, counting William Guy, the captain, Arthur Pym, and Dirk Peters, formed a body of thirty-two men, armed with guns, pistols, and knives. The dog Tiger accompanied them.

On reaching the narrow gorge leading to the village,

preceded and followed by the numerous warriors of Too-Wit, the little company divided, Arthur Pym, Dirk Peters, and Allen (the sailor) entering a cleft in the hill-side, with the intention of crossing it to the other side. From that moment their companions were never to see them more.

After a short interval a shock was felt. The opposite hill fell down in a vast heap, burying William Guy and his twenty-eight companions.

Twenty-two of these unfortunate men were crushed to death on the instant, and their bodies would never be found under that mass of earth.

Seven, miraculously sheltered in the depth of a great cleft of the hill, had survived the catastrophe. These were William Guy, Patterson, Roberts, Covin, Trinkle, also Forbes and Sexton, since dead. As for Tiger, they knew not whether he had perished in the landslip, or whether he had escaped. There existed in the right side of the hill, as well as in the left, on either side of the fissure, certain winding passages, and it was by crawling along these in the darkness that William Guy, Patterson, and the others reached a cavity which let in light and air in abundance. From this shelter they beheld the attack on the *Jane* by sixty pirogues, the defence made by the six men on board, the invasion of the ship by the savages, and finally the explosion which caused the death of a vast number of natives as well as the complete destruction of the ship.

Too-Wit and the Tsalal islanders were at first terrified by the effects of this explosion, but probably still more disappointed. Their instincts of pillage could not be gratified, because some valueless wreckage was all that remained of the ship and her cargo, and they had no reason to suppose that any of the crew had survived the cleverly-contrived collapse of the hill. Hence it came about that Arthur Pym and Dirk Peters on the one side, and William Guy and his companions on the other, were enabled to remain undisturbed in the labyrinths of Klock-Klock, where they fed on the flesh of bitterns—these they could catch with their hands—and the fruit of the nut-trees which grow on the hill-sides. They procured fire by rubbing pieces of soft against pieces of hard wood ; there was a quantity of both within their reach.

After a whole week of this confinement, Arthur Pym and the half-breed had succeeded, as we know, in leaving their hiding-place, securing a boat, and abandoning Tsalal Island, but William Guy and his companions had not yet found an opportunity to escape.

After they had been shut up in the labyrinth for twenty-one days, the birds on which they lived began to fail them, and they recognized that their only means of escaping hunger—(they had not to fear thirst, for there was a spring of fresh water in the interior of the hill)—was to go down again to the coast, lay hands upon a native boat, and get out to sea. Where were the fugitives to go, and what was to become of them without provisions ?—these were questions that had to be asked, and which nobody could answer. Nevertheless, they would not have hesitated to attempt the adventure if they could have a few hours of darkness ; but, at that time of year, the sun did not as yet go down behind the horizon of the eighty-fourth parallel.

Death would probably have put an end to their misery had not the situation been changed by the following events.

On the 22nd of February, in the morning, William Guy and Patterson were talking together, in terrible perplexity of mind, at the orifice of the cavity that opened upon the country. They no longer knew how to provide for the wants of seven persons, who were then reduced to eating nuts only, and were suffering in consequence from severe pain in the head and stomach. They could see big turtles crawling on the beach, but how could they venture to go thither, with hundreds of natives coming and going about their several occupations, with their constant cry of *tékéli-li?*

Suddenly, this crowd of people became violently agitated. Men, women, and children ran wildly about on every side. Some of the savages even took to their boats as though a great danger were at hand.

What was happening?

William Guy and his companions were very soon informed. The cause of the tumult was the appearance of an unknown animal, a terrible quadruped, which dashed into the midst of the islanders, snapping at and biting them indiscriminately, as it sprang at their throats with a hoarse growling.

And yet the infuriated animal was alone, and might easily have been killed by stones or arrows. Why then did a crowd of savages manifest such abject terror? Why did they take to flight? Why did they appear incapable of defending themselves against this one beast?

The animal was white, and the sight of it had produced the phenomenon previously observed, that inexplicable terror of whiteness common to all the natives of Tsalal.

To their extreme surprise, William Guy and his companions recognized the strange animal as the dog Tiger.

Yes! Tiger had escaped from the crumbling mass of the hill and betaken himself to the interior of the island, whence he had returned to Klock-Klock, to spread terror among the natives. But Tiger was no mere phantom foe; he was the most dangerous and deadly of enemies, for the poor animal was mad, and his fangs were fatal!

This was the reason why the greater part of the Tsalal islanders took to flight, headed by their chief, Too-Wit, and the Wampos, who are the leading personages of Klock-Klock. It was under these extraordinary circumstances that they abandoned their island, whither they were destined never to return.

Although the boats carried off the bulk of the population, a considerable number still remained on Tsalal, having no means of escape, and their fate accomplished itself quickly. Several natives who were bitten by Tiger developed hydrophobia rapidly, and attacked the others. Fearful scenes ensued, and are briefly to be summed up in one dismal statement. The bones we had seen in or near Klock-Klock were those of the poor savages, which had lain there bleaching for eleven years!

The poor dog had died, after he had done his fell work, in a corner on the beach, where Dirk Peters found his skeleton and the collar bearing the name of Arthur Pym.

Then, after those natives who could not escape from the island had all perished in the manner described, William Guy, Patterson, Trinkle, Covin, Forbes, and Sexton ventured to come out of the labyrinth, where they were on the verge of death by starvation.

What sort of existence was that of the seven survivors of the expedition during the eleven ensuing years?

On the whole, it was more endurable than might have been supposed. The natural products of an extremely fertile soil and the presence of a certain number of domestic animals secured them against want of food; they had only to make out the best shelter for themselves they could contrive, and wait for an opportunity of getting away from the island with as much patience as might be granted to them. And from whence could such an opportunity come? Only from one of the chances within the resources of Providence.

Captain William Guy, Patterson, and their five companions descended the ravine, which was half filled with the fallen masses of the hill-face, amid heaps of scoria and blocks of black granite. Before they left this gorge, it occurred to William Guy to explore the fissure on the right into which Arthur Pym, Dirk Peters, and Allen had turned, but he found it blocked up; it was impossible for him to get into the pass. Thus he remained in ignorance of the existence of the natural or artificial labyrinth which corresponded with the one he had just left, and probably communicated with it under the dry bed of the torrent. The little company, having passed the chaotic barrier that intercepted the northern route, proceeded rapidly towards the north-west. There, on the coast, at about three miles from Klock-Klock, they established themselves in a grotto very like that in our own occupation on the coast of Halbrane Land.

And it was in this place that, during long, hopeless years, the seven survivors of the *Jane* lived, as we were about to do ourselves, but under better conditions, for the fertility of the soil of Tsalal furnished them with resources unknown in Halbrane Land. In reality, we were condemned to perish when our provisions should be exhausted, but they could have waited indefinitely—and they did wait.

They had never entertained any doubt that Arthur Pym, Dirk Peters, and Allen had perished, and this was only too true in Allen's case. How, indeed, could they ever have imagined that Pym and the half-breed had got hold of a boat and made their escape from Tsalal Island?

So, then, as William Guy told us, not an incident occurred to break the monotony of that existence of eleven years—not even the reappearance of the islanders, who were kept away from Tsalal by superstitious terror. No danger had threatened them during all that time; but, of course, as it became more and more prolonged, they lost the hope of ever being rescued. At first, with the return of the fine season, when the sea was once more open, they had thought it possible that a ship would be sent in search of the *Jane*. But after four or five years they relinquished all hope.

There is no need for dwelling on this period, which extends from the year 1828 to the year 1839. The winters were hard. The summer did indeed extend its beneficent influence to the islands of the Tsalal group, but the cold season, with its attendant snows, rains, and tempests, spared them none of its severity.

During seven months Captain William Guy had not lost one of those who had come with him safe and sound out of the trap set for them at Klock-Klock, and this was due, no doubt, to their robust constitutions, remarkable power of endurance, and great strength of character. Alas! misfortune was making ready to fall on them.

The month of May had come—it corresponds in those regions to the month of November in northern lands—and the ice-packs which the current carried towards the north were beginning to drift past Tsalal. One day, one of the seven men failed to return to the cavern. They called, they waited, they searched for him. All was in vain. He did not reappear; no doubt he had been drowned. He was never more seen by his fellow-exiles.

This man was Patterson, the faithful companion of William Guy.

Now, what William Guy did not know, but we told him, was that Patterson—under what circumstances none would ever learn—had been carried away on the surface of an ice-block, where he died of hunger. And on that ice-block, which had travelled so far as Prince Edward Island, the boatswain had discovered the corpse of the unfortunate man almost decomposed by the action of the warmer waters.

When Captain Len Guy told his brother of the finding of the body of Patterson, and how it was owing to the notes in his pocket-book that the *Halbrane* had been enabled to proceed towards the antarctic seas, William Guy hid his face in his hands and wept.

Other misfortunes followed upon this one.

Five months after the disappearance of Patterson, in the middle of October, Tsalal Island was laid waste from coast to coast by an earthquake, which destroyed the south-western group almost entirely. William Guy and his companions must soon have perished on the barren land, which no longer could give them food, had not the means of leaving its coast, now merely an expanse of tumbled rocks, been afforded them in an almost miraculous manner. Two days after the earthquake, the current carried ashore within a few hundred yards of their cavern a boat which had drifted from the island group on the south-west.

Without the delay of even one day, the boat was laden with as much of the remaining provisions as it could contain, and the six men embarked in it, bidding adieu for ever to the now uninhabitable island.

Unfortunately a very strong breeze was blowing; it was impossible to resist it, and the boat was driven southwards by that very same current which had caused our iceberg to drift to the coast of Halbrane Land.

For two months and a half these poor fellows were borne across the open sea, with no control over their course. It was not until the 2nd of January in the present year (1840) that they sighted land—east of the Jane Sound.

Now, we already knew this land was not more than fifty miles from Halbrane Land. Yes! so small, relatively, was the distance that separated us from those whom we had sought for in the antarctic regions far and wide, and concerning whom we had lost hope.

Their boat had gone ashore far to the south-east of us. But on how different a coast from that of Tsalal Island, or, rather, on one how like that of Halbrane Land! Nothing was to be seen but sand and stones; neither trees, shrubs, nor plants of any kind. Their provisions were almost exhausted; William Guy and his companions were soon reduced to extreme want, and two of the little company, Forbes and Sexton, died.

The remaining four resolved not to remain a single day longer in the place where they were doomed to die of hunger. They embarked in the boat with the small supply of food still remaining, and once more abandoned themselves to the current, without having been able to verify their position, for want of instruments.

Thus had they been borne upon the unknown deep for

twenty-five days, their resources were completely exhausted, and they had not eaten for forty-eight hours, when the boat, with its occupants lying inanimate at the bottom of it, was sighted from Halbrane Land. The rest is already known to the reader of this strange eventful history.

And now the two brothers were at length reunited in that remote corner of the big world which we had dubbed Halbrane Land.

CHAPTER XXV.

"WE WERE THE FIRST."

TWO days later not one of the survivors from the two schooners, the *Jane* and the *Halbrane*, remained upon any coast of the Antarctic region.

On the 21st of February, at six o'clock in the morning, the boat, with us all (we numbered thirteen) in it, left the little creek and doubled the point of Halbrane Land. On the previous day we had fully and finally debated the question of our departure, with the understanding that if it were settled in the affirmative, we should start without delay.

The captain of the *Jane* was for an immediate departure, and Captain Len Guy was not opposed to it. I willingly sided with them, and West was of a similar opinion. The boatswain was inclined to oppose us. He considered it imprudent to give up a certainty for the uncertain, and he was backed by Endicott, who would in any case say "ditto" to his "Mr. Burke." However, when the time came, Hurliguerly conformed to the view of the majority with a good grace, and declared himself quite ready to set out, since we were all of that way of thinking.

Our boat was one of those in use in the Tsalal Archipelago for plying between the islands. We knew, from the narrative of Arthur Pym, that these boats are of two kinds, one resembling rafts or flat boats, the other strongly-built pirogues. Our boat was of the former kind, forty feet long, six feet in width, and worked by several paddles.

We called our little craft the *Paracuta*, after a fish which abounds in these waters. A rough image of that denizen of the southern deep was cut upon the gunwale.

Needless to say that the greater part of the cargo of the *Halbrane* was left in our cavern, fully protected from the weather, at the disposal of any shipwrecked people who might chance to be thrown on the coast of Halbrane Land. The boatswain had planted a spar on the top of this slope to attract attention. But, our two schooners notwithstanding, what vessel would ever venture into such latitudes?

Nota Bene.—We were just thirteen—the fatal number. Perfectly good relations subsisted among us. We had no longer to dread the rebellion of a Hearne. (How often we speculated upon the fate of those whom he had beguiled!)

At seven o'clock, the extreme point of Halbrane Land lay five miles behind us, and in the evening we gradually lost sight of the heights that variated that part of the coast.

I desire to lay special stress on the fact that not a single scrap of iron entered into the construction of this boat, not so much as a nail or a bolt, for that metal was entirely unknown to the Tsalal islanders. The planks were bound together by a sort of liana, or creeping-plant, and caulked with moss steeped in pitch, which was turned by contact with the sea-water to a substance as hard as metal.

I have nothing special to record during the week that succeeded our departure. The breeze blew steadily from the south, and we did not meet with any unfavourable current between the banks of the Jane Sound.

During those first eight days, the *Paracuta*, by paddling when the wind fell, had kept up the speed that was indispensable for our reaching the Pacific Ocean within a short time.

The desolate aspect of the land remained the same, while the strait was already visited by floating drifts, packs of one to two hundred feet in length, some oblong, others circular, and also by icebergs which our boat passed easily. We were made anxious, however, by the fact that these masses were proceeding towards the iceberg barrier, for would they not close the passages, which ought to be still open at this time?

I shall mention here that in proportion as Dirk Peters was carried farther and farther from the places wherein no trace of his poor Pym had been found, he was more silent than ever, and no longer even answered me when I addressed him.

It must not be forgotten that since our iceberg had passed beyond the south pole, we were in the zone of eastern longitudes counted from the zero of Greenwich to the hundred and eightieth degree. All hope must therefore be abandoned of our either touching at the Falklands, or finding whaling-ships in the waters of the Sandwich Islands, the South Orkneys, or South Georgia.

Our voyage proceeded under unaltered conditions for ten days. Our little craft was perfectly sea-worthy. The two captains and West fully appreciated its soundness, although, as I have previously said, not a scrap of iron had a place in its construction. It had not once been necessary to repair its seams, so staunch were they. To be sure, the sea was smooth, its long, rolling waves were hardly ruffled on their surface.

On the 10th of March, with the same longitude the observation gave 7° 13′ for latitude. The speed of the *Paracuta* had then been thirty miles in each twenty-four hours. If this rate of progress could be maintained for three weeks, there was every chance of our finding the passes open, and being able to get round the iceberg barrier; also that the whaling-ships would not yet have left the fishing-grounds.

The sun was on the verge of the horizon, and the time was approaching when the Antarctic region would be shrouded in polar night. Fortunately, in re-ascending towards the north we were getting into waters from whence light was not yet banished. Then did we witness a phenomenon as extraordinary as any of those described by Arthur Pym. For three or four hours, sparks, accompanied by a sharp noise, shot out of our fingers' ends, our hair, and our beards. There was an electric snow-storm, with great flakes falling loosely, and the contact produced this strange luminosity. The sea rose so suddenly and tumbled about so wildly that the *Paracuta* was several times in danger of being swallowed up by the waves, but we got through the mystic-seeming tempest all safe and sound.

Nevertheless, space was thenceforth but imperfectly lighted. Frequent mists came up and bounded our outlook to a few cable-lengths. Extreme watchfulness and caution were necessary to avoid collision with the floating masses of ice, which were travelling more slowly than the *Paracuta.*

It is also to be noted that, on the southern side, the sky was frequently lighted up by the broad and brilliant rays of the polar aurora.

The temperature fell very perceptibly, and no longer rose above twenty-three degrees.

Forty-eight hours later Captain Len Guy and his brother succeeded with great difficulty in taking an approximate observation, with the following results of their calculations:

Latitude: 75° 17′ south.
Latitude: 118° 3′ east.

At this date, therefore (12th March), the *Paracuta* was distant from the waters of the Antarctic Circle only four hundred miles.

During the night a thick fog came on, with a subsidence of the breeze. This was to be regretted, for it increased the risk of collision with the floating ice. Of course fog could not be a surprise to us, being where we were, but what did surprise us was the gradually increasing speed of our boat, although the falling of the wind ought to have lessened it.

This increase of speed could not be due to the current for we were going more quickly than it.

This state of things lasted until morning, without our being able to account for what was happening, when at about ten o'clock the mist began to disperse in the low zones. The coast on the west reappeared—a rocky coast, without a mountainous background; the *Paracuta* was following its line.

And then, no more than a quarter of a mile away, we beheld a huge mound, reared above the plain to a height of three hundred feet, with a circumference of from two to three hundred feet. In its strange form this great mound resembled an enormous sphinx; the body upright, the paws stretched out, crouching in the attitude of the winged monster which Grecian Mythology has placed upon the way to Thebes.

Was this a living animal, a gigantic monster, a mastodon a thousand times the size of those enormous elephants of the polar seas whose remains are still found in the ice? In our frame of mind we might have believed that it was such a creature, and believed also that the mastodon was about to hurl itself on our little craft and crush it to atoms.

After a few moments of unreasoning and unreasonable fright, we recognized that the strange object was only a great mound, singularly shaped, and that the mist had just rolled off its head, leaving it to stand out and confront us.

Ah! that sphinx! I remembered, at sight of it, that on the night when the iceberg was overturned and the *Halbrane* was carried away, I had dreamed of a fabulous animal of this kind, seated at the pole of the world, and from whom Edgar Poe could only wrest its secrets.

But our attention was to be attracted, our surprise, even

our alarm, was evoked soon by phenomena still more strange than the mysterious earth form upon which the mist-curtain had been raised so suddenly.

I have said that the speed of the *Paracuta* was gradually increasing; now it was excessive, that of the current remaining inferior to it. Now, of a sudden, the grapnel that had belonged to the *Halbrane*, and was in the bow of the boat, flew out of its socket as though drawn by an irresistible power, and the rope that held it was strained to breaking point. It seemed to tow us, as it grazed the surface of the water towards the shore.

"What's the matter?" cried William Guy. "Cut away, boatswain, cut away!" shouted West, "or we shall be dragged against the rocks."

Hurliguerly hurried to the bow of the *Paracuta* to cut away the rope. Of a sudden the knife he held was snatched out of his hand, the rope broke, and the grapnel, like a projectile, shot off in the direction of the sphinx.

At the same moment, all the articles on board the boat that were made of iron or steel—cooking utensils, arms, Endicott's stove, our knives, which were torn from our pockets—took flight after a similar fashion in the same direction, while the boat, quickening its course, brought up against the beach.

What was happening? In order to explain these inexplicable things, were we not obliged to acknowledge that we had come into the region of those wonders which I attributed to the hallucinations of Arthur Pym?

No! These were physical facts which we had just witnessed, and not imaginary phenomena!

We had, however, no time for reflection, and immediately upon our landing, our attention was turned in another direction by the sight of a boat lying wrecked upon the sand.

"The *Halbrane's* boat!" cried Hurliguerly. It was indeed the boat which Hearne had stolen, and it was simply smashed to pieces; in a word, only the formless wreckage of a craft which has been flung against rocks by the sea, remained.

We observed immediately that all the ironwork of the boat had disappeared, down to the hinges of the rudder. Not one trace of the metal existed.

What could be the meaning of this?

A loud call from West brought us to a little strip of beach on the right of our stranded boat.

Three corpses lay upon the stony soil, that of Hearne, that of Martin Holt, and that of one of the Falklands men.

Of the thirteen who had gone with the sealing-master, there remained only these three, who had evidently been dead some days.

What had become of the ten missing men? Had their bodies been carried out to sea?

We searched all along the coast, into the creeks, and between the outlying rocks, but in vain. Nothing was to be found, no traces of a camp, not even the vestiges of a landing.

"Their boat," said William Guy, "must have been struck by a drifting iceberg. The rest of Hearne's companions have been drowned, and only these three bodies have come ashore, lifeless."

"But," asked the boatswain, "how is the state the boat is in to be explained?"

"And especially," added West, "the disappearance of all the iron?"

"Indeed," said I, "it looks as though every bit had been violently torn off."

Leaving the *Paracuta* in the charge of two men, we again took our way to the interior, in order to extend our search over a wider expanse.

As we were approaching the huge mound the mist cleared away, and the form stood out with greater distinctness. It was, as I have said, almost that of a sphinx, a dusky-hued sphinx, as though the matter which composed it had been oxidized by the inclemency of the polar climate.

And then a possibility flashed into my mind, an hypothesis which explained these astonishing phenomena.

"Ah!" I exclaimed, "a loadstone! that is it! A magnet with prodigious power of attraction!"

I was understood, and in an instant the final catastrophe, to which Hearne and his companions were victims, was explained with terrible clearness.

The Antarctic Sphinx was simply a colossal magnet. Under the influence of that magnet the iron bands of the *Halbrane's* boat had been torn out and projected as though by the action of a catapult. This was the occult force that had irresistibly attracted everything made of iron on the *Paracuta*. And the boat itself would have shared the fate of the *Halbrane's* boat had a single bit of that metal been employed in its construction. Was it, then, the proximity of the magnetic pole that produced such effects?

An antarctic mystery.

At first we entertained this idea, but on reflection we rejected it.

At the place where the magnetic meridians cross, the only phenomenon produced is the vertical position of the magnetic needle in two similar points of the terrestrial globe. This phenomenon, already proved by observations made on the spot, must be identical in the Antarctic regions.

Thus, then, there did exist a magnet of prodigious intensity in the zone of attraction which we had entered. Under our eyes one of those surprising effects which had hitherto been classed among fables was actually produced.

The following appeared to me to be the true explanation.

The Trade-winds bring a constant succession of clouds or mists in which immense quantities of electricity not completely exhausted by storms, are stored. Hence there exists a formidable accumulation of electric fluid at the poles, and it flows towards the land in a permanent stream.

From this cause come the northern and southern auroras, whose luminous splendours shine above the horizon, especially during the long polar night, and are visible even in the temperate zones when they attain their maximum of culmination.

These continuous currents at the poles, which bewilder our compasses, must possess an extraordinary influence. And it would suffice that a block of iron should be subjected to their action for it to be changed into a magnet of power proportioned to the intensity of the current, to the number of turns of the electric helix, and to the square root of the diameter of the block of magnetized iron. Thus, then, the bulk of the sphinx which upreared its mystic form upon this outer edge of the southern lands might be calculated by thousands of cubic yards.

Now, in order that the current should circulate around it and make a magnet of it by induction, what was required? Nothing but a metallic lode, whose innumerable windings through the bowels of the soil should be connected subterraneously at the base of the block.

It seemed to me also that the place of this block ought to be in the magnetic axis, as a sort of gigantic calamite, from whence the imponderable fluid whose currents made an inexhaustible accumulator set up at the confines of the world should issue. Our compass could not have enabled us to determine whether the marvel before our eyes really was at the magnetic pole of the southern regions. All I can say is, that its needle staggered about, helpless and useless. And in fact the exact location of the Antarctic Sphinx mattered little in respect of the constitution of that artificial loadstone, and the manner in which the clouds and metallic lode supplied its attractive power.

In this very plausible fashion I was led to explain the phenomenon by instinct. It could not be doubted that we were in the vicinity of a magnet which produced these terrible but strictly natural effects by its attraction.

I communicated my idea to my companions, and they regarded this explanation as conclusive, in presence of the physical facts of which we were the actual witnesses.

"We shall incur no risk by going to the foot of the mound, I suppose," said Captain Len Guy.

"None," I replied.

"There—yes—there!"

I could not describe the impression those three words made upon us. Edgar Poe would have said that they were three cries from the depths of the under world.

It was Dirk Peters who had spoken, and his body was stretched out in the direction of the sphinx, as though it had been turned to iron and was attracted by the magnet.

Then he sped swiftly towards the sphinx-like mound, and his companions followed him over rough ground strewn with volcanic remains of all sorts.

The monster grew larger as we neared it, but lost none of its mythological shape. Alone on that vast plain it produced a sense of awe. And—but this could only have been a delusion—we seemed to be drawn towards it by the force of its magnetic attraction.

On arriving at the base of the mound, we found there the various articles on which the magnet had exerted its power; arms, utensils, the grapnel of the *Paracuta*, all adhering to the sides of the monster. There also were the iron relics of the *Halbrane's* boat, all her utensils, arms, and fittings, even to the nails and the iron portions of the rudder.

There was no possibility of regaining possession of any of these things. Even had they not adhered to the loadstone rock at too great a height to be reached, they adhered to it too closely to be detached. Hurliguerly was infuriated by the impossibility of recovering his knife, which he recognized at fifty feet above his head, and cried as he shook his clenched fist at the imperturbable monster,—

"Thief of a sphinx!"

Of course the things which had belonged to the *Hal-*

brane's boat and the *Paracuta's* were the only articles that adorned the mighty sides of the lonely mystic form. Never had any ship reached such a latitude of the Antarctic Sea. Hearne and his accomplices, Captain Len Guy and his companions, were the first who had trodden this point of the southern continent. And any vessel that might have approached this colossal magnet must have incurred certain destruction. Our schooner must have perished, even as its boat had been dashed into a shapeless wreck.

West now reminded us that it was imprudent to prolong our stay upon this Land of the Sphinx—a name to be retained. Time pressed, and a few days' delay would have entailed our wintering at the foot of the ice-barrier.

The order to return to the beach had just been given, when the voice of the half-breed was again heard, as he cried out:

"There! There! There!"

We followed the sounds to the back of the monster's right paw, and we found Dirk Peters on his knees, with his hands stretched out before an almost naked corpse, which had been preserved intact by the cold of these regions, and was as rigid as iron. The head was bent, a white beard hung down to the waist, the nails of the feet and hands were like claws.

How had this corpse been fixed to the side of the mound at six feet above the ground?

Across the body, held in place by its cross-belt, we saw the twisted barrel of a musket, half-eaten by rust.

"Pym—my poor Pym!" groaned Dirk Peters.

He tried to rise, that he might approach and kiss the ossified corpse. But his knees bent under him, a strangled sob seemed to rend his throat, with a terrible spasm his faithful heart broke, and the half-breed fell back—dead!

The story was easy to read. After their separation, the boat had carried Arthur Pym through these Antarctic regions! Like us, once he had passed beyond the south pole, he came into the zone of the monster! And there, while his boat was swept along on the northern current, he was seized by the magnetic fluid before he could get rid of the gun which was slung over his shoulder, and hurled against the fatal loadstone Sphinx of the Ice-realm.

Now the faithful half-breed rests under the clay of the Land of the Antarctic Mystery, by the side of his "poor Pym," that hero whose strange adventures found a chronicler no less strange in the great American poet!

CHAPTER XXVI.

A LITTLE REMNANT.

THAT same day, in the afternoon, the *Paracuta* departed from the coast of the Land of the Sphinx, which had lain to the west of us since the 21st of February.

By the death of Dirk Peters the number of the passengers was reduced to twelve. These were all who remained of the double crew of the two schooners, the first comprising thirty-eight men, the second, thirty-two; in all seventy souls. But let it not be forgotten that the voyage of the *Halbrane* had been undertaken in fulfilment of a duty to humanity, and four of the survivors of the *Jane* owed their rescue to it.

And now there remains but little to tell, and that little must be related as succinctly as possible. It is unnecessary to dwell upon our return voyage, which was favoured by the constancy of the currents and the wind to their northern course. The last part of the voyage was indeed accomplished amid great fatigue, suffering, and danger, but it ended in our safe deliverance from all these.

Firstly, a few days after our departure from the Land of the Sphinx, the sun set behind the western horizon to reappear no more for the whole winter. It was then in

The *Paracuta*.

the midst of the semi-darkness of the austral night that the *Paracuta* pursued her monotonous course. True, the southern polar lights were frequently visible; but they were not the sun, that single orb of day which had illumined our horizons during the months of the Antarctic summer, and their capricious splendour could not replace his unchanging light. That long darkness of the poles sheds a moral and physical influence on mortals which no one can elude, a gloomy and overwhelming impression almost impossible to resist.

Of all the *Paracuta's* passengers, the boatswain and Endicott only preserved their habitual good-humour; those two were equally insensible to the weariness and the peril of our voyage. I also except West, who was ever ready to face every eventuality, like a man who is always on the defensive. As for the two brothers Guy, their happiness in being restored to each other made them frequently oblivious of the anxieties and risks of the future.

Of Hurliguerly I cannot speak too highly. He proved himself a thoroughly good fellow, and it raised our drooping spirits to hear him repeat in his jolly voice,—

"We shall get to port all right, my friends, be sure of that. And, if you only reckon things up, you will see that we have had more good luck than bad. Oh, yes, I know, there was the loss of our schooner! Poor *Halbrane*, carried up into the air like a balloon, then flung into the deep like an avalanche! But, on the other hand, there was the iceberg which brought us to the coast, and the Tsalal boat which brought us and Captain William Guy and his three companions together. And don't forget the current and the breeze that have pushed us on up to now, and will keep pushing us on, I'm sure of that. With so many trumps in our hand we cannot possibly lose the game. The only thing to be regretted is that we shall have to get ashore again in Australia or New Zealand, instead of casting anchor at the Kerguelens, near the quay of Christmas Harbour, in front of the Green Cormorant."

For a week we pursued our course without deviation to east or west, and it was not until the 21st of March that the *Paracuta* lost sight of Halbrane Land, being carried towards the north by the current, while the coast-line of the continent, for such we are convinced it is, trended in a round curve to the north-east.

Although the waters of this portion of sea were still open, they carried a flotilla of icebergs or ice-fields. Hence arose serious difficulties and also dangers to navigation in the midst of the gloomy mists, when we had to manœuvre between these moving masses, either to find passage or to prevent our little craft from being crushed like grain between the millstones.

Besides, Captain Len Guy could no longer ascertain his position either in latitude or longitude. The sun being absent, calculations by the position of the stars was too complicated, it was impossible to take altitudes, and the *Paracuta* abandoned herself to the action of the current, which invariably bore us northward, as the compass indicated. By keeping the reckoning of its medium speed, however, we concluded that on the 27th of March our boat was between the sixty-ninth and the sixty-eighth parallels, that is to say, some seventy miles only from the Antarctic Circle.

Ah! if no obstacle to the course of our perilous navigation had existed, if passage between this inner sea of the southern zone and the waters of the Pacific Ocean had been certain, the *Paracuta* might have reached the extreme limit of the austral seas in a few days. But a few hundred miles more to sail, and the iceberg-barrier would confront us with its immovable rampart, and unless a passage could be found, we should be obliged to go round it either by the east or by the west.

Once cleared indeed—

Ah! once cleared, we should be in a frail craft upon the terrible Pacific Ocean, at the period of the year when its tempests rage with redoubled fury and strong ships dread the might of its waves.

We were determined not to think of this. Heaven would come to our aid. We should be picked up by some ship. This the boatswain asserted confidently, and we were bound to believe the boatswain.

. . . .

For six entire days, until the 2nd of April, the *Paracuta* held her course among the ice-barrier, whose crest was profiled at an altitude of between seven and eight hundred feet above the level of the sea. The extremities were not visible either on the east or the west, and if our boat did not find an open passage, we could not clear it. By a most fortunate chance a passage was found on the above-mentioned date, and attempted, amid a thousand risks. Yes, we required all the zeal, skill, and courage of our men and their chiefs to accomplish such a task.

At last we were in the South Pacific waters, but our boat had suffered severely in getting through, and it had sprung more than one leak. We were kept busy in baling out the water, which also came in from above.

The breeze was gentle, the sea more calm than we could have hoped, and the real danger did not lie in the risks of navigation. No, it arose from the fact that not a ship was visible in these waters, not a whaler was to be seen on the fishing-grounds. At the beginning of April these places are forsaken, and we arrived some weeks too late.

We learned afterwards that had we arrived a little sooner, we should have met the vessels of the American expedition.

In fact, on the 1st of February, by 95° 50′ longitude and 64° 17′ latitude, Lieutenant Wilkes was still exploring these seas in one of his ships, the *Vincennes*, after having discovered a long extent of coast stretching from east to west. On the approach of the bad season, he returned to Hobart Town, in Tasmania. The same year, the expedition of the French captain Dumont d'Urville, which started in 1838, discovered Adélie Land in 66° 30′ latitude and 38° 21′ east longitude, and Clarie Coast in 64° 30′ and 129° 54′. Their campaign having ended with these important discoveries, the *Astrolabe* and the *Zélée* left the Antarctic Ocean and returned to Hobart Town.

None of these ships, then, were in those waters; so that, when our nutshell *Paracuta* was "alone on a lone, lone sea" beyond the ice-barrier, we were bound to believe that it was no longer possible we could be saved.

We were fifteen hundred miles away from the nearest land, and winter was a month old!

Hurliguerly himself was obliged to acknowledge that the last fortunate chance upon which he had counted had failed us.

On the 6th of April we were at the end of our resources; the sea began to threaten, the boat seemed likely to be swallowed up in the angry waves.

"A ship!" cried the boatswain, and on the instant we made out a vessel about four miles to the north-east, beneath the mist which had suddenly risen.

Signals were made, signals were perceived; the ship lowered her largest boat and sent it to our rescue.

This ship was the *Tasman*, an American three-master, from Charlestown, where we were received with eager welcome and cordiality. The captain treated my companions as though they had been his own countrymen.

The *Tasman* had come from the Falkland Islands where the captain had learned that seven months previously the American schooner *Halbrane* had gone to the southern seas in search of the shipwrecked people of the *Jane*. But as the season advanced, the schooner not having reappeared, she was given up for lost in the Antarctic regions.

Fifteen days after our rescue the *Tasman* disembarked the survivors of the crew of the two schooners at Melbourne, and it was there that our men were paid the sums they had so hardly earned, and so well deserved.

We then learned from maps that the *Paracuta* had debouched into the Pacific from the land called Clarie by Dumont d'Urville, and the land called Fabricia, which was discovered in 1838 by Bellenny.

Thus terminated this adventurous and extraordinary expedition, which cost, alas, too many victims. Our final word is that although the chances and the necessities of our voyage carried us farther towards the south pole than hose who preceded us, although we actually did pass beyond the axial point of the terrestrial globe, discoveries of great value still remain to be made in those waters!

Arthur Pym, the hero whom Edgar Poe has made so famous, has shown the way. It is for others to follow him, and to wrest the last Antarctic Mystery from the Sphinx of the Ice-realm.

THE END.

Reprint Publishing

For People Who Go For Originals.

This book is a facsimile reprint of the original edition. The term refers to the facsimile with an original in size and design exactly matching simulation as photographic or scanned reproduction.

Facsimile editions offer us the chance to join in the library of historical, cultural and scientific history of mankind, and to rediscover.

The books of the facsimile edition may have marks, notations and other marginalia and pages with errors contained in the original volume. These traces of the past refers to the historical journey that has covered the book.

ISBN 978-3-95940-191-3

Facsimile reprint of the original edition

www.reprintpublishing.com

www.ingramcontent.com/pod-product-compliance
Lightning Source LLC
LaVergne TN
LVHW020657110826
845149LV00012B/2026

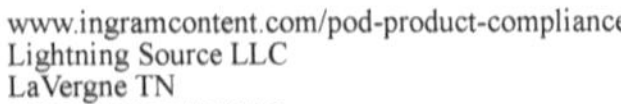